Bone by Bone

Gary Krist

Bone by Bone

S T O R I E S

HARCOURT BRACE & COMPANY

New York   San Diego   London

Copyright © 1994 by Gary Krist

Library of Congress Cataloging-in-Publication Data
Krist, Gary.
Bone by bone: stories/by Gary Krist. —1st ed.
p.   cm.
ISBN 0-15-182064-3
I. Title.
PS3561.R565B6   1994
813'.54—dc20   93-4865

Designed by Camilla Filancia
Printed in the United States of America
First edition   A B C D E

For Anna Chang-Yi

Contents

Acknowledgments

I would like to thank the editors of the magazines in which these stories, sometimes in slightly different form, first appeared:

"Baggage"	*Gentleman's Quarterly*
"Eclipse"	*Ladies' Home Journal*
"Uncle Isaac"	*Tikkun*
"Hungry"	*Western Humanities Review*
"Ghost Story"	*The Hudson Review* (as "Bleeders")
"Giant Step"	*The Hudson Review*
"Numbers"	*Western Humanities Review*
"Bone by Bone"	*The Quarterly*
"Unique Szechuan II"	*Boulevard*

I would also like to thank The National Endowment for the Arts, for financial support, Martha Browne, for perspicacity above and beyond the call of duty, and Robert Wright, for intelligent commentary and just enough philosophical rope to hang myself with.

PART ONE

Baggage

THE DOORCHIME goes all morning, like a prize-fight bell announcing rounds.

The first ring is Deeker. "Hey Pip," he says, standing out on the brownstone stoop. He's wearing a black wool hat and paint-spattered jeans—moving clothes. There's a little shaving cut over his Adam's apple. "Am I the first?" he asks.

"You're the first."

"Good." He pushes past me into the front hall. I can smell Old Spice on his collar, Deeker's idea of a classy scent ever since high school. "You took the seat off the lift? We'll need room on the staircase."

"All taken care of."

Deeker nods. He sprints up the stairs and then stops short in the open doorway to the apartment, nearly causing me to run into the back of his sweat-mottled T-shirt. "Check out this Japanese gum," he says, holding out a neat little packet covered with merry cartoon figures.

I pull a tiny wrapped slab from the pack.

"They call it Stress-Age gum," he goes on. "Tests your pH level. Chew it for three minutes and see what color it turns."

Deeker flies to Japan six times a year on business. He advises Japanese advertising firms on the use of Occidentals in their ads. They pay him for this.

"Can we please go in?" I ask him then.

Deeker steps into the apartment and looks around. "Wonderful, wonderful. Everything in boxes."

The doorchime goes again. "Don't touch anything yet," I say, and head back downstairs to the front door.

Della and a heavy woman with short-cropped black hair are holding hands out on the stoop. Della's my assistant from work. The other woman I don't know. They're both wearing overalls. "That your truck?" Della asks as I pull open the door. She's pointing at the grimy red van at the curb.

"That's it."

"Who's the ghoul reading wrestling magazines in the front seat?"

"The official driver. He comes with the van, but he doesn't help with the loading or unloading. It's the rules."

Della grimaces. "Bizarre."

"I'm Annbeth," says the other woman, sticking out her hand. "I'm Della's girlfriend."

I shake Annbeth's round knot of a hand. Della, her hair pulled back in a ponytail, gives me a peck on the temple.

"Glad to see you're both dressed for it," I tell them.

Annbeth says: "We know what has to be done."

We go upstairs and find Deeker pacing around the dining room, already organizing boxes. "We got how many coming today?" he asks, pressing his toe to a carton that says "Living Room: Candlesticks/Magazines/Teapot."

"Two more, and maybe Bill from next door."

I introduce the women. Deeker gives them both some Stress-Age gum.

The early sun, meanwhile, angles into the tall back windows, fixing us in diagonal blocks of amber. October.

"So where's Gail?" Della asks, chewing.

"In the front bedroom," I say. "It's sort of a low profile day today."

Della nods. Nobody says anything for a few seconds. I probe their silence for any hint of censure, like a worried home-owner sniffing for gas.

The doorchime again, thank God.

It's Michele from work and Hank from aerobics, standing outside the front door, peering in through the spotted glass panes. Michele is a fellow account executive. Hank does something with real estate. "We saw each other on the F train," Michele says as I let them in. "Hank remembered me from your Christmas party."

"That hair," Hank says. "Not something you forget."

Michele has pounds of frizzy red hair. All the women I know, in fact, have emphatic hair. Even Gail.

I shepherd them through the front hallway. "We're all up in the dining room, getting organized," I say, following their feet up that old, crooked stairway. Their eyes, I notice, avoid the shiny new chairlift track running under the wooden ban-ister.

"Jesus Christ, what's with this gum?" Della shouts just as we come in. She's got a bright green pebble of it in the palm of her slender hand.

"Let me look," says Deeker. He examines the gum. "Green means you're too tired. Get some rest. See, mine's pink, mean-ing my pH is in balance. Very low stress."

We all check the color of our gum. Mine is green.

"Should I even bother to ask what's going on?" Michele says to me.

Annbeth slaps her knee. "Pink!" she crows, displaying her gum. She seems to derive enormous satisfaction from the fact that the wad in her hand is a glossy shade of rose.

"The Japanese are amazing," Deeker goes on. "Like I said to Pip here, who else would think of diagnostic gum?"

"It's their savings rate that impresses me," says Michele.

"Didn't I hear somewhere that they used to eat the brains of live monkeys?" Hank asks the room. Then he turns to me. "And why does he call you Pip, anyway?"

I can see that this could get out of hand. "Look," I say, glancing at the clock over the kitchen doorway—the clock that's staying. "I'm paying for the van by the hour . . ."

"Uh-oh," says Michele, "the serious voice."

We start moving boxes. Deeker, taking charge, assigns Hank and Annbeth to the back of the truck, to stack boxes as we bring them down. He informs them that we want to make just one trip, so they should stack carefully. "I do everything carefully," Hank says tartly. He grins at Annbeth. "My little cross to bear."

The rest of us do the moving. We carry the boxes one by one down the stairs, out the front door and down the ramp I installed last year for Gail's wheelchair, onto the sidewalk, to the back of the van. Deeker sings as he carries, doing a Springsteen imitation that is just good enough to warrant our tolerance. It all goes quickly. Michele, Della, and I smile or make little jokes as we pass each other on the way in or out, like acquaintances meeting on the street for the second time that day.

On one trip, I find Hank leaning around the back of the truck, pointing something out to Annbeth. I follow the line of his hand to the bedroom window, where Gail is now, waiting for this to be over. Annbeth looks embarrassed, then angry, when she sees me. I pretend I don't notice. Maybe Della didn't tell her whom they'd be helping to move today—a man leaving his crippled girlfriend, a man even Della is having a hard time making excuses for.

Meanwhile, the driver—bearded and fat—sits in the front seat, looking up from his magazine occasionally to stare at us through the hazy mirror on the side door of the truck.

"He looks kind of like God, doesn't he," Michele remarks as we're heading back into the building. "Either God or an ax-murderer, something like that."

"I think I'd prefer to face an ax-murderer today. Less judgmental."

Her eyes cut over to me. "Second thoughts?"

"No, definitely not," I say. "But I guess I didn't think I was going to feel this . . . isolated."

"Isolated," Michele repeats, examining the word.

By eleven we've moved all the portable items; still to load are the few large pieces of furniture coming with me—my reading chair, the scratched file cabinet, and the enormous mission-oak armoire that Gail and I bought at an antiques store on Atlantic Avenue years ago.

Deeker, of course, has an opinion on how we should proceed. "Pip," he says, standing in front of the white-brick fireplace that never worked, "you and me on the very attractive, very heavy armchair, and the ladies on the lighter cabinet."

"The ladies?" Della says.

"The ladies will take the very heavy armchair, thank you," Michele says.

The two of them step over to the armchair, lift it, and carry it carefully out of the room.

"Don't say I never saved you any labor," Deeker says then, pursing his lips in that way he's always had.

"You did that on purpose."

He shrugs. "Manipulating people is my business."

"For that you take the cabinet by yourself," I tell him. I'm serious.

He looks at me and sighs. Then he bends over to grab

the cabinet from the bottom. I can see the faint gleam of scalp beneath ropy strands of his black hair. "You're going bald, you know, Deeker. You're starting to look just like that Driver's Ed teacher, what was his name, Mr. Bok."

The eyes look up at me from under his elegantly arching eyebrows. "Glass houses, my boy, glass houses." He grunts as he wrestles the cabinet onto his outthrust hip. I watch silently as he tries to maneuver his body and the cabinet through the doorway into the hall. "You're enjoying this, aren't you," he sputters.

"Tell them all to come in now." I pat the top of the metal cabinet, making a dull, hollow sound. "We'll need everybody for the armoire."

The five of them come back laughing about something the van driver has said. Apparently he told them they should have loaded the big pieces of furniture first and saved the boxes for last. "Thank you for your input," Annbeth replied, and slammed a box of books up against the back of his seat.

"There's still gobs of room in there," Della says, "so fuck him."

"I wouldn't rile the man," I warn her. "Michele says he's probably an ax-murderer."

The doorchime goes.

Silence.

"Oh God," Hank says, "he's coming after us with his ax!"

Actually, it's only Bill from down the block. He's standing outside the open front door, peering in with his wire-rimmed glasses. He's wearing brand-new jeans and a brand-new lumberjack shirt, pinched with sharp creases. "Peter," he says, "my apologies, but I had to take care of something at the hospital this morning. It looks like I'm too late to help on this end."

"Well, we've just got one more thing to move."

"But I'll certainly help you unload at the other end," he

assures me, preceding me up the stairs. Bill, unlike the others, has no qualms about staring at the greased track of the chairlift. He's a doctor, after all. He knows all about Gail's disease—all about the slow deterioration of motor abilities, the deceptive remissions. He knows all about me, too, I suppose. He can probably isolate and identify whatever infirmity it is in me that's making me do this, making me leave her, making me run.

I follow Bill into the apartment and introduce him around the room. Deeker even shakes his hand. "We're trying to figure out how to get this *armoire*"—he emphasizes my French pronunciation of the word—"through that doorframe."

"Ah," Bill says, then clears his throat.

Della pulls on one of the armoire's cracked porcelain handles. "Can we take these doors off?" she asks.

Once everyone's attention is on the armoire, Bill pulls me aside. "Gail?" he asks me in a whisper.

"In the bedroom," I answer in a normal voice.

He nods his head gravely. "Understood."

We move the armoire. It takes all seven of us—four on the ends, Deeker underneath lifting with his back, Della and Hank directing from front and behind. Three times it almost tips over, and once we put a scrape in the outside door the size of a clamshell. By the time we finally hoist the thing up onto the truck and wedge it back against the boxes, Deeker and I are shedding dollops of sweat onto the metal floor of the truck.

"Lunch break!" Deeker shouts.

I look at my watch. I've ordered three pizzas for 11:30. Perfect timing. "You all go in and help yourself to the beer in the fridge. I'll get the pizzas from the corner."

Michele slips over to me. "Want some company?"

"Actually, no," I say, surprising myself a little.

"Fine," she answers quickly. I've surprised her, too.

"It's just that I, kind of, don't."

"It's fine, Peter, fine," she says, trying to figure me. "I'll just stay here and talk soulfully with your doctor friend."

The back door of the truck rumbles as Deeker slides it shut. I watch them all pile into the building, pull the front door closed, and snap the anchoring pegs into place. Della waves to me through the thick glass pane to the right of the door.

"Leave it unlocked!" I tell her.

I take a breath and then walk down my block to get the pizzas. It's turning chilly. The leaves of the London plane trees have already reached their exhausted shade of green, the color they turn just before edging into brownness and falling. I look for a particular tree—the one just after the hydrant—that has the phrase "Onyx Rules" carved into the bark. Trees were why Gail and I came to Brooklyn in the first place. For trees and lots of room and a place to be alone together as her health got worse. Fighting multiple sclerosis together among the historic brownstones. It seemed a frightening idea at the time—but just frightening enough to be romantic and right. That was the way we thought then.

Hank is in the middle of a story when I get back. He's sprawled on the floor, leaning against the brown steamer trunk in the living room. The rest are scattered around the room, all of their legs pointing toward Hank like spokes. I wonder who, if any of them, has been in to see Gail while I was gone.

"Naturally," Hank goes on as I put the pizzas on the table, "since I've only ordered an appetizer and I'm alone, the waitress thinks I'm some kind of out-of-town pauper who can't afford a main course, so she's rude, she practically throws the eggplant in my lap, so I think, no tip for you, my dear, but then I think, oh God, if I don't leave a tip, it'll just confirm what she already thinks of me, so I've got to, you know, give her a tip, a big one, but then, damn it, I'd just be rewarding rudeness."

"So what did you do?" Annbeth asks him.

"I'm trapped. What *can* I do? So I just sit there. Then it comes to me . . ."

"What?"

"The check. But I'm still trapped."

"I tell you what I'd do," Deeker says, pointing with his bottle of beer. "I'd leave money on the table for the eggplant, then take two or three dollar bills, rip them in half in front of the waitress, and hand the right halves to her on my way out."

Everybody stares at him. "Correct me if I'm wrong, Peter," Michele says to me, "but I'd guess that Deeker would indeed do just that."

"He would."

Deeker puts his arms out—Ecce Homo style—and shrugs innocently.

"Seems to me you'd both be out three bucks," Della says, struggling to her feet.

Just then, the enormous figure of the driver appears in the doorway of the dining room, practically filling it. He's wearing a grimy unzipped jacket and worn chinos. Two lines of sweat run down from his temples, draining into his dark, close-cropped beard. "Excuse me," he says. "Can I use your phone a minute?"

It's a full second before I come to. "There's one in the kitchen," I say. "Through there."

He nods and then makes his way toward the back of the apartment, causing the half-empty bookcases to sway.

"Maybe he's calling his accomplice for another ax," Michele whispers to me over the pizza boxes.

"We're too many for him, maybe," Hank says. "One look at Deeker and he knew he'd need help to do us all in."

Deeker recognizes the irony, but looks pleased in spite of himself. "Must've been that he saw me carry that cabinet by myself."

"We were *all* impressed by that, honey," says Della.

I rip open the pizza boxes. Aromatic steam rises up among us, filling the room with warm, comforting smells. We each grab a slice and a napkin and head back to the living room, this time breaking up into separate conversations. "So tell me, Bill . . ." I hear Michele saying as she steers him toward the couch.

"We'll be moving soon?"

I turn, and it's the driver behind me, hands on his thick hips.

"Right after we eat," I tell him. Then: "Listen, why don't you have a piece of pizza with us? There's plenty to go around."

"Hey, thanks," he says, "but I didn't earn it. My job's still coming up."

"This pizza doesn't have to be earned," I say.

He hesitates.

"Yeah, come on, Driver," Deeker yells from the living room. "Try the mushroom."

The huge man coughs once into his hand and then shrugs. He tears off a slice of extra-cheese from the semicircle of pie.

"Let me get you a beer to go with it," I say, heading toward the kitchen.

"No beer when I'm driving," he says, "but if you got a Diet Coke or something."

I come back with the soda, and the driver's already sitting on the floor of the living room, talking to my friends. He's explaining why the company rules won't allow him to help load and unload the van. "We broke too many things," he says, a comma of mozzarella punctuating the side of his red-lipped mouth. "One guy sued. So now we just drive. It's kind of embarrassing."

"We understand," Michele tells him.

"Most people got lots of friends to help them, anyway." He looks up at me as I hand him the soda. "Like you."

They all look at me for a second.

"Say shucks," says Deeker.

We, all eight of us, just occupy the half-filled room for a second. Again, I'm straining to hear something that may not be there—the hesitation, the unspoken reproach. Can friends be so forgiving, so loyal? A horn blows in the street outside.

"I want to go in for a minute," I tell them. "You all go out to the van when you're done. I'll be a couple minutes."

I head down the lightless hallway to our bedroom at the front of the apartment. The door is closed. The plankwood floor at my feet glows dully with light from the wide space under the door. Moving quickly, I touch the crystal doorknob and go in without knocking.

Gail is pulled up to the front window, reading. The light, much whiter now, washes across her shoulder-length straw-colored hair. She looks up when I come in. The wheelchair creaks as she moves—that luxuriant, smoky rasp of leather against metal.

"All done?" she asks.

I close the door behind me. "They're finishing up the pizza and then we're going." I step across the room and lower myself onto the unmade bed, right across from her. The mattress gives beneath me; I've already forgotten how soft this mattress is.

"So," she says.

"I promised you, no speeches."

"Did I make the same promise?"

I laugh. "No, I guess not." I rub my hand back and forth on the rough surface of the emerald wool blanket.

"A couple of things," she begins, closing the book in her lap. "My mother will pick up the extra wheelchair at your parents' on Thursday. And as far as the mail goes, do I write 'Please Forward' or save it for you to pick up?"

It's a loaded question, I suppose. I look down at the blanket under my hand. The coarse green weave reminds me of farmland as seen from an airplane window. "I'll let you know about that. I'll call."

We sit for a moment, a few moments, a minute. Our bodies seem to want the time to reorient themselves to each other, as if something physical needs to happen, an adjustment.

"When does your mother arrive?" I ask finally.

Gail does her comic grimace, looking a little relieved. "She wants to stop off at some furniture outlet first. She needs a chaise longue for the back yard at home. She says she'll be here by four."

"And Ellen?"

"The movers are coming tomorrow at eight in the morning, God save me." She lifts the book from her lap and places it on the cold radiator under the window. "It'll be like college again, rooming with Ellen. And Eberson seems willing to put her name on the lease."

"That's great," I tell her. "Perfect."

"Perfect," she says.

"I should go now." I get up from the bed and lean over to kiss her. She reaches up and embraces me briefly. I can detect the subtle palsy in her movements, the worsening stiffness. I let go of her shoulders. This is what it feels like to be despicable, I say to myself. But even now, as I'm leaving, I can't quite believe it. I just wasn't strong enough for this, I tell myself. It's as simple as that.

Gail sinks back into the groaning leather of her wheelchair. She smiles. She claims to understand me, to forgive me, though I'm not sure she really does. I've never been entirely certain of what Gail really thinks.

I turn and step toward the door.

"The seat," she says as I turn the knob. "Don't forget to put the seat back on the lift before you leave. And put back the other wheelchair downstairs."

My last duties. "Right." I turn to look at her again, but her face has already shifted to the white light of the window. "Call you next week." I open the door, step into the hallway, and pull the door shut behind me.

They're all out in the van, waiting for me. I can see from their faces—the expressions of nervous expectation—that they're waiting for a sign. "Everything's OK," I tell them. Michele nods, seeming encouraged if not convinced. Della sticks out her arm to help me up into the back of the truck. The vast space is only partially filled with boxes and my furniture. The rest is people.

"Hey," I say, slipping toward the front of the truck to talk to the driver. "What do you say I drive?"

The driver frowns at me. "Against the rules," he says.

"I drove a rig twice this size one summer," I lie. "I can handle it."

The driver hesitates a moment but then shrugs. "What the hell," he says. He opens the door, steps down to the sidewalk. As I slip into the warmth of the worn vinyl seat, he goes around the truck and climbs in the back.

I turn the key. The engine stumbles to attention, and I hear the back door of the truck shunt into place. "We're set!"

Michele shouts from behind. I rev the engine and maneuver the long, unwieldy stick into first. The truck lurches ahead as we start off.

"There's play in that clutch!" the driver yells to me over the engine noise. "You got to get used to it."

I nod and pull the stick down into second. The truck lurches less this time.

Bill, beside me in the passenger seat, smiles and braces his bony hand against the dash. I can tell from his face that he's also performing a last duty here. After this, his debts of friendship will be paid. He won't have to pretend to be sympathetic anymore. Maybe that's what they all think. Maybe I'll never hear from any of them again. They'll forget they even knew me.

I press down on the accelerator. The engine bellows like something feral and eager beneath me. The truck is a monster, I tell myself. And an image comes to me—of this wild-eyed, unkempt, unrepentant monster, this appalling creature that has managed to devour my friends, my furniture, my life. "It's a monster!" I shout aloud, feeling joyful now, feeling invincible, as if I myself were the awful beast pawing down that street, searching for the nearest highway out of there.

Eclipse

*T*HE OWNER wants nobody by the windows today,"
says the waiter in a smoker's voice. He's wearing one of those
plastic pocket guards—ENGLEWOOD TOOL AND DIE printed
across the top, just above the tips of the pens. "We don't want
any lawsuits. With the eclipse and all." The man is serious.

"What about her?" I ask. I point to the old woman in
polka dots sitting at the window booth two places down. She's
all alone, staring into the plate glass with an empty coffee cup
in her hand.

The waiter shrugs. "This is the owner says, not me."

"C'mon, Dad," says Kenny, my oldest.

"It's ridiculous."

"It's fine, Dad. Let's go." Kenny rolls his eyes at his
brother. I embarrass him now.

"Well kids," I say finally. "The owner suggests one of those
booths in the corner."

"I *told* you it was dangerous," says Alex, my youngest, as
they slide out of the window booth. "Mrs. Zeltner says you
can go blind."

"That's only if you stare at it, Numb Nose."

"Revise that," I warn.

"That's only if you stare at it, *Alex*."

"But the owner said."

"The *owner*," Kenny says, eyes rolling again.

So I guide my pair of offspring past the waiter, deeper into the diner. Their heads bob against my open palms, heads like mine—too round, maybe; hair the color of year-old newspaper.

At the safe booth in the back, the waiter takes our order: three plates of home fries and scrambled, toasted English, cranberry juice. Alex asks for extra ketchup. "Ketchup's on the table," the waiter drones, clicking his ballpoint and sheathing it in his pocket guard like a rapier.

We settle, my sons and me. That other sun, not yet blocked, glares through the windows far behind us. "So I brought us some supplies," I say, untying my knapsack. "Essential stuff. For our expedition."

I'm happy. This is my Saturday—our Saturday. I have it all planned. Breakfast at our usual place. Overpeck Creek for the event itself. Then a drive into the city, the 1 P.M. show at the Hayden Planetarium, a late lunch at a hot dog cart in the park. My kids are mine until dinnertime.

"Eclipse hats," I announce then, pulling them out of my knapsack.

"Eclipse hats!" Alex shouts. I push one of the blue, long-brimmed baseball caps down over his ears. He laughs and touches the button on top of the hat like something magic.

"Specially designed to prevent that inadvertent glance upward." I plop another cap on Kenny's head and put on my own. "Don't leave home without it."

"What's that one?" Alex asks, pointing to the fourth cap.

"That was Annie's." Annie, their sister. "Nobody told me about this rehearsal she had today."

Kenny takes off his cap and gives his little brother a look.

"What else you have?" Alex, uncomfortable, asks.

I miss only one beat before reaching into the knapsack

again. "Observation devices," I say. "Untested, but theoretically they should work."

"That's cardboard," Kenny complains. The waiter comes by then and slides a plate of English muffins in front of him.

"Don't let the simplicity fool you. Galileo tested gravity with just a cannonball and a feather."

"How do they work?" asks Alex, one hand still on his cap.

I push aside my napkin and silverware to make room. We can hear the comforting clatter of thick dishes in the kitchen behind us. "The top piece, see, has a hole in it—a tiny, precision-drilled pinhole. You hold this top piece up, at an exact distance above the other, and the light enters the pinhole and projects a small image of the sun onto the bottom piece here." Alex is nodding his head in confusion. "Now, today we're only getting what they call a partial eclipse—ninety percent. It'll look something like a crescent moon."

"God," says Alex.

Kenny is looking skeptical but vaguely interested. He picks up an English muffin. "It's like a camera, Alex," he explains to his brother.

"You made these?" Alex asks me.

I smile. "In cooperation with NASA, yes."

Alex pulls his hand away from the cardboard. "God."

Kenny makes a noise. "He's joking, clamhead, don't you get it?"

"Hey, Ken—"

"I *know*," says Alex, quietly mortified. I can see his scalp blushing furiously under his thin, light hair.

We sit for a second. Kenny bites into his English muffin with a loud crunch. Then: "Hey Alex, look," he says, holding up the muffin. "My muffin's got an eclipse, see?"

Alex reluctantly looks up, then giggles. Kenny glances at me to see if he's made good.

"You're both out to breakfast," I say, bopping them each over the head with a piece of high-technology cardboard.

"That guy's playing with fire, man." Kenny points his stripped willow branch and then starts whipping the tall grass in front of him. "He looks up at that kite and it's good-night ladies."

Some guy is flying one of those black plastic kites that you can make dip and dive. The thing rattles in the wind like a log fire. I warn the kids not to look up at it.

"Good-night mister," says Alex, crouching next to me to watch the cardboard I'm manipulating. All three of us in our eclipse hats.

"We're getting something here, look," I say. We just have a dent in our little spot of light, but I'm excited myself.

"Lemme see." Alex moves forward, bumping the cardboard with the brim of his hat. I gather him between my arms, set his head under my chin, and realign the cardboard. Alex's hard scalp radiates heat, as his mother's always did. He smells like her, too—bay leaves. Kenny stands above us, whip in hand, watching.

"This is an actual image of what's happening now. The sun disappearing behind the moon."

Alex's head nods. "It's bending the sun like that?"

"Kenny," I say, preempting.

"No, *Alex*, it's just moving in front of it." Then, to me: "I wasn't gonna say anything." He whips the tip of his sneaker.

"He calls me stuff," says Alex.

"Hey, let's watch this astronomical event here, kids. Happens five times in your life if you're lucky, right?" We keep quiet and watch the blob of light change—agonizingly—into something like a distorted oval with two bumps in its side. The wind gusts, meanwhile, making the willows down by the creek throw their branches like ribbons. I can feel Alex's small hot body shift against my chest.

"So what's this play Annie's in?" I ask quickly.

"What play?" asks Alex, preoccupied with the cardboard.

I look up at Kenny. "Just some play," he lies, badly, then turns to stare at nothing in the grass ten feet away. Dirty trick, yes, but I had to make sure.

"You guys'll just have to tell her about this."

We take a break later, to give the instruments a rest. We're down by the creek. Kenny has his shoes off. He's wading in the glossy, ankle-deep water, trying to catch minnows with his hands. Alex is moving along the mud bank with his arms spread wide to shepherd the fish toward his brother.

"So how's Mom these days?" I shout over to them.

"She picks us up at school," Alex says. I turn this sentence over in my mind, checking for some kind of reproach. Does he think that *I* should pick them up at school?

"She likes her new job," Kenny says. "She sets up meetings for the mayor now, you know."

"I know."

"Dad knows about Mom," Alex says, trying for his brother's tone.

"Hey, is it me or is it getting darker?" The boys both freeze where they are. The light is changing. The willows, the water, the highway bridge behind it all suddenly look like something out of a Flemish painting—squat, sitting more heavily in place. "We must be reaching maximum blockage," I say.

The kids drag themselves out of the water and up the bank to me. "Can I?" Alex asks. I give him the two pieces of cardboard and guide his hands to the right focal length.

"It's like a fingernail or something!" Kenny shouts. "Like when you cut your fingernails?"

We can really see that little black disk moving now, eating up more and more of the sun. "Keep those hat brims down, men," I warn.

We watch for another five or ten minutes, until Alex's arms get tired and start swaying the image all over the cardboard. Kenny is whipping the grass again with his willow branch. Alex's head turns under my chin. He's looking at the creek. "It smells like crab shells here," he says.

Time to move on.

"Kenny uses deodorant now," Alex confides to me as we file out of the planetarium after the special eclipse show. His brother is ahead of us on the steps, out of earshot.

A little twinge of regret, sorrow. My son is old enough to use deodorant. "Happens to the best of us," I say. I'm still groggy, wondering if planetarium shows were this dull when I was young. I even dozed off once or twice, what with the darkness and the soft seats and that melodious, godlike voice all around. I think Kenny slept too. He stretches and yawns as he stands at the exit to wait for us. Stretches the way I do, elbows out, hands laced behind his neck.

"Now you can both understand what we saw this morning, right?"

No response.

OK, enough education for one day. "So who could use a hot dog in the park?"

We find a cart out near Sheep Meadow and eat some chili dogs. Then we kick off our shoes and walk through the rich hot grass. Sheep Meadow is jammed. We have to thread through knots of people, canteloupe- and nut-colored in the sun, lying on towels, listening to the radio, reading. We get to a less crowded place under some trees and collapse onto the grass. I lie back for a second, but then sit up, waving away a few fluorescent gnats that come to investigate.

Good a time as any, I think to myself. "Hey, men, see that brown building over there through the trees?"

Both heads turn to follow the line of my arm. The place looks empty and forbidding in the afternoon sun, the windows like dark holes. "I'm moving into that building next month."

"Moving?"

"Which one?" Alex insists.

"I'm only moving into the city to be closer to my work. I'll still be able to see you guys twice a week, don't worry."

"That's Dad's new building," Alex announces, not worried.

I swallow once, hard. They don't even *seem* upset. I should be relieved, I guess.

"Hey, check out this dog," Kenny says. He's running toward one of those glossy red dogs—Irish setters?—that you see in ads for scotch. The dog, catching sight of him, meets him halfway on the grass in an ecstasy of welcome. "All *right*," Alex says, following his brother.

The owners, a young, prosperous-looking couple with a spacey two-year-old between them, walk up—good shoes, good haircuts, the woman with glasses around her neck on a green string. She looks up at her husband. "You were right," she says, about some observation he must have made, and he smiles.

And God, he *is* right, I tell myself suddenly. Everything is right—the dog, the shoes. Why hadn't we ever had a dog? Why hadn't I run out to the pound one day and picked up a schnauzer or a beagle, never mind some sleek, magnetic animal like this? We lived in the suburbs, had a yard even.

The dog has knocked Alex to the ground. "Shasta!" the

man says, springing forward and hauling the dog back by the collar. Alex is crying when I lift him. There's a little curl of grass clinging to his wet cheek. "You're all right, trooper," I tell him.

"Sorry about that," the man says, trying to hold the excited animal. "He gets rambunctious."

"We're all right," I say. Alex is trembling in my arms. Even Kenny is cowed. He has himself on the other side of my legs from the dog. "That thing's too happy," he says, voice a little shaky with awe.

"I want to go back," demands Alex.

"Oh, c'mon, trooper," I say. "Relax, we're fine. Nobody's hurt." I reset the eclipse hat on his head. "Just a little local fauna."

"I want to *go*," Alex insists, pulling off the hat.

Kenny is holding me by the belt. "You know how he gets, Dad. He wants to go home to his little room."

I look at my older son. He wants to go too. That martyred tolerance around the eyes.

OK, so we drive back over the bridge.

Call it an early night.

The sun is still high over the rooftops when we turn into the old street. Alex, recovered now, is sitting between Kenny and me on the front seat. He has the bent-up pieces of cardboard in his hands, holding them as if they contained some kind of major scientific secret.

We pull up at the house. Looking down the alley, I can just make out Abby in the backyard, hovering over a smoky barbecue grill. My wife. Yes, I tell myself, a dog would have been perfect here. Something small, short-legged, loyal, and slightly ridiculous. A dog we could have laughed at in a kind, good-natured way.

"Hey men, one more piece of equipment I've been saving." I reach over the headrest and grab the knapsack.

"Uniforms!" Alex shouts as I take out the T-shirts and display them. I SURVIVED THE ECLIPSE, in red and yellow letters. I ironed the letters on myself.

"Thanks, Dad." They both lean toward me and let me kiss them on the head. Then they slide over to the car door and get out.

"I'll see you Wednesday night," I say. "Tell Annie we missed her today."

They cross in front of the car, Alex's hair just visible over the hood. "Your mother's in the back, by the way."

They change course, head toward the alley, waving.

"Tell her I said hello!"

"She knows you always say hello," says Kenny, without looking back.

I watch my two sons running down the alley toward the yard, trailing the cardboard and T-shirts behind them.

My hand is on the ignition key.

No, I say, maybe aloud. I open the car door and climb out. The sunshine glints off the hood of the car. It's turned almost balmy.

I make the decision not to check my hair in the side mirror of the car. But I do tuck my shirt more neatly into the waistband of my pants. Then I turn and follow my sons down the alley.

The back yard reveals itself slowly around the edge of the house—Abby bending to kiss her returning boys, little Annie looking at the hamburgers smoking on the grill. I'm almost around the corner when I see the man in the lawn chair under the stunted peach tree. He's older than me, graying, but handsome in a coarse, craggy way. On his lap is a blue, unfamiliar platter on which he's arranged large pink disks of ground beef.

The man looks up, sees me. An uncertain but welcoming smile appears on his face. He doesn't know me. He must think I'm one of the neighbors. One of Abby's neighbors stopping by for a drink. To meet him.

I nod. He looks down to put aside the platter of meat. He's about to get up from the chair. "Abby," he is saying.

Before he can look up again, I step back—breathing— and disappear behind the edge of my old brick house.

Uncle Isaac

ON THE WAY to pick up Uncle Isaac for his semiannual dental checkup, Michael Spielberg stopped on the Avenue to buy flypaper. He had a little difficulty finding some at first. The man in the hardware store said they hadn't carried flypaper since 1978, and the apathetic teenager at the Rite-Aid just looked at him as if she had never heard the word before (which, now that he thought about it, could possibly have been the case). But Michael persisted, retracing his steps up and down the busy commercial street crowded with early holiday shoppers. He knew that when his Uncle Isaac asked for flypaper, it was flypaper that Uncle Isaac wanted.

Finally, in the chaotic back aisles of the County Discount—among the half-unwound balls of string and the plastic water pistols in rainbow colors—he found a dusty roll of the paper, wrapped, appropriately enough, in brittle, fly-specked cellophane. "You're lucky," said the wiry middle-aged woman who checked him out, "we usually only sell this in summer." Her hair was a muddy red color that somehow reminded Michael of tropical river deltas. He thanked her kindly, and told her not to bother putting the roll into a bag.

His task accomplished, Michael walked back to his car and drove the rest of the way to his uncle's. Uncle Isaac lived in a pleasant garden-apartment complex not far from the school where Michael taught seventh-grade geography. The low brick buildings were surrounded by London plane trees—large, elegant trees that in summer shaded a central courtyard and a small fountain illuminated by colored lights. Now, on this last day of November, the trees were skeletal but still impressive, the bark shearing off in curved, brittle chunks.

Michael climbed the five brick steps to his uncle's front door and knocked. After a moment, he heard a voice calling, "It's open!" from deep within the apartment, muffled by several layers of wall.

Michael sighed. Despite numerous lectures over the years about burglars and psycho killers, Isaac persisted in keeping his door unlocked. But Michael refused to resign himself to his uncle's intransigence. Turning the knob, he entered the apartment and locked the door firmly behind him.

"I'll be a few minutes yet," said Uncle Isaac from another room. "Did you get what I asked for?"

Michael held up the roll of flypaper, as if his uncle could see through walls. "It took me three tries! Nobody stocks this stuff anymore. They all wanted to sell me No-Pest Strips!"

"Aaak! Chemicals!" Michael could hear his uncle banging around in his bedroom closet. By the sound of it, Uncle Isaac would be late again—his usual fifteen or twenty minutes.

Michael shook his head. He crossed the apartment and put the flypaper on the gray Formica counter that divided the dining nook from the kitchenette. Three large-format cameras stood on tripods in a corner of the room, looking like hopeless three-legged extraterrestrials. Uncle Isaac, formerly a studio photographer specializing in baby pictures, had stopped taking photographs years ago—ever since his unsuccessful cataract operation—but he still liked to be surrounded by his gear.

"Call me old-fashioned," Uncle Isaac said then, continuing

the conversation as he came out of the bedroom, "but I don't trust those No-Pest Strips. Besides, I like to watch my flies dying slowly. I think starvation is an appropriate death for vermin, don't you?"

Uncle Isaac was a short man—five-foot-five, if Michael had to guess—with a bulbous nose and a slight potbelly. He was wearing one of his more emphatic outfits today: a royal-blue turtleneck with matching jacket and pants, rose-tinted glasses, and a large brass medallion around his neck. The medallion, which Uncle Isaac had picked up at a market in Cancún years ago, depicted a gold sun surrounded by a border of zodiac signs.

He had a pair of white calfskin loafers in his hand. "I've just got to put these on and do a few more things and then we can go," he said.

"What time is the appointment?"

"Not till two-fifteen, but we can be late. God knows I've sat around in that man's reception room enough times waiting for *him*. All of that laughing gas must have done something to the old bird's sense of time."

"I like your shoes," Michael said.

Uncle Isaac flashed him a bright, ironic smile. "Thanks, they're new." He collapsed into the couch and started putting on the shoes. "Your Uncle Howard thinks they're hideous."

Uncle Howard, Isaac's older brother, lived in a high-rise old-age home across town. Of Michael's three maternal uncles, Uncle Howard was the most conservative, the most likely to disapprove of things like white calfskin shoes. Uncle Isaac and his younger brother Sam usually made Howard miserable, taunting him with their unapologetic flamboyance, but they both loved him fiercely and were clearly in awe of his position as the family patriarch.

"Since when have you listened to fashion advice from Uncle Howard?" Michael asked, glancing briefly at his own shoes—oxblood loafers whose studied casualness he liked.

Uncle Isaac, having slipped into the new shoes, pulled up his socks and glanced at his nephew. "Who says I listen to him? No, child, your eldest uncle still wears the clothes he wore back in the forties, after the war. The more successful he became, the less his wardrobe changed. Rumor has it there's an old portrait of Howard in his attic that keeps getting nattier." Isaac snorted at his own joke, which was not new. "What do I owe you for the flypaper?" he asked.

"My treat," Michael said, staring fondly at his uncle. Isaac already owed him a thousand dollars, so another $1.95 hardly seemed to matter. Michael had lent him the money—secretly—that spring. In earlier years, of course, Uncle Isaac had been a great philanthropist, giving large chunks of his income to all sorts of lefty causes (including, to Uncle Howard's annoyance, a radical kibbutz somewhere in the Negev), but nowadays Uncle Isaac couldn't afford to be so generous. His nephew knew for a fact that he often fell behind in his rent.

"You're so good to me," Isaac said, getting up from the couch. He clapped his chubby hands once and rubbed them together. His problem eye looked lurid and enormous behind the thick tinted lens of his glasses. "OK, I'll just find my wrap and we'll be gone."

Isaac got his coat, an incongruously drab mackintosh, from the hall closet and slipped into it. Then he pulled a blue fisherman's cap over his thin reddish-gray hair. "Ready," he said in satisfaction to his nephew, "and hardly late at all."

They left the apartment and walked out to the car. As they descended the stairs from the raised courtyard to the street, Michael noticed a brittleness, a cautious hesitancy, in his uncle's step. He was tempted to grab the older man's elbow as they went down, but didn't. Uncle Isaac, he knew, was sufficiently embarrassed by the fact that he now had to be driven everywhere. The thought that he also had to be helped down stairs would probably not be pleasant for him.

They settled into Michael's battered Corolla and waited while Michael raced the engine to warm it. Uncle Isaac pulled on a pair of suede gloves, his breath vaporizing in the cold, closed space of the car. "So tell me about your love life," he said then, flashing his nephew an impish grin.

Michael laughed aloud—a hearty, spontaneous laugh that felt good in his chest. "You're a very nosy person, Uncle," he said.

"Of course I am. It's part of my charm."

Michael reached forward and wiped his side of the windshield with a bare hand. "I'm seeing somebody," he said. "This woman who also teaches at my school. Karen."

"Oh," Isaac said, pursing his lips, "a woman."

Michael frowned. "Let's not start that again."

"Start what? If you insist on perpetuating this myth of bisexuality—"

"*You* say it's a myth—you and your queenie friends."

"Watch your tongue," Uncle Isaac said, slapping his nephew backhand on the arm. He was enjoying this. "A bisexual is somebody who can't make up his mind. That is all."

"You can't imagine it yourself," Michael said, enjoying it somewhat less, "so you don't believe in it. You probably don't believe in heterosexuality either." Michael looked over at his uncle, who was just sitting quietly now, his eyebrows up and a faint, knowing smile on his lips. "Sexuality," Michael intoned carefully, and with quotation marks, "is a continuum."

"Aaagh!" his uncle cried. He covered his ears with his gloved hands. "You sound like that brother of yours. What does he call himself nowadays?"

Michael looked out the windshield. "Pansexual," he said.

"Pansexual!" Uncle Isaac shook his head at the roof of the car.

Michael's brother Josh, an artist/plumber's assistant, lived in the city. Two years ago, Josh decided to dye his hair platinum and wear only white clothing. His studio in Chelsea was now all-white as well, with no furniture except for a few wispy canvas chairs and dozens of silver-framed mirrors. "To be honest," Michael said finally, "I think Josh has no sexuality at all. I think he's asexual."

Uncle Isaac nodded. "I agree with you there, child." He put his fingertips up to his bad eye and carefully rubbed it, his gold pinky ring catching the winter light. Then: "Pansexual! Sounds like something to do with little boys playing flutes, if you ask me."

The two men looked at each other. Almost in unison, they began snickering, their shoulders bobbing cheerfully. It went on like that for seconds, almost a minute, until Michael, wiping his eyes, said, "Put on your seat belt, you old thing," and slowly pulled the car away from the curb.

Michael found a parking place in the large Shop-More lot behind the dentist's office. Dr. Shriver, whom every member of the Ellerman and Spielberg families had patronized for years, practiced in a street-level storefront a few steps off a major shopping avenue. The street was almost identical to the one Michael had scoured earlier in search of flypaper, only this one, a few miles south, was in an older, more congested part of the New York metropolitan sprawl. Dr. Shriver's office held horrifying childhood memories for Michael, and even now he couldn't help shuddering at the thought of that anonymous waiting room. The image of its coarse brown carpeting, antiseptic-smelling rest room, and rack of bent-up, months-old magazines still held for him a stubborn aura of sheer terror.

Uncle Isaac, as if sensing something of Michael's revulsion, paused as they approached the small maroon awning. "What time is it?" he asked, glancing nervously up the street. Above, dark tentacles of cloud were creeping stealthily across a gray sky. It would rain soon.

"Just past two," Michael said.

"Well, then, we're early. Let's not give the smug man that satisfaction. I have to pick up some tomatoes anyway."

"Tomatoes?"

"Whatever. Come along, there's that Shop-More back there. We can go in from the street up ahead." Uncle Isaac, hunching his raincoat higher on his round shoulders, pushed past his nephew and started for the street. He stopped when he noticed that his nephew was not following. "Come *along*, will you, child? He won't see us until two-forty-five no matter what time we decide to waltz in there."

Michael, recognizing the justice of this, heaved an exaggerated sigh and followed his uncle's hurrying figure to the corner.

"This way," Isaac said, barely pausing.

They made their way down the busy avenue, Uncle Isaac taking the center of the sidewalk with the regal confidence of a parade float. Michael caught a few people staring—a teenaged mother with a tiny child on her arm, an older man outside a barber shop who gawked at them with unconcealed amazement. Uncle Isaac seemed not to notice. His uncle walked in public, Michael thought, with the same self-conscious casualness that he had seen in celebrities on the streets of New York. The thought made him suddenly, irrationally, proud.

The automatic door of the Shop-More hissed as it opened for them. "Now make yourself useful, Michael," Uncle Isaac said, looking around, "Find the produce aisle for me."

Michael read down the line of signs his uncle could not see. "Aisle Seven. At the end," he told him finally.

They pushed past several overloaded carts and found themselves in front of a wall of vegetable and fruit bins. Michael was surprised at the quality of the cold-weather produce—rows and rows of smooth-skinned eggplants, oranges, apples, each touched by a spot of reflected light. He remembered something he had told his geography students one day, how any aisle in any American supermarket represented the produce of countless countries and climates. "Modern transportation!" he had exclaimed at the front of the class, trying to infect them with a little enthusiasm for the world. "We live in an age of variety, of diversity, of plenty! Do you realize that?" They all just slumped lower in their seats, looking down at their textbooks for the answer.

"Oh, these tomatoes look dreadful!" Uncle Isaac said now, clucking his tongue. He picked up a few of the lumpy pink spheres and tossed them higher on the pile. "Absolutely awful! Oh young man!" He went up to a blond-haired man, hardly young, who stood in shirtsleeves and loosened tie at the swinging doors to the storeroom. The man was chatting with the scale clerk, an enormous Hispanic teenager. "Are you the manager?" Uncle Isaac asked.

The blond man turned and saw Uncle Isaac. A faint grin creased his face. "Yeah, I'm the manager. What can I do you for?"

"Have you had a look at those tomatoes? They're a disgrace!"

Michael saw the manager sneak a quick, conspiratorial look at the scale clerk. "Are they really? Well that's a shame, a damn shame."

"Aren't there any others?"

"We only got the kind of tomatoes you eat," the man said, sending the scale clerk at his shoulder into giggles.

Isaac spun around, stepping back toward his nephew. "We'll get nothing sensible from them, clearly," he said, only slightly flustered.

"Hey," the manager called out after him. "Nice shoes."

Michael glared back at the two men, a band of anger tightening around his ribs.

"Forget it, forget it," Uncle Isaac said to him. He turned his nephew bodily toward the front of the store. "Come on, Michael. I'll live without tomatoes for a day." He pushed his nephew through the checkout lines to the exit.

It was 2:20 when they got back to the maroon awning in front of the dentist's office. "Well, we'll have to wait after all," Uncle Isaac complained. He nodded politely when Michael opened the door for him. "What a well-brought-up boy you are," he said, letting his nephew know that everything was just fine.

The waiting room, Michael noticed immediately, was as it had always been, only now, in honor of the season, a yellowing poinsettia sat in a pot on the central table. The room was empty except for a small child—a preschool girl in a neat white shirt and tiny overalls. "My mommy's inside," the girl said to them as they entered, to make sure they knew.

"I'm delighted to hear it, sweetheart," Uncle Isaac said, honoring her with his most charming avuncular smile. Michael helped him off with the old mackintosh and hung it in the closet, jangling the metal hangers. Then he took his uncle's cap. "Mr. Ellerman?" the receptionist asked from the sliding glass window.

"In the flesh," Uncle Isaac said. He stepped over to the window. "You're new here, aren't you? I haven't seen you before."

The receptionist, a tired-eyed brunette with studious, black-framed glasses, nodded. "My third week." Then, in an awkward, businesslike tone, she said: "Dr. Shriver can see you right away."

Uncle Isaac's eyes grew large. "Be still, my heart!" he said, putting a hand to his chest. "My ears must be deceiving me."

"Yes, but—" The receptionist shuffled a few papers on her desk. "We have a new prepayment policy. I'll have to ask you for a check in advance of treatment."

"Well, dear," Uncle Isaac began calmly. He leaned against the sill and put his head through the open window, making his sun medallion clatter on the wall. "I'm afraid I haven't brought a check with me. No one told me of this new policy."

"We accept Visa and MasterCard."

Uncle Isaac threw up his hands. "I have nothing with me, I'm afraid. You'll just have to trust me this once."

"There is already an outstanding balance of $147.48, past due."

Uncle Isaac's jaw stiffened. "May I speak to Dr. Shriver, please?" His voice began to take on the high-pitched, droning quality that Michael recognized as a harbinger of trouble.

"Just a moment," the receptionist said. Her hand went up to the window and slid it shut. "Harridan," Uncle Isaac said under his breath, but then turned to the little girl on the couch. "I didn't mean you, dear."

"Uncle Isaac," Michael said, moving closer to his uncle, "I've got a few checks with me . . ."

"Don't even think about it, Michael." He twisted his gold chain around his index finger, thinking. "I'll talk with Shriver and everything will be all right. Hunky-dory."

After a moment, the door to the inner office opened. Dr. Shriver, a graying but still trim figure in a spotless white coat, stood rubbing his hands together. "Hello, Isaac," he said. "And Michael, how are you?"

Michael nodded and mumbled something, feeling the old uneasiness.

"Dr. Shriver—" Isaac began.

The dentist held up his two palms. "Let's talk about this in my consulting room, shall we?" He stepped to the side and gestured for Isaac to come into the inner office.

Uncle Isaac turned to Michael. "Wait here!" he commanded. Then he hurried past Dr. Shriver into the shiny corridor beyond. Dr. Shriver smiled once at Michael and let the door shut behind him with a tiny whoosh.

Michael, trying to calm his own agitation, took a seat in the armchair across from the little girl. She had opened a magazine on the glass-topped table and was now kneeling in front of it, turning pages. Michael watched her, rubbing his forehead, his uncle's cap on his knees. He was worried. It was obvious that Uncle Isaac was floundering. He had worked for himself for most of his life; his photo studio on the Avenue could not have been particularly lucrative. Michael wondered if his uncle had put aside a retirement nest egg. Then he wondered if he was giving money to obscure causes again. The family would be furious.

The little girl across the table sighed and turned another page. Michael saw the magazine she was reading: *Cosmopolitan*. This observation made him slightly ill. He wondered if children still read the magazines he had read in dentists' offices as a child—*Ranger Rick,* and *Highlights for Children,* with the Goofus and Gallant comic strip. He remembered once telling an uncle—it may have been Isaac—that he liked the naughty Goofus better than the perfectly-mannered Gallant, that Goofus was smarter, not such a goody-two-shoes. He remembered the uncle approving, smiling and patting him on the shoulder, saying that Michael was right, absolutely right, to think so.

Suddenly the door to the inner office sprang open again. Uncle Isaac came cruising through, his teeth grasping one side of his lower lip, his medallion clanging. "Uncle Isaac?" Michael asked, rising from his chair.

Isaac made a beeline for the closet and began fooling with his mackintosh on the hanger.

"Here, let me get that," Michael said.

"I've got it, I'm fine, I'm fine. Put your own coat on." Isaac grabbed the cap from his nephew's hand and pulled it down around his florid ears.

"Uncle—"

"Don't say a word!" he commanded. He pushed past his nephew and pulled open the door. "Bye now," the little girl called out from the couch.

Outside, freezing rain had started to fall. It pattered the sidewalk like tiny white spitballs, bouncing on the concrete. Michael hurried down the street after his uncle, who despite his age was moving at an impressive clip around the building toward the parking lot.

"Uncle Isaac," Michael shouted after him. He thought of the image they must be creating—two grown men slipping on the slick pavement, holding onto car hoods for support.

Finally they reached Michael's car. "You've locked the goddamned door!" Isaac wailed, pulling at the handle. Michael quickly unlocked the passenger door and opened it for his uncle, who lowered himself into the front seat. He waved Michael away impatiently. "I can close it myself, thank you."

Michael rounded the front of the car and got in on the driver's side. Frozen rain sizzled on the metal roof.

"Say nothing," Isaac pronounced then. "Start the car and drive me home and say nothing."

Michael stared across at his uncle for a long moment before obeying. He turned on the wipers, which swept away the half-melted pellets of rain with an almost brutal efficiency.

"Uncle Isaac, you need money," Michael said.

Uncle Isaac sat with his arms crossed over his chest. The windshield wipers began making lewd rubbery sounds as they swept over the glass. "Of course I need money."

Michael nodded at the windshield. "I can help you out," he began. "We can arrange something."

"That's exactly, *precisely*, what that dentist said to me!" Isaac shouted. He pulled off his cap and knocked the wetness from it. "Damn you and him both."

"There's a difference," Michael said. "I'm family."

"I don't care, I don't care, I don't care." Isaac was biting the thumb of his suede glove.

"I could lend you another thousand . . ."

"Why is the automatic assumption that I need your concern?" Isaac screamed toward the ceiling, clenching his fists at his temples.

"What's wrong with you?" Michael shouted.

"Nothing, nothing," Isaac said, calmer now. He took off his glasses and began cleaning them with a scrap of tissue. "I'm a blind old man, that's all. That's what's wrong with me."

Michael watched his uncle rubbing furiously at the lenses.

"Drive away now," Uncle Isaac said. "I'm ready to go now."

After a moment, Michael obeyed. But when he put the car into drive and tried to pull away, the front left wheel flapped and rumbled. "Shit," he muttered.

"Oh lovely," Uncle Isaac said. "Now we've got a flat tire on top of it all."

Michael turned off the engine. "I'll work as fast as I can," he said quietly. "But it's going to take a few minutes. A few minutes minimum."

When Michael was five years old, the summer before he entered kindergarten, the Ellerman family threw an informal reunion in the back yard of Michael's uncle Howard. This was when all of the Ellerman siblings lived in houses—two-bedroom ranches and small colonials, all within a ten-minute walk of one another. Grandma Ellerman, seated majestically in a lawn chair, presided over the occasion, while Howard and his best friend Pete turned hamburgers and sausages on the grill. It was a hot day—the Fourth of July—and people passed the afternoon drinking beer, playing lawn darts, and listening to Howard's collection of Peggy Lee recordings on his cheap stereo with one burned-out speaker.

Uncle Isaac took pictures that day. He hovered at the periphery with his cameras and tripods, "capturing moments," as he called it. He caught Michael's mother sitting at the picnic table with her boss from the board of education; he caught Uncle Sam holding three-year-old Josh on his shoulders. Afterwards, as the sun got lower and the party began winding down, Isaac asked Michael if he wanted to help develop the pictures. Michael, who was getting bored with the reunion anyway, agreed, and so the two of them walked the few short blocks to Isaac's house.

In the basement darkroom, after Isaac had gone through the boring process of developing the film, Michael stood beside his uncle in the eerie red glow of the safelight. Isaac was taking some of the more promising negatives and printing them on 8 × 10 paper. Michael watched as his uncle projected the images—unrecognizable in negative—onto the stiff sheets of glossy paper. He would project each negative for seconds at a time, occasionally dodging or burning in parts of the image with gestures that seemed almost dancelike to the young boy. After exposing a few dozen sheets, Isaac turned off the enlarger and handed the blank sheets to Michael. "Just stick them one by one into that developer tray, child," he said quietly, "and see what happens."

Michael did what he was told. And after a few moments, he was amazed to see figures appearing on the paper out of nowhere. Likenesses of his family—scenes he had witnessed just an hour earlier—assembled themselves, emerging from the white mists. Michael began laughing. "It's remarkable, isn't it?" his uncle said, standing behind him. Michael threw more sheets into the developer, one after the other, the images appearing faster and faster. He couldn't stop laughing. It was all so astonishing, that his uncle could do this thing, this magic. His own Uncle Isaac.

Now, as he began changing the flat tire on his car in the Shop-More parking lot, Michael found himself thinking about that Fourth of July. He recalled most vividly the surge of rapture he felt, watching those pictures develop. It was the same feeling he now tried to instill in his geography students. That hunger for the world around them. The delighted surprise of what is.

"Are you sure you've got that jack-thing positioned properly?" Uncle Isaac asked, hovering behind him as Michael spun off the lug nuts with a cross-shaped wrench.

"It's fine. Why don't you go shopping or something?"

"Hold on. Something's happening at the supermarket. Over behind Shriver's building. Looks like a demonstration brewing."

Michael stopped work to see what his uncle was talking about. Isaac was right. There seemed to be a crowd assembling, mostly teenagers, unfurling makeshift banners and handing around placards. Michael could just make out what a few of them said: MORE WORK, LESS PAY—NO WAY!! and SHOP-MORE EQUALS SHOP-POOR!

"It's a picket," Michael said. "Somebody's on strike."

"Indeed." Uncle Isaac pulled his cap lower over his ears and buttoned up his mackintosh. "You get back to that tire, child. I'll amuse myself."

"Just be careful," Michael said. "They look pretty rowdy. And the whole parking lot is like a sheet of ice."

"I'll skate, then," Uncle Isaac answered, stepping awkwardly toward the little crowd.

It took Michael fifteen minutes to change the tire. When he had pounded the hub cap back into place, he straightened up and looked around for his uncle. Isaac was not difficult to find. His rotund form in the cap and raincoat was clearly distinguishable from those of the two dozen or so lanky, leather-jacketed teenagers. It looked like Uncle Isaac was arguing with a few of them, waving his arms energetically. The teenagers around him seemed on the verge of turning ugly.

"Oh God," Michael muttered to himself, hurrying across the parking lot to his uncle.

One of the teenagers was shouting as Michael approached. "Fuckin' right!" the boy was saying. He held a piece of a brick in his hand. "The bastards won't listen to anything else!"

A couple of the others picked up stones and bottles and pieces of shattered crates that lay strewn around the Shop-More's dumpsters. They moved forward, toward, then past Uncle Isaac. As Michael broke into a trot, a few of them started heaving rocks and sticks at the large windows of the Shop-More. Most of the debris bounced off the heavy plate glass, but then, with a splintering crash, one of the poster-covered windows collapsed. Someone on the street screamed.

"Uncle Isaac!" Michael said, reaching his uncle at last. "Let's get out of here!"

The teenagers were louder now. Three of them began turning over the huge green dumpsters. Another big window, struck by a brick, shattered to the ground.

"Uncle Isaac!"

His uncle was watching with gloved hands pressed delightedly to his mouth. People were streaming in panic out the front entrance of the Shop-More. Then, as Michael watched in disbelief, Uncle Isaac bent over shakily and picked up a small stone. He made as if to throw it at the Shop-More, but he stopped.

"What the hell are you doing?" Michael shouted, grabbing his uncle's arm. "Are you crazy?"

But Uncle Isaac pulled away. His cheeks were flushed; his breath created puffs of vapor around his head. "Leave me alone, child," he whispered, stooping to pick up another, bigger stone. "Can't you see I'm starting something?"

Uncle Isaac turned and tossed the stone straight at one of the back windows of Dr. Shriver's office. It passed through the smoked pane, leaving a hole the size of a golf ball. "Louder, boys!" he shouted then to the rioting teenagers. "Louder! Let them know you're there!"

—for A.B., in memoriam

Ever Alice

*T*HE FIRST THING she ever did to me was ruin Emily Dickinson.

I was splayed over one of those electric blue chairs in the town library, flipping through *The Collected Poems*. She appeared suddenly—all eyes and auburn hair—and eased herself onto the low oak table in front of me. "Did anyone ever tell you," she said, crossing those muscular, ivory-toned legs, "that any poem by Emily Dickinson can be sung to the tune of 'The Yellow Rose of Texas?'"

The legs were distracting, but I managed: "Texas?"

"Try it. Take any first stanza." She sang, softly, leaning forward: *"Hope is the thing with feathers / That perches in the soul . . ."*

She smelled of violets, olive oil, bitter lemon. As I watched her sing, my tongue felt like a thick, squat creature in my mouth.

—And she was right?

—What do you mean, right?

—About Emily Dickinson.

—Of course she was right. Give or take a syllable here and there. That's the point.

—(singing experimentally) *Be-ee-cause I could not stop for*

Death / He kindly stopped for me; / The carriage held but just ourselves / And Immortality. Remarkable.

—Not the word I'd use.

—But why would someone do that? It's like planting a virus.

—That's why someone would do it.

—(singing) *Success is counted sweetest / By those who ne'er succeed* . . .

—You see what I'm talking about.

—(still singing) *I had been hungry all the years; / My noon had come, to dine* . . .

—Stop it.

—. . . *I, trembling drew the table near* . . .

—Stop, damn it.

We slept together that night. My house. She made me lie face down on the mattress. She was running the edge of her top teeth over the cobbles of my backbone. Her long hair brushed over my shoulders and trickled down my ribs. I felt the heat of her, the short rough triangle of hair, on the back of my thighs. She was whispering something, but I couldn't make out what it was.

After a while, I turned over. I had to. I was forgetting what she looked like. She sat back against her haunches, annoyed. Her hair seemed different in that light, darker somehow. Her eyes wouldn't meet mine.

"Why won't you tell me your name?" I asked her.

She laughed—a curt, coaxing laugh. "I *have* told you my name," she said, starting to massage the front of my thighs. "Alice. A is for Alice. You just forgot."

—And was that true?

—That she'd already told me her name? I guess so. I'm

not really sure. When she said it, it sounded familiar, so maybe she had. I'm not sure.

She left before midnight. I had fallen asleep—we'd drunk a couple of bourbons in bed—and when I woke up, she was just pulling a black cotton sweater over her bare breasts. She was dressed. I was surprised.

"You're leaving?" I asked.

She grabbed her watch off the bureau and began strapping it around her thin wrist. "It's gotten colder. Mind if I borrow a jacket?"

She had already taken the jacket from the hall closet, my brown leather bomber. It lay at the bottom of the bed, weighing down my feet like a pet.

"Sure," I said, though I didn't want her to take it. It was the jacket I always wore. Wool lining, and the shell felt like warm skin to the touch. "I want to see you again," I said.

She smiled. She picked up the jacket and shouldered into it, her slim body disappearing into the folds. "I've left my number on the pad by the phone. Don't call between 10 and 3 in the afternoon." She came over and sat on the edge of the bed. I felt her hand on my crotch through the sheet. She ran the other hand over the nape of my neck. "Call me," she said, but then she was gone. She didn't kiss me. I heard her moving down the hallway toward the front door. She was humming something I didn't recognize.

—You never found the phone number.

—I looked all over. At first I thought the slip of paper might have blown behind something when she opened the front door. It was windy that night. So I checked under the furniture. I even pulled up the rug near the phone table. Nothing.

—So she lied.

—So the phone number wasn't there. I couldn't contact her.

—Basically, what you're telling me is she stole your jacket.

—She didn't steal my jacket. I still have the goddamn jacket.

—You got it back from her?

—I got it back. Eventually.

—(pause) Do you have a picture?

—I took a couple shots of her, later, a week or so later. But I never got them developed.

—Why not?

—Because they're still in the camera.

—The camera that's missing.

—The camera that's missing.

I couldn't sleep for several nights. My head was full of vague, fleeting aches, like half-thoughts. And every time I went to the library, I found myself looking around for her. I thought I saw her once, a figure browsing deep in the stacks, but when I went back there, it was someone else, someone much younger, who didn't even look like her. I couldn't concentrate. Shit, I thought, I've got a book to write, I can't fool around like this. I've got to get back to work.

Then, one evening the following week, she was there, in the parking lot, leaning against my car. She was wearing the leather jacket and smiling at me knowingly. The light from the neon street lamp was strange—bone-colored and shadowy— a mugger kind of light. "I've been waiting for a half hour," she said as I came up to the car. She pelvised away from the fender and grabbed me, slipping her hands under the unbuttoned sides of my winter coat. She grabbed the edges of my shoulder blades with her fingertips. "I missed you," she whispered.

I kissed her, hard. When I pulled away, she had her eyes closed, like some college freshman. A thought flashed across my mind: Is she making fun of me?

A car pulled out of a space behind us, raking us with headlights.

"I couldn't find the number you left," I said after a moment. "I looked everywhere. I even—"

Her fingers pressed against my lips, stopping them. "Don't apologize," she said. She shifted in my arms, the leather jacket creaking lushly. "There's absolutely nothing to explain. I understand."

—So she turned it around on you. She made it seem like it was your choice that you didn't call her.

—I didn't think it was worth going into right then. I mean, there she was, waiting for me. For godsake, she'd waited half an hour!

—She said.

—Her face was cold. I remember thinking that as I kissed her. Her lips were white-cold.

—And then you took her home again.

—She followed me in her car.

—Wait. Her own car was there in the lot?

—Yes.

—Then why didn't she wait for you in her car? Out of the wind and cold?

—Christ, you're determined to think that she was hatching some kind of plot, aren't you.

—I'm just trying to figure what she was thinking. I'm trying to get at her motivations.

—She didn't wait in her car, OK? She waited outside. My leather jacket is warm.

—And so she followed you home, the same way she did the first time.

—The same way.

—And did you get her license plate number this time?

—(silence)

—You got it, didn't you?

—(pause) I got it.

—Well, there.

—I got it and wrote it down on a business card. I wrote it on two different cards and kept a copy in the car.

—You were getting suspicious.

—I was getting careful.

We ate dinner in bed. Lamb curry, which we had delivered from the Indian place near the train station. We ate everything with our fingers, the cartons resting against our chests as we lay back against the down pillows. When we were finished, I licked off an oval of curry sauce that had dripped onto her left breast—a second nipple—and then the two of us just lay there, like full-bellied lions after the kill. I wondered then how I could have doubted her. Her body gave off this gorgeous warmth. She lay there with her eyes closed, smiling faintly, as if listening to something. Then she belched—loudly—and it seemed to surprise her. She laughed, and rubbed her belly up and down, slowly. She was staring at me now.

I took a slow breath. "What do you do?" I asked her. "Tell me about yourself. What you do for a living."

She sighed, looking down frankly at the tips of her breasts, as if my question were some kind of obscure betrayal. "It's hard to explain," she said.

"Try."

She turned to her side, facing me. Her hair spread across her chest like an open fan. I could see the pulse beating in a tiny hollow at the base of her neck. "I find out things about people," she said. "A kind of investigator, I suppose. For a couple of lawyers in the city."

"Find out things like what?"

"Oh, not secret dark pasts, necessarily. Just things. Whatever there is to know about a person. You'd be amazed how useful certain kinds of information can be in the right hands."

I was watching her closely. "I'm not sure I—"

"Look," she interrupted, shifting on the bed. "You find out a man has a drinking problem, or that he has this thing for little boys, or that he's giving someone money, secretly. That kind of information can be *used*."

"In a lawsuit?"

"In whatever." She reached out and ran her hand over the angular curve of my pelvis. Her hand was warm, hot even. "It's a stupid job, really. I just do it for the money. It doesn't mean a thing."

I put my hand over hers, stopping it in mid-caress. "I've never heard of anything like it," I said, shivering suddenly.

"Are you all right?" she asked. A little ridge of concern appeared between her eyebrows. "You look pale. And your skin feels strange."

It was as if her words released illness into my body. A bubble of nausea burst in my chest, shaking my entire body. I barely made it to the bathroom.

—You were sick.

—The Indian food. There must have been something wrong with it.

—Was she sick then, too?

—I'm not used to the spices. My eating habits tend to be pretty tame. I never eat Indian food normally.

—And what did she do?

—That's just it. She cried. She came into the bathroom, sat down on the edge of the bathtub in the darkness, and wept.

—I don't understand.

—She kept saying that it was her fault, that she was responsible. She said she'd make it up to me.

—She was responsible?

—I missed some of it. Maybe I didn't hear right. But then she crouched behind me. I felt her thighs clasping my hips, her breasts easing up against my shoulders. She held my head between her hands. After my retching was over, she wiped my mouth with a bath towel. She was murmuring something, soothing sounds, into my ear.

—Could you make out what she was saying?

—Nothing. She was saying nothing. It was just sounds, that's all. Like what you'd say to a crying baby.

—And what happened then?

—We stayed there on the floor of the bathroom, on the cold tiles, for a while. She held me. The only light was from the bedroom.

—But she didn't stay with you that night either.

—She said she had to go. I was feeling drained anyway. All I wanted to do was sleep.

—So she left, leaving no number again.

—No, actually, I *found* the number next morning, the original number. It was under the telephone itself, on the back of a little card.

—You hadn't looked there before?

—I must not have. I mean, it was there.

—But do you remember looking under the phone before?

—Maybe I did. I don't know. But it was there.

The next day I had to take the train into the city. I still felt a little unsteady, but the major illness had passed. I was meeting with somebody about my book, and by the time we got to the restaurant, one of those expensive northern Italian places, I was ravenous. I ate everything—the whole basket of bread, the lion's share of the antipasto, even what was left of my companion's entree.

Afterward, since I was in the city, I decided to do some shopping. I bought myself some books, a pair of running shoes, and a little Indonesian wood sculpture—a frog with pink wings—that caught my fancy. I also bought something for her. I saw this leather jacket in a window, it looked almost exactly like mine. "Here's something I know she'll like," I told myself as I handed my credit card to the cashier. The jacket was expensive—more than I could afford, really—but I wanted to do something for her. For Alice.

I got home after dark. I let myself into the house clumsily, juggling packages in my arms. A light was on in the living room. It was her, sitting knees to chest on the Haitian cotton couch, dressed in nothing but my blue terrycloth robe. She was clipping her toenails.

—Clipping her toenails?!
—As if she lived there. As if we were married or something.
—But how did she get in?
—She broke in.
—(silence)
—The back door. She broke in.

"I'll pay for the window," she said, angered by my incredulous expression. "You shouldn't have a window in a door anyway, especially a back door. Somebody could just break the window, reach in, and undo the deadbolt."

"Somebody did."

"I did. But next time it could be a burglar. You should replace the window with a wood panel. Or get a new lock, something that can only be opened with a key, even from the inside."

"You seem to know a lot about it."

"It's common sense."

"You do a lot of breaking and entering in your job, I guess."

"Don't be a shit, okay?" She sighed and got up from the couch. She came over and kissed me, grabbing the lapels of my coat. "I was freezing outside," she said, in a different, softer voice. "And besides, I wanted to do something for you. I wanted to surprise you."

"Do what?" I asked.

"You don't notice?" She stepped back and swept her hand around the room. "I cleaned up. I vacuumed. You had nothing in the kitchen cabinets, so I shopped for you. I did your laundry."

And it was true. My house was immaculate. The furniture gleamed. The carpet was spotless. Lulling dinner smells emanated from the kitchen.

"I thought you would like it," she said. "Was I wrong?"

"You're cooking?"

She smiled oddly, sheepishly. "A pot roast. With mashed potatoes and broccoli. American food."

We sat down to dinner—at the table in the dining room, which I never use normally. We ate the pot roast, the mashed potatoes drenched in gravy, the tiny florets of steamed broccoli. She had baked bread, and we ate that too. Alice laughed through dinner. She held the glass of red wine against her cheek, so that it cast a ruby glow on her chin and neck. She told me about her day. There had been some amusing woman in the supermarket, she said. The woman was complaining, to no one in particular, about the quality of the flank steak. Apparently, she was rummaging through the packages of meat in the refrigerator case, muttering. Alice had to reach past her to get the pot roast. "You wonder what can make a woman behave that way," Alice said, dipping her head hungrily toward a forkful of mashed potatoes.

—She was eating too?
—What do you mean?
—Was there anything she gave you to eat that she didn't eat herself?
—She ate everything.
—And you weren't sick afterward?
—(pause) No. Not in the way you mean.
—In what way, then?
—(more decisively) No. I wasn't sick. I wasn't sick in any way.

It was later, over coffee, that I decided to give her the gift. "I'm sorry I didn't have time to wrap it," I said, getting up from the table. I pulled the box from my pile of packages near the front door. "I didn't know I'd be seeing you tonight."

"I didn't expect this," she said, obviously pleased. "You bought me a present."

I put the box on the table in front of her, among the crumbs and spills of dinner. She lay her hands flat on top of it for a moment. "A present," she whispered, and again I was momentarily uncertain: Is she making fun of me?

"Open it," I said.

She did. She pulled off the top and tore away the tissue paper. But when she saw what was inside, she stopped. She sat back against her chair, shoulders drooping. "I don't understand," she said. "You gave me something like this already."

It took me a moment. "I gave you—?"

"The leather jacket. The one I've been wearing. Why are you giving me another one?"

"I never *gave* you that jacket."

Her eyes shot toward mine. "What are you trying to do here? You want the other jacket back?"

"Of course I want it back! I lent it to you that night, when it was cold. You asked me to lend you something warm!"

She rose from the table. "I can't believe you're saying this. This is cowardly."

"Alice!"

But she was already past me. She stalked down the hallway to the bedroom. I followed. By the time I reached the bedroom, she had already shucked off the terrycloth robe and was stepping into a skirt.

"You're lying!" I shouted at her. "You're just blatantly lying!"

"I don't need this kind of shit," she muttered, zipping up the skirt at her hip. She tried to push past me to get at the rest of her clothes, but I didn't budge. I was livid. I wasn't even thinking straight. I pushed her onto the bed. I pushed her down and got on top of her.

—You forced yourself on her?

—It didn't get that far.

—You realized what you were doing.

—I don't know. She went limp. I was trying to hold her

down when suddenly she closed her eyes and just went blank. It was like she was unconscious or something.

—Was she?

—No, no. Nothing like that. It was something she just did, to stop me.

—And it worked?

—Yes.

"I'm sorry," I said, getting up from the bed. I backed away, disgusted with myself. "I'm sorry. I don't know what to say."

She sat up and stared at me. She was rubbing her bare left breast. I had hurt her, I think.

"I was angry." I turned away and stared at nothing. "Please don't leave," I said. "Please."

I heard her behind me rummaging through her clothes. She was getting dressed.

"If you leave, we'll never see each other again. I know that. You know that."

"I won't leave," she said finally, from behind me.

I turned. She was fully dressed now—skirt, blouse, shoes.

"There's still dessert," she said, smiling crookedly. "I've made something special."

I didn't know how to respond. I felt lightened somehow, like a prisoner suddenly and unexpectedly free of his restraints. I held out my arms to her.

"Later," she said, then gestured with a toss of her head to the doorway.

Smiling, I left the bedroom, and she followed behind me. At the end of the hallway, just as I was stepping into the living room, I turned to look at her. I just caught sight of the bat descending toward my head.

—The baseball bat.

—The one I kept in the closet in the spare bedroom. For burglars. She must have planned it all in advance. She must have found the bat before I got home and planted it somewhere in the bedroom. Under the bed, maybe.

—So she knocked you out.

—Cold.

—(trying to suppress a smile) I'm sorry. I know it's not funny. You could have been seriously hurt.

—It *is* funny. Ridiculous. But no, I wasn't hurt.

—But you were out for a while.

—Several hours, actually.

—(pause) And then, when you came to, you had your vision.

It must have been a little before dawn. I was still lying there on the floor, when I became aware of something—a faint, blue, prickly light occupying the living room. The light got brighter, until there were tiny sparks igniting everywhere, touching the edges of the furniture, the rug, the doorways. I tried to get up, but I couldn't move. The blue sparks were all around me.

"Don't worry," a voice said then. The voice was silent— I knew that—but I could understand what it was saying. It wasn't a man's voice, or a woman's either. "Give me all," it said. "Give me all."

And that was it. It was over. The next thing I remember was that the sun was up. Amber light seeped into the living room windows, spreading rhododendron shadows across the carpet in front of my eyes.

I got slowly to my knees. My head was pounding, so I had to move gradually. The baseball bat stood against the wall near the front door.

The house was a disaster. The couch was overturned, the television screen smashed, my CDs strewn all over the floor. She had pulled the curtains from the windows, bending the rods into wild configurations.

I struggled to my feet. On the side table was a note, scribbled in large, block letters. I picked it up and read it: "Leftovers from dinner in the fridge. Ever, Alice."

—And that was the last of her?

—That was the last. I tried the phone number she left—about a dozen times over the next days—but there was never any answer. I'm not even sure it's a real number.

—And the license plate number?

—Well, I followed up on that, too. But they can't give me any information unless I file an official complaint. Assault or something.

—Which you won't do.

—Which I can't do. Remember what preceded it.

—But she ransacked your home!

—Nothing was missing, nothing I could put my finger on, at least. Yes, the camera was gone, but that had gone missing earlier. And some notes for my book, but I might have just lost them in the library.

—But you think she took something.

—I know she took something. I'm certain of it.

—And you've never seen the blue light again? Or heard the voice?

—I knew you would fix on that. I knew it would skew your reading of the whole affair.

—Nonsense. I was just asking. (pause) And what about the leather jacket?

—I have two now. She left both of them.
—Ah.
—But I only wear one of them. The one she wore.
—The one you lent her.
—Yes. The one that holds her scent.

Hungry

1.

WHEN MR. MEDWIK at the Hart Memorial Funeral Home refused to upgrade my title from Assistant to Associate Embalmer, I knew that it was time for me to go to Alaska. I decided—on the spot—to give notice, pile everything I owned into the back of my orange Toyota Corolla, and just drive away. When I informed my mother of this plan (she also worked at Hart, as a part-time greeter/mourner), she threw a quick *sotto voce* tantrum at the back of the Blue Room, causing the attendees at one Edward Bledsoe's wake to twist in their seats and glare. Finally, after she calmed herself, she touched her breastbone, took a deep breath, and asked if she could go with me. I said okay.

2.

That evening my mother and I went home early to look at a map of Alaska. We opened the 1967 Standard World Atlas that she had appropriated from the library when I was in third grade and had to write a report on Paraguay. The state appeared on a double-page spread, with all of the important towns lost in the depths of the binding.

"Here's a place called Farewell," I said. "That would be appropriate."

"Like hell it would," my mother answered. "Never say good-bye, that's my motto." She frowned in concentration, pressing on the thick pages until the binding crackled. "Now here's something: Platinum. Right on a thingie called Good-news Bay. Talk about good omens . . ."

"Nothing on the coast," I told her. "Alaskan coastal towns are full of fishermen. Fishermen die at sea, so their bodies are usually lost. I wouldn't be able to get a job in my field."

My mother stared at me hard, her heavy, afternoon-funeral makeup dense around the eyes and mouth. "You've really thought this through, haven't you."

"I've done some thinking."

"So you probably have a town picked out already. You're just humoring me with this atlas."

"Well, there *is* a place . . ." I admitted. Actually, I'd had a town in mind for some time—the key element in a half-formed plan of escape I'd been concocting for over a year now. The East, I'd decided, was too crowded for me, too full of town councils and Boards of Ed and co-op committees. I wanted out. "It's called Hungry."

"Hungry? As in Hungry for Love?"

"No. As in Hungry for Fresh Air and Open Spaces. As in Hungry for Something Better out of Life."

My mother thought about this for a moment, biting her perfectly pared thumbnail. Finally, she nodded. "I like it. I like the sound of it. We'll do well there, I know it."

We closed the atlas. "Hungry, Alaska," she said wistfully, sitting back in her chair. She kicked off one of her high heels and then nudged off the other with the tip of her black-stock-inged foot. My mother had good, shapely legs—the legs of a twenty-year-old. Her best asset, she always said. Although my mother had worked in funeral homes for most of her life, she'd also freelanced in her youth for something she called a "businessman's escort service." She'd built a career on those legs.

"So we're moving to Hungry," I said, feeling the full weight of our decision for the first time.

"So we're moving to Hungry," she confirmed. "But first, we're getting drunk."

3.

A soft summer evening. My mother and I nursed double old-fashioneds out on the back lawn of our townhouse co-op complex. We did have a screened-in porch attached to our unit, but I'd heard that the mosquitoes in Alaska were as big as finches; since I thought we should practice enduring insect pests, we'd taken the pitcher of drinks and a couple of folding chairs out to the dark stretch of grass between the co-ops and the parking lot. Dreary, damp-eyed businessmen, a common species in our part of Westchester, were arriving home late from their jobs in the city. We watched them pull themselves out of their mournful Volvos and—neckties loosened, brief-cases hanging mutely from their hands—walk up the concrete paths toward home.

"Hey!" my mother shouted to one of them. "You look like you could use a drink!"

The man waved, uncertain whether he knew us.

"Come on over! It's cocktail hour!"

The man pretended not to understand. "Nice night!" he said heartily, then ducked behind a forsythia.

My mother rolled her eyes. "The men in Alaska," she said, "had better be livelier than these poor sods."

"They will be. They'll all be miners and wilderness guides and bush pilots. Rugged individualists."

"What's a bush pilot? Sounds dirty."

"A bush pilot," I intoned, "is someone who flies mail and

supplies to remote places in the Interior. By reputation, bush pilots are supposed to be resourceful, brave, and reckless."

"Mmm. I like the sound of that." My mother giggled and then, cursing, swatted a mosquito on her bare thigh. She was on her third old-fashioned.

"We'll have to sell the co-op," I told her.

"Ha! Won't the board be thrilled about that!" she cried. My mother and I were not popular members of our cooperative. Although we had given them our usual story about my father being dead, the hapless victim of a tractor collision in our native Nebraska, rumors to the contrary had begun circulating in the last six months. One of my mother's old escort regulars from Albany had seen us two days before Christmas at the Shop-Rite. He was down here visiting his sister, and when he saw my mother at the artichoke bin, he apparently felt no compunction about blowing our cover. For all I know, this man could have been my father.

Anyway, by New Year's morning the gossip had reached the board of the Woodland Whispers Cooperative. Several of our more conservative neighbors seemed to regard us now with high suspicion. One old Italian widow had even taken to crossing herself every time she passed our unit.

"You think they'll miss us?" I asked.

"I tell you who *I'll* miss," she said, pressing a finger to my forearm for emphasis. "Nobody."

"Nobody at all?" I asked. "What about Bear?"

My mother's expression turned complicated in the dim moonlight. She looked down into her drink and nodded her head. "Okay. Right. I'll miss Bear."

Bear was our colleague at the funeral home. He was hired to vacuum and dust and refill the tissue dispensers, but he would also pallbear in a pinch, which is how he got his name. Bear was about thirty-five (ten years my senior) and slightly retarded. He lived with his aging uncle Woody above the real estate office on Old Post Road.

"There are some things I'll miss," I said, twirling the ice in my glass. "Bear among them. But there's a lot more about this place that I'll be glad to leave behind."

I could feel my mother's eyes on me in the darkness. "We've been happy here," she said quietly, "for the most part." Then: the faint tinkle of ice in her glass as she lifted it to her lips.

A bat swooped suddenly between us, pinwheeling in the air for insects. I could feel the wind of it on my face.

"Christ!" my mother cried out. She dropped her drink onto the lawn, spattering my pants leg with spots of old-fashioned. "What the hell was that?"

My heart was beating faster in my chest. "A sign," I told her. "A good one."

And I truly believed it was. No, I told myself, no second thoughts. It was time to burn some bridges.

4.

I should mention at this point a fact that people seem to find relevant about me—namely, that I am fat. Not grotesquely so, not even abnormally so, but definitely, unambiguously fat. There are smooth, serpentine rolls around my waist which have been there for as long as I can remember. All of my belts come from a big-and-tall-man mail-order house in Jasmine, Florida.

In fourth grade, just when I was beginning to balloon, several of my classmates invented a rhyme about me: "Frank, Frank, big as a bank, Went for a swim but then he sank." That was when I made a conscious decision to be smart—as revenge.

I began reading—just about anything I could get my hands on. I read Emerson, Zane Grey, my mother's Silhouette romances, and everything in the Everyman Pocket Library. In school, meanwhile, I was collecting as many D's as A's. This would puzzle my mother, but the explanation was clear to me. Several of my teachers, I knew, felt that fat boys, particularly fat boys who answered too many questions, shouldn't get high grades. It was a matter of aesthetics.

A month after I took my PSATs, my guidance counselor, a Mr. Davidson Robie, called me into his office to deliver my scores in person. I had received twin 80's on the math and verbal sections, something that no one in the Albany school system had done for five years. "Your grades," the man said, "might be a problem, but with scores like these, you might just have your pick of colleges. What do you think of Yale?"

Sighing, I told him what I had decided just a few weeks earlier—that I was not going to college. I told him that I had accepted a job as an embalmer's assistant at the local funeral home (a place called Ornstein's, my first job in the industry). This position, I told him, was only part-time now, but would become full-time at the end of the term, and I wasn't yet sure if I'd be returning for my senior year.

"Ha ha!" he said, forcing a laugh at what he thought was a somewhat protracted and not very funny joke. When he finally realized that I was serious, he took off his glasses. "Um," he said, "do you mind if I speak to your mother about this?"

That night, Mr. Robie called my mother. They spoke for almost an hour. By the end of the conversation, the gloves, to use my mother's description, were off. Mr. Robie kept telling my mother that I should go to Yale; my mother kept telling Mr. Robie that he should go to hell. She'd come into contact with plenty of college boys in her day, she told him, and she was more than sympathetic to my desire to give organized higher education a skip. I'd be better off, she said, hanging around with corpses than with college sophomores (not to mention college professors, who occupied a tier of existence in her personal chain-of-being somewhere between personal injury lawyers and the lesser slime molds).

They left the issue unresolved, Mr. Robie threatening to get the principal involved, my mother counterthreatening to pull me out of school immediately. Not that it mattered, in the end. As it turned out, the entire issue became academic. Because in May of that year, my mother and I were run out of town.

I should explain. It was, of course, a well-known fact in our part of the capital city just exactly who and what I was. The absence of a paternal authority in my life, in fact, had been the explanation provided by some of my teachers for what they perceived as my inability to accept direction. My classmates were somewhat less tactful. They frequently exercised their creativity in coming up with clever little names for my mother and me, names which would then be muttered within my hearing in math class or on line at the school cafeteria. It was all harmless enough, I suppose—until, one night, on my way back home from a movie (I was alone), I passed the high school gym, where our basketball team had apparently just won an important game. Several of our home-team supporters stumbled on me in the parking lot of a dark A&P and, making reference to my parentage, proceeded to beat me up. I tried to fight back, but, being fat, not to mention one boy against five, I could do little. I was left bleeding beside the night watchman's Grand Am—broken nose, fractured wrist, and three bruised ribs—where I lay for several hours before lifting myself up and dragging myself home.

Naturally, my mother wanted to press charges. I just wanted out of there. We argued for days. I won. So we moved south, to Westchester, where I could finish high school as an unknown. That was really all I ever wanted—to be left alone.

I've never asked for more than that from anyone, even my mother.

A footnote: The day before we left Albany, the windows of several houses in our neighborhood were found mysteriously broken. No one could determine exactly who was responsible for the vandalism. But I did find a few bricks in the trunk of my mother's Caddy as I was loading it with our luggage. When I asked her about them, she shrugged. "I keep them there for ballast," she explained, smiling her ambiguous smile.

The next day we left Albany for good, driving fast.

5.

"Ahoy, Frank!" my mother called from the top of the basement stairs. It was the day after our decision to drive to Hungry, during the overlap of our shifts at the funeral home. We had both given Medwik the customary two-weeks' notice and were putting in a few extra hours to improve our cash flow for the trip. My Toyota would need a tune-up before any attempt at the Alaska-Canada Highway.

"I'm down here!" I shouted back. "I'm working on somebody!"

I heard the click of her high heels, then saw, in superb sequence, her ankles, those good, black-stockinged legs, and the bottom of her black silk dress, all descending the stairs. My mother, at forty-seven years of age, was both the youngest and the sole female greeter/mourner at Hart. Her sexiness—there was nothing else to call it—was stubborn and difficult to mask, but she *could* look grave, concerned, and dignified at a funeral, which is why Medwik had hired her. Also a factor, undoubtedly, was her willingness to accompany him to dinner when he needed to impress a business associate.

"Hi," she said. "Having fun?"

"Yes, lots." I was preparing an injection, filling the large syringe with pungent formaldehyde.

"Anybody I know?" she asked.

I stepped aside to let her see. It was Beulah Lancaster, the editor of *Suburban Simmerings*, the local alternative newspaper. She had died of a stroke, I was told, while protesting the inauguration of a toxic dump.

"Good God," my mother said, recoiling. "Isn't this the woman who rejected that 'Radical Catholicism As Subversive Act' thingie you wrote last year?"

"Yes," I said, pressing the needle firmly into Miss Lancaster's bare, helpless neck.

My mother turned away. "Can you take a break for a minute or two? I'd like to talk to you."

I finished the injection and wiped my hands on an old rag. My supervisor, Willard, the chief embalmer, could finish up on Beulah tomorrow. Like most bosses, Willard always wanted to have what he called "the last word" on any given project, although this apparently did not preclude allowing me to do most of the work.

I pulled the sheet over Beulah's face. My mother was across the room, examining the glass-fronted chest full of chemical bottles. "So what's up?" I asked.

She turned. "I've been thinking," she said. "And I think maybe we're being selfish."

I felt a pressure in my ears. The phrase "I think we're being selfish," with its implication that we were now going to *stop* being selfish, had, in my experience, almost invariably preceded my mother's most self-serving proposals. "What do you mean, selfish?" I asked.

"Well, damn it, here we are, getting ready to set off on the adventure of a lifetime and escape this idiot town and start life over, and there are people we care about right here who are trapped just as much as we—"

"You want to take Bear with us," I said flatly.

"Well, the thing is, hon, if we sell your Toyota instead of my Cadillac, which is so old that we'd probably get nothing for it anyway, but it's roomy enough for a whole army, and really, when you think of the long trip to Alaska, who wants to spend days in a subcompact with no leg room, not to mention the low suspension that probably wouldn't survive the unpaved roads once we got there, why, it just makes a hell of a lot of sense." She crossed her arms and stared at me.

"Is that sentence finished?" I asked.

"He would be lost without us."

"But what about his uncle?"

"Woody could come too."

I wiped a line of sweat from my forehead. My sleeve smelled of embalming chemicals, and curry from the takeout lunch I'd had at noon. "Okay," I said.

My mother's face blossomed into a smile. She leaned forward and kissed me on the forehead. "You're a good man, Frank."

"I'll ask them about it tonight," I said. "I'll see what Woody has to say."

My mother tossed her dark hair back over her shoulders. "Woody says he likes the idea in theory, but he wants to discuss some details with you."

I stared at her. "You've already talked to them."

"I knew you'd say yes, so I decided to save some time." She stood with her hands on her hips. "Oh, come on, Frank. You're an open book to me. Most men are."

"I'm not most men."

She smiled. "No, thank God for that." Then she swung around and headed toward the stairway, looking around the room with an expression of slight distaste. "They're expecting you at eight tonight," she said, laughing musically. "Bring the atlas. And make sure to wash your hands before you go."

6.

I went to see Bear and his uncle Woody in their minute three-room apartment over the Hyacinth Real Estate office. They had lived there together ever since Bear's parents died in what the local newspapers described, with typical originality, as "a fiery New Year's crash" on the New York Thruway. The Dugger family had been a force in local retailing (they owned the long-defunct Sweater Barn on Old Post Road) until about the early 1970's, when the big malls started to pull business away from downtown areas. The family, falling on hard times, began to disperse. Woody and Bear, in fact, were the only Duggers left in the county.

Uncle and nephew were listening to music—Mel Torme's "Greatest Hits," their favorite—when I arrived at their apartment. Bear pulled open the door, hitting me instantly with a virtual wall of hep crooning. "TURN IT DOWN, UNCLE!" he shouted over his shoulder. Bear then just smiled at me, forgetting to invite me in.

The sonic bulwark disappeared, leaving a faintly audible resonance on the carpetless stairwell. Old Woody cruised into the living room, stooped but lively.

"Sorry, Frankie," he said, coming up beside Bear. "We're doing some celebrating here. This Alaska idea's got us all steamed up."

"When do we leave?" Bear asked, hugging me suddenly.

"Let the man come in first, Beebee," Woody scolded. "We were just frying up some home fries. Want some?"

"I would," I answered. The smell was heavenly.

"In the kitchen."

Woody led the way into their spotless white kitchenette. Pans, pots, and colanders hung like silver planets from the ceiling and walls. Along one side of the room was a narrow Formica counter and two butcher-block stools. A several-days'-old helium balloon (Woody had just celebrated his seventieth birthday) hovered at about knee-level near the refrigerator, skittering away under the counter like a miserable old dog accustomed to frequent whippings.

"Sit down, sit down, take a load off," Woody said, picking up a spatula. The potatoes were sizzling luxuriously in a pan on the stove.

I eased onto one of the stools. As I did, Bear slipped the atlas from my hands and opened it on the counter. "First of all," Woody began, but Bear, flipping through the maps, interrupted: "Is there a funeral home? I want to work in a funeral home."

Bear's enthusiasm for the business was well known at Hart Memorial. It was understood by everyone who worked there that he was not to be left alone with the deceased.

"There is a funeral home," I assured him. "I checked it with directory assistance."

"And a hospital?" Woody asked. "And a video store?"

"I'm not sure. But there must be." Actually, I had intentionally not overresearched the amenities of Hungry. All I needed in a town, I thought, was a funeral home and a Catholic church. And besides, this trip was supposed to be a spontaneous act of defiance, of independence; I didn't want to spoil it by being too careful.

When I explained all of this to Woody, however, he seemed skeptical. "I'll do some reading and calling around just to be sure," he said.

Bear was still flipping the pages of the atlas. "Let's look at it on the map. Show me."

I took the atlas and turned to the Alaska spread. There were already fingerprints visible over the Aleutians, from all of the pawing my mother and I had done the last few days.

"Yes!" Bear cried when he followed my finger to the right place. "Those are mountains!"

"Bear thinks Westchester's too flat," Woody explained to me. "He says he always wanted to live in the mountains."

"I always wanted to live in the mountains. I love mountains."

"Well then, you'll be living in the mountains."

Woody turned off the flame under the home fries. "These are nicely burned, I guess. Beebee, how about you find us a bottle of wine from the rack in my bedroom?"

"Something bubbly?" Bear asked.

"There's some nice Cold Duck, I think."

Bear catapulted out of the kitchen. When he was gone, Woody came over to me, the frying pan gurgling in his hand. "Frankie, listen," he said, speaking softly. "Let me ask you a question. What do you think, you personally, about how Bear will make out in Alaska? I mean socially-wise."

I sat with the question for a moment. I could understand Woody's concern. Bear had not always gotten the best reception in these parts. There were a couple of local restaurants, in fact, that had made it plain that Bear, who had a tendency to raise his voice when he was enjoying himself, would not be welcome during peak meal times.

"I don't know what to tell you," I said finally. "From what I understand, these little backwoods towns are pretty laissez-faire."

"Laissez-faire?"

"Live and let live. Nobody will bother you, is what I think. Everyone will be too busy surviving the winter, making sure the wolves don't get into the root cellar. That's the beauty of Alaska."

Woody was nodding his head doubtfully. "You think so?" he said, worrying the home fries with his spatula. "You think so?"

That's when Bear returned, carrying champagne.

7.

Word got around the community that we were leaving. The idea of our trip seemed to touch something in people, at least in certain people. At the local Rite-Aid, where I was buying extra pairs of tube socks for the trip, the cashier eyed me for a moment before saying: "You're parta that group driving up to Canada, aren't you."

"Alaska," I told her.

"Gawd, I'd love to go with you, I really would. Get out of this old sweatshop." She shoved the package of socks into a paper bag and then patted it shut. "No need to pay for that, sweetie," she whispered, winking. "He"—and here she tossed her head toward the one-way mirror above the pharmacy counter—"can certainly afford it. And you'll want those socks for the long winters up there, Lord love you."

Epatha Waters, my mother's hairdresser, also expressed interest in the trip. Epatha, a statuesque black woman who never wore fewer than six pairs of earrings at a time, told my mother that she had a sister in Anchorage. She'd always wanted to try her luck up there, but was afraid to do it on her own. Could she tag along behind us in her Buick?

"She wouldn't be a bother at all," my mother said that night, as I massaged her feet in the living room. She was lobbying with surprising vehemence for Epatha's inclusion in our plans. I think she liked the idea of having someone in

Alaska who knew her hair. "It would be an extra car, think of that. And Epatha's sister might be a good connection. Someone who knows the ropes up there."

I didn't say anything for a minute, just studied the foot-massage diagram that my mother had cut out of one of her magazines. She had come home from work with a slight neck-ache, so I was trying to give special attention to the pad of her third left toe, which the diagram listed as corresponding to the cervical vertebrae. As I kneaded the elegant little toe, I marveled at how vulnerable my mother's foot looked at the end of her sleekly muscled leg. Holding its delicate warmth in my hands filled me with an obscure protective melancholy.

"Please," my mother urged quietly, from above me.

I looked up at her. "You know I won't object."

She sighed impatiently. "I know you won't object. But I don't want you just not to object, I want you to want her to come. Okay?"

I looked down at her feet in my hands. She wriggled her toes once, coaxing me. What could I say? I said okay.

Then, the next afternoon at the funeral home, Henry, the delivery boy from the Indian takeout next door, refused to take the tip I offered. He hovered for a while on the threshold, then asked if he could speak with me privately. "That man my boss is a monster," he whispered. "I must go with you to Alaska. You must take me with you."

His eyes were arguments in themselves. Henry was fourteen and beautiful—ink-black eyes, milk-chocolate skin, fine-boned hands. He had immaculate white fingernails, and that stoic, wounded look I can't seem to turn away from.

I sighed. How could I deny someone escaping from an overbearing boss? Besides, he'd probably be good company for Epatha in the Buick.

8.

"Have you packed your mukluks yet?" my mother asked, checking through her master list. It was two days before the closing on our co-op, three days before our planned departure to the Great White North.

"There is apparently no store in Westchester County that carries mukluks," I told her, not for the first time.

"You checked Loehmann's?"

"We probably won't even need mukluks," I went on. "To be honest, I'm not even sure exactly what they are."

"Epatha says they're fur boots of some kind. She says her ex-husband had a pair, but the dog gnawed them to shreds after she spilled some chicken gravy on them. She says we'll need them in Alaska."

"Epatha can certainly take mukluks if she likes," I snapped. I was being testy, I knew it, but I had reason. There were now ten of us bound for Hungry. In the two weeks since Epatha and Henry joined our group, it had been further expanded by Epatha's elderly mother, the unemployed construction worker who bought my Toyota Corolla, the organist from St. Mary of the Rocks (the church I frequented), and the jazz critic from *Suburban Simmerings*, which had folded suddenly upon its editor/publisher's untimely death. Our initial carload was turning into a caravan.

"Fine," my mother said finally. "I'll cross mukluks off the list." She put a dark line through the word on her pad and then took a satisfied sip of her drink. "She also said something about grizzly repellent."

"There is no such thing as grizzly repellent. That's an old superstition."

"How do you know? Epatha says."

"Epatha says," I said.

"Well, she at least has a sister in the state. You've never even been there."

I stopped packing. Massaging my temples, I sank onto the couch, which my mother had just sold to the mailman that morning.

"Tired?" she asked, coming over and putting a cool hand on my forehead.

"Too many loose ends," I answered. "Miss Guglielmo says she doesn't want to go in the same car as Ernesto, and now she wants to ride with us."

"But there's no room. She can go in Epatha's car."

I shook my head. "Henry's in that car. Miss Guglielmo and Henry apparently had a falling out once about some samosas. He refuses to ride with her."

"It's not a big problem," my mother said, putting that cool hand to her own forehead. "Maybe that man what's-it can take her in the Toyota."

"Breeden is his name. We can ask." I turned and met her eyes. "This is getting complicated," I said. "I had no idea there were so many people in this town who wanted to get out of it."

My mother smiled. "We're probably eroding the tax base. The town may try to prevent us all from leaving."

"No big taxpayers in our group," I said. "The town will probably be happy to see us leave."

My mother put a hand under my chin. "This means a lot to everybody, I want you to know. You've given a lot of people hope."

"I haven't done anything. I just decided to get out."

"It was enough. One person taking action."

I got up from the couch. This was not what I wanted to hear. "I'll call Breeden and ask if Miss Guglielmo can ride with him. Somehow, I can't imagine them having much to talk about for 4,500 miles."

"They'll find something. Who knows? Maybe they'll fall in love."

I smiled. "You're an old romantic, you know that?"

"I'm not an old anything, thank you," my mother said. She got to her feet and drained the rest of her drink. "And besides, I have my eye on this Breeden myself. It gets cold at night in Alaska, you know."

I shook my head and made for the front door.

"Where are you going?"

"To church," I said. "I'll pray for you."

9.

I first became a Catholic in the seventh grade. Not that there was anything even remotely religious in my upbringing; my mother always claimed to be a pagan (which she was), and had raised me accordingly. But one week, during a particularly boring series of shop classes, I read St. Ignatius Loyola's *Spiritual Exercises* (Everyman Library Volume 73) and was deeply impressed. So I started making tentative visits to St. Joseph's in Albany. I liked what I saw—the incense, the dark, ecstatic pain of all the artwork, the mesmerizing repetitiousness of the prayers. Before long, I was a regular. Without telling my mother anything about it, I arranged to join the Church. I took my First Communion on the day after my twelfth birthday, along with six overdressed and lavishly taffetaed Hispanic girls, all of them shorter than me by at least a foot. Later that afternoon, I told my mother what I had done.

"You joined *what*?"

"St. Joseph's. I'm a member of the Catholic Church now."

"You mean *the* Catholic Church?"

"Yes," I said, my confidence faltering a bit at the vehemence of her disbelief.

"You mean the same Catholic Church that thought up the Spanish Inquisition? The same one that forces poor women to have children they can't take care of? That *is* the Catholic Church you mean, right?"

That afternoon, I experienced my first religious crisis.

What can I say in my defense? I recognize the contradictions inherent in what I believe. I recognize them and embrace them. And to be perfectly honest, I find the Catholic mass one of the most moving experiences to be had in contemporary life. The exquisite ritual of it all sucks me in—the blood, the drama, the ultimate satisfying conclusion. Like billions of people before me, I find the whole thing darkly comforting. I go to mass and feel insignificant for a half-hour. I go to mass and feel cleansed.

St. Mary of the Rocks, the church I had attended for the last five years, was a modern structure, a sleek glass pyramid standing amid Japanese maples at the end of a wooded cul-de-sac. It had been built in the 1960's, when church attendance was high and architects self-indulgent. The tall airy interior was nearly always full of sun, the floor patterned with lozenges of red, blue, and green light from the abstract stained-glass windows of the nave. It was not a small church, but its popularity had declined in recent years. On Sunday mornings nowadays, there was usually about one person for every ten places in the pews.

I entered the church and, wetting my fingers with holy water, crossed myself. The church was nearly empty; two old women were praying loudly in a side chapel, while the sexton, a muscular 50's-ish man named Herb, swept up around the rack of votive candles. I nodded hello to him as I made my way to the confession booths.

The light was on at Father Payson's usual booth, so I slipped in. The closed space reeked of raspberry tobacco, from the priest's pipe. He wasn't supposed to smoke in the confessional, but he often sat in there for hours without a single soul coming to confess. Smoking, he said, helped him pray.

As I sat down, I heard the pipe being hurriedly tapped out on the other side of the opaque screen.

"It has been five days since my last confession," I began. "Bless me, Father, for I have sinned, though exactly how is difficult to explain."

Fragrant silence for a moment. Then Father Payson's voice: "You're not sure if what you've done is a sin?"

"Well, no. What I'm not sure of is exactly what I've done."

The priest sighed. "This is Frank Corey, isn't it. You're talking about the trip to Alaska you're organizing."

I thought this line of questioning a bit unprofessional for a priest, not to mention inaccurate (I wasn't *organizing* anything), but I said yes.

"You know," he went on after a moment, "Elaine Guglielmo is the best organist we've had here in some time."

"I'm sorry."

"We'll have a difficult time replacing her."

"I'm sorry."

He laughed. "Don't be sorry," he said. "Getting away will probably do the old girl a world of good. She hasn't been the same since her sister died, God rest her soul. So what's your problem?"

I sat back and stared up at the mahogany ceiling of the confession booth. How to put it into words? "I didn't mean it to turn into this," I said finally. "This trip to Hungry, I mean. I just wanted to do something for myself."

"Ahh, you're being selfish is what you're saying."

"No," I answered quickly. At least I didn't *think* I was

being selfish. Alaska was not something I wanted to hoard for myself. There was enough of it, presumably, to go around.

The priest cleared his throat. "All right, not selfish. How about afraid? Are you afraid of this trip?"

I looked down at my plump, dishearteningly dimpled hands. "No. Not that either."

I heard rustling on the other side of the screen, then a match scraping into flame. Father Payson was lighting up again. I had annoyed him.

"Look," he said, after what smelled like several copious puffs, "I'm not sure you grasp the concept of this booth. You're supposed to come in here and tell me about your sins. I'm supposed to listen and make them go away. It's simple. The Catholic Church is not in the business of providing therapy."

"I'm not looking for therapy," I insisted.

"Then what is it you're looking for?"

I couldn't answer him at first. Without really thinking about it, I said: "A little quiet, maybe."

"Well," Father Payson said, "we've got a nice rose garden behind the refectory. You have my permission to sit there for an hour or two. In the meantime, have you done anything that *really* needs absolution? You haven't touched yourself or anything recently?"

"What? Oh. No."

"Too bad. Well, say four Hail Marys for stealing my organist. Come to think of it, say a few more for that mother of yours. And, Frank?"

"Yes."

"Try not to lose the joy of it. Lighten up is probably what I'd say to you, in a different context." He paused a moment. I heard the snap of another match popping into flame. "Okay," the priest said finally, "get out of my confessional now. Make room for real sinners."

I did, though reluctantly. I didn't feel satisfied, as I should have when leaving the confessional. I wanted him to say more.

On my way out of the church, Herb, the sexton, came up to me, the sleeves of his corduroy shirt rolled up to the top of his gently sagging biceps. "About this trip to Alaska," he began.

"Okay," I said, not even waiting for him to finish the request. "Okay, okay, okay, okay. Okay?"

He seemed taken aback. "Great," he said. "I'll have a car, so don't worry about finding me a seat. And I was thinking of asking my friends Elissa and Steve . . ."

And so we became thirteen—twelve plus me. Like Christ and his disciples. "Shit," I said aloud when this thought came to me. I excused myself and hurried down the aisle.

"I'll call you," Herb said, confused, transfixed in the speckled light of the nave.

10.

"We could spend the fifth night in Belfield, North Dakota," my mother said, leaning over the AAA map of the North Central United States. Her wet, newly washed hair fell from her shoulders and pattered the map in front of her. "There's a Motel 6 right on I-90. They'd probably be able to take all of us, unless there's a cattle ranchers' convention or something."

"Everyone can fend for themselves," I answered. "If there's no room, some can go on ahead to Medora or Beach."

"We stick together, Frank. That's a given. If there's not enough room in Belfield, we all move on."

It was the afternoon before our departure. We had spent the morning at a lawyer's office, closing on our co-op, severing our last connections to the state in which I was born. Now my mother was putting together a last-minute itinerary. Epatha and some of the others wanted a definite plan, so that no one would get lost on the way. I had refused to do one myself. The whole point of the trip, I insisted, was to get away without a plan, to be spontaneous, to live the heady danger of root-lessness. You don't make motel reservations for that kind of trip.

But no one else saw it that way. And they all wanted a say in planning the route. Herb wanted a stop in Topeka to visit his mother. Miss Guglielmo had a sister in Seattle. Henry had always dreamed of seeing Disneyland.

"Butte, Montana, would be good for the sixth night," my mother went on. "That would give us time to fit in Yellow-stone. Breeden knows a good place to eat there."

The phone rang.

"That'll be Breeden now," my mother said. "He's getting stuff to eat and drink for the party tonight." My mother had planned a going-away party for all of us in the basement of Hart Memorial. Medwik knew nothing about it yet.

I made my way through suitcases and boxes to the phone. The caller was indeed Breeden.

"Hi, Frank? Question for you. Should I get one case of Coke, one of Sunkist Orange, and one of Dr Pepper, or one of Coke, one of Orange, and one of Sprite? Or maybe a half-case of Sprite and a half-case of Dr Pepper?"

"Breeden," I began.

"And on the cold-cut issue. Turns out Herb's friend Elissa is a vegetarian. And Henry won't eat anything that comes from a cow, right? And Ernesto, is he Jewish?"

"Whatever you get will be fine, Breeden."

"Come on, Frank. I need a little help here. And there's a line of people waiting for this phone."

"Ma," I said, holding out the receiver to her.

Sighing, she got up from the table and took it from me. "Okay, what's up?" She made a face at me while Breeden explained his problem. "Well, I say get half-cases of everything, including seltzer, because Woody won't drink anything with sugar. Yes, Ernesto is Jewish, but he eats everything. And we can get some crudités for the vegetarians. We'll make onion dip here. We were just going to throw out the mix anyway. Got it? Good. Bye."

She hung up. "Not so very difficult, was it?" My mother returned to her map. "Frank," she said after a moment. "Come here, hon." She patted the box on the floor next to her, the one labeled NONFICTION: GOULD TO MCPHEE.

I sat down. She began rubbing my shoulders, her thumbs pressing deep into the soft flesh. "You've lost some weight in the past week," she said.

"I'll put it back on before winter. Like a bear."

She chuckled, and then pulled the short hairs on the nape of my neck. "Do you remember, when you were five or six and Zoe and I would take you to the ice-cream store on Front Street in Albany?"

"Zoe?"

"The girl who used to work for the same service I did? Long blond hair, thinnish nose."

"Oh right, right. She never wanted me to call her Aunt."

"Exactly. We took you every Sunday night to the Dairy Queen—were they called Dairy Queens in those days?—and we always ordered you a banana sundae, with chocolate sauce, and then watched you eat it. We couldn't get any for ourselves, we had our figures to watch, but we got almost as much pleasure just watching you eat yours. You had such a big appetite then."

I couldn't really place the memory she was talking about, but I nodded my head. I wanted her to go on.

"And every time," she said, "afterwards, we'd walk home together through the streets of Albany, you between us, holding hands with both of us. Men in cars would slow down as they passed, shouting out the window, asking if we needed a ride, and every time you'd look at them and say, in that tiny five-year-old voice, 'They're with me.' It was hilarious. Even the men had to laugh. That firm little voice. 'They're with me.' "

"I guess I cramped your style."

She dug her thumbs in, sending a spasm of pain down my backbone. "I have never, in twenty-five years, for a single moment, regarded you as an obstacle or burden of any kind. Remember that."

"I will."

She stopped massaging my shoulders. "I sometimes wonder if I should've married after I had you. There was no shortage of opportunities, you know."

"Why didn't you?"

"Oh, I don't know. I thought I could do a better job of bringing you up by myself. If you'd've had a father, who knows? You might have grown up to become a banker or something. I don't think I could have stood that."

She grabbed the map again and spread it out on the table. "Now, seeing as I've gotten you all relaxed, what do you think about Butte as an overnight stop for day six?"

Sighing, I got up from the box and, leaning over my mother's shoulder, examined the map. "Well, if we skip Yellowstone, we can probably make it as far as Coeur d'Alene. This isn't a sightseeing trip, after all."

My mother thought about that for a moment. Then she crossed out Yellowstone on her legal pad. "Coeur d'Alene it is," she said. "Breeden will be disappointed, though."

"You think so?"

"Probably. A little."

I closed my eyes for a moment. I could hear the absence

of ticking from the hallway clock we had sold to our next-door neighbor. "So Breeden will be disappointed," I said finally, pulling the legal pad toward me.

11.

Herb's young friend Steve had filled the embalming syringes with spiced rum punch. "Open wide," he kept saying, squirting little streams of the stuff into people's mouths. When he tried it on Epatha's mother, though, she pushed him into the chemical cabinet, making the bottles clink ominously.

"Mother!" Epatha scolded from across the room. She turned to me, her earrings tinkling. "Sorry about that. The woman gets rambunctious."

"It's fine," I assured her. "As long as the people upstairs don't hear anything." There was an important wake going on in the Green Room of Hart Memorial. One of the local captains of industry, the owner/founder of Gallo Pool and Fountain Cleaners, Inc., had had an embolism at a Chamber of Commerce meeting. Mr. Medwik, attending the same meeting, was able to offer the services of Hart Memorial on the spot. He considered it a coup. So now, while we soon-to-be Alaskans partied downstairs, the cream of the cream of north-central Westchester County stalked the Green Room upstairs, networking around the old man's coffin.

"Hey Frank!" Herb called out from the snacks table. "Elissa and I have an idea. We're going to start a freelance proofreading service up in Hungry. Elissa's a copy editor."

"Great," I said, wondering how much call for proofreading there would be in the frozen tundra.

"We've got a name for it too," Elissa added in her gravelly alto. "Galley Slaves of Hungry!"

"Why on earth would they call it that?" Miss Guglielmo whispered to me, her breath redolent of rum.

"Excuse me," I whispered. I slipped away to find my mother, whom I hadn't seen for the better part of an hour. There were a few last-minute details I wanted to discuss with her.

I found her, finally, in the refrigerated vault beyond the stockroom, making out with Breeden.

"Sorry, hon," she said, straightening her blouse. Her lipstick was smeared, giving her the appearance of a little girl who had filched some cherry Kool-Aid. Breeden, meanwhile, looked away in embarrassment, at the shrouded figure that was my last act as an employee of Hart Memorial.

"Can I speak to you a minute, Mother?" I said.

"Mother? When have you ever called me Mother?"

"I'll go check on the clam dip," Breeden said quickly.

After he had closed the door behind him, my mother and I stared at each other in the dim light. "Are you mad at me?" she asked, vapor creeping from her mouth in the cold air.

"What possible right could I have to be mad at you?" I said, trying not to be mad at her. "I just wish this had happened a little sooner. I might have been able to get more money from him for the Toyota."

She smiled. "Oh good. You're *not* mad." She put her arm around me. She was wearing a black silk blouse and, God knows why, her funeral pearls. "Isn't he cute? But don't worry. I won't ask him to share our igloo, at least not yet." She squeezed my shoulder. "Speaking of igloos, Woody has a problem he wants to talk to you about. He's worried about the availability of housing in Hungry, now that so many people are coming with us."

"I've thought of that," I said. "If there's not enough room, the younger ones can make do with tents until something is built. Or we'll get Quonset huts. I think you can order them by mail."

"Quonset huts," my mother said dreamily. "At my age, I never imagined I'd ever be living in a Quonset hut."

"I wanted to tell you, I finally got in touch with Ramona, the woman who runs Hungry Dry Goods. I gave her the final total of our party, so she'll know how much extra stuff to order from her distributor." I checked the item off on my mental list, then said: "Ramona also thought she could use some extra help with the books, just twelve hours a week or so. Interested?"

My mother bared some eye white in my direction. "You got me a job?"

"If you want it. Think of it this way, you'll probably be the only professional accountant in the country living in a Quonset hut."

My mother kissed me. "So that leaves just Miss Guglielmo and Ernesto without a job up there."

"I'll see what I can do."

There was a knock on the door of the vault. "I'll get it," my mother said.

It was Henry, standing hand in hand with a small, doe-eyed Indian boy who couldn't have been more than nine or ten. "May we come in?" Henry asked.

"Please," my mother said, gesturing them in my direction.

Henry stepped into the vault, the boy in tow behind him. "This is my cousin Harold," Henry said. "Harold is the third son of my mother's favorite sister."

No, I told myself, there has to be a line drawn somewhere. "Henry," I said. "We've got too many already."

Henry frowned. "The boy's family won't miss him very much," he said. "And we've been making plans—"

"I'm sorry, there's just no room. I'm very sorry."

Henry was undeterred. He took a short breath and then announced: "If Harold can't go, I can't go."

I closed my eyes for a moment, then opened them. I looked at the boy, his slender wrists and neck, the eyes that wouldn't meet mine. "I'm sorry," I said finally.

"Fine," Henry said. Turning and grabbing Harold's hand, he left, pulling the door shut behind him.

My mother was watching me from across the vault. Shifting weight on her high heels, she said, "There would've been room in Herb's car. But, of course, it's your decision." She took a few steps toward me, her heels clicking on the cement floor.

"He's a boy. They'd probably arrest us for kidnapping. Carrying a minor across state lines."

She stopped a few feet away from me. "As you say," she whispered. Then she turned away and headed for the door.

I sat in that vault for another five minutes, feeling the chill seep into the folds of my clothing. I wasn't sure what I had just done, but I was sure I didn't like it. I leaned back and filled my lungs with cold air. The vault smelled of alcohol and pancake makeup, as it always did. I wondered if the vault of the funeral home in Hungry would smell like this. The owner, a man called Klanzer, had told me over the phone that they didn't even have to refrigerate their vault. The foundation was built low into the permafrost, so the entire room worked like an icebox.

Feeling suddenly exhausted, I got up. I pushed past the shrouded gurneys and slipped out the back door for some air.

A group of men—guests from the Gallo wake—were standing around in the parking lot outside, wearing dark suits and smoking cigarettes. I watched them huddling together, whispering, telling the jokes that men always told at wakes. The light from the funeral home spilled out the back door, throwing their shadows far across the rain-slicked parking lot.

I passed them quickly, trying not to be noticed. But then

I turned and looked back at them. I knew these men. They were the kind who used to visit the Albany whorehouses at night and then shut them down the next morning, for corrupting public morals. The men who did favors for each other, who looked the other way when necessary, who knew what it took to get things done. The movers and the shakers.

No, I told myself as I watched them. I spun around again and stared across the parking lot. No, I repeated silently, go back to the beginning. I felt the key to my mother's Cadillac in my trouser pocket. And there, in a corner of the lot, was the old car itself, sitting wet and cool and patient, like the easy answer to a difficult question. Start again, I said, almost aloud. Begin at the beginning.

The car was uncharacteristically clean; all of the old clothing and books and half-used cosmetics that usually cluttered the back seat had been packed into the U-Haul that now stood in our driveway at Woodland Whispers. The plan was to hitch the trailer to the Caddy tomorrow morning and take off, before sunrise.

I slipped into the expansive front seat and started the engine. The atlas—the one my mother once stole for me—lay on the passenger seat, ready for tomorrow's trip. I picked it up and opened to a page at random, letting my finger fall where it may. Goldfield, Nevada. I smiled. The kind of name my mother would like.

I put the car into reverse and pulled out of the parking space. As I did, the headlights swept across a figure in the middle of the asphalt lot—my mother, in her pearls, staring at me. I pulled up beside her and rolled down the window.

"You're leaving us, aren't you," she said, pulling an errant strand of hair behind her ear.

"I have to. You understand, I think."

She heaved a breath and looked back at the lights of the

funeral home. The men were gone. "This won't work without you. It'll fall apart. I know it."

I watched the milky specter of my hand gripping the top of the enormous steering wheel. For a moment, I considered asking my mother to come with me, but decided against it. Of course. "Maybe it's better if it does fall apart."

"Maybe." She looked down at me. "You'll tell me where I can send your luggage?"

I nodded. "And I'll send you five hundred for the car."

"Make it eight hundred," she said.

"Six-fifty."

"Eight hundred."

"Okay."

"Well," she began slowly. Then, suddenly, she leaned over and kissed me, hard, through the open window. I could taste the wax of her lipstick, the faint trace of spiced rum punch. "I'll let you know if anything happens with Breeden," she said. She looked down at me. "I like him."

I shifted the car into drive. "Good-bye."

She nodded. "Right. Drive carefully. And remember that the left windshield wiper doesn't work."

It was midnight when I reached the first long straightaway of Interstate-80. I had just crossed the edge of the New York metropolitan sprawl, at the place in New Jersey where the highway fans out to three lanes, then four, then five. The Cadillac felt like a part of me, an extension of my arms and legs. All I had to do was touch the pedal, and it would leap forward, eager for the long glide west.

PART TWO

The Erikson Stories

Ghost Story

*T*HE NIGHT of my father's first business trip, my mother turned up at my bedroom door around midnight. My light was off, but I wasn't asleep and she knew it. She stood silhouetted in the doorway, wearing her tattered flannel pajamas, her dark hair pulled back into a youthful ponytail. I watched her from the bed through slitted eyes. She had one of her golf clubs with her—a heavy-headed putter, nearly unused, which she held against her shoulder like an infantryman's rifle. In her other hand were two steak knives and the red plastic flashlight from the master bathroom. She seemed to be having difficulty holding onto it all.

My mother sighed pointedly and leaned against the doorjamb. The flashlight clicked on and off, once. She sighed again.

"Can't sleep?" I asked from the shadowy bed.

She nodded. "It's ridiculous, of course. We both know there's nothing down there." She clicked the flashlight on again, playing its beam idly across my desktop, over a pile of textbooks and my collection of plastic Apollo rockets. In the corner beyond the desk was a colonial-style brass lamp that she examined briefly before turning the beam on my face.

"Sorry," she said, dousing the flashlight.

A dark pellet of afterimage floated in front of my eyes. "You heard something downstairs?" I asked her.

"Maybe."

I lay in bed for a few seconds, silent.

"He would say there's nothing down there, wouldn't he?" my mother stated then.

"You're not really scared," I told her.

She looked at me oddly, as if considering the truth of what I had just said. "The situation," she began, "is what makes me scared. The three of us alone in this house without your father." She pushed away from the doorjamb and stepped toward my bed. "Here," she said, holding out the putter by the shaft. "And I've got some knives for me and Elise. The set your Aunt Rita gave us as a wedding present."

I sat up in bed and reached for the putter. What we were both thinking of—what neither of us would admit to thinking of—was the fact that this same Aunt Rita had been burglarized just three months before. Her house in Riverdale had been broken into by some drunk teenagers looking for vodka and a few things to sell. Rita and her husband, Deems, had come home from vacation to find the cushions on the sofa slashed, crumbs of glass crackling underfoot as they walked.

"Just for our peace of mind," my mother went on. The shaft of the club was warm against my palm, not like metal at all. "Now let's go wake your sister."

I followed my mother out of the room. We edged quietly along the upstairs corridor and stepped through Elise's half-open door. My sister's room was swimming in a soft, orange glow from the nightlight above the bureau. The poorly taped edges of her posters—lurid group pictures of The Monkees, The Dave Clark Five—curled away from the walls, throwing small triangular shadows at the corners.

"You won't be able to wake her up," I said, almost in a normal voice. Elise, two years younger than me, was a heavy sleeper, never easy to rouse.

My mother leaned over Elise's bed and lifted her out from under the covers. "Come on, sweetheart," she whispered, setting the small body on its feet. She pressed the handle of a steak knife into my sister's unresponsive hand.

"Let's leave her up here," I said. "She's asleep."

My mother shot me a quick, angry look. "This is something we do together, the three of us. Understand?"

The suddenness of the rebuke surprised me, shut me up. I touched the head of the putter to my sister's cream-colored rug. There were socks—small, white ankle socks—all over the floor.

"Now follow me," my mother said, still whispering. We crept behind her—my sister slowly coming awake—out of the room and down the hallway. At the top of the carpeted stairs, my mother stopped us and signaled silence with the steak knife. "Make a lot of noise now," she said. "Talk to me."

I looked at her blankly. "Won't he hear us then?"

"Talking will keep us safe," she answered quickly. "Besides, there's no he to hear us. We're just putting our minds at rest." My mother wet her lips with her tongue. "Now talk," she said. "Tell me about school, your teacher, whatever."

I nodded, took a breath, and then began with the first thing that came to mind: "OK, this new guy Cory—"

"Louder!" she whispered.

"This new guy Cory counts the Sea Train trucks passing by the classroom window."

My mother nodded at me in encouragement. She began slowly descending the steps, shepherding Elise and me behind her.

"Anderson Avenue is on their route, I guess. He keeps count from lunchtime to three o'clock, and makes a mark on his notebook for each one. I sit behind him."

We reached the bottom of the stairs, already beyond the

glow of light from the upstairs hall. My mother turned the flashlight on and put her hand—the handle of the steak knife clicking against her wedding ring—on my sister's narrow back.

"He's from somewhere south," I went on, trying to make my voice sound natural as we moved across the dark living room. "So I told him about going to Grandma's in El Paso, how we all liked it there. And about those spiky yucca plants I liked."

We reached the front closet. Without thinking, I stopped talking when my mother's hand touched the knob; I forgot even to lift the golf putter.

She pulled open the door.

"Nothing there," I said after a moment.

My mother played the light up and down the racks of clothing—our winter coats, our torn rubber boots, the box containing the slide projector we never used. They all looked slightly mysterious in the weak light of the flashlight beam, but they were safe, quiet objects, objects we knew.

My mother closed the door. "Of course," she said. Her body seemed to slump in relief. Then, collecting our weapons and pushing them out of sight under the mahogany end table, she took our hands and led us to the living room. She collapsed onto the couch and pulled us down on either side of her. "There, I told you it was nothing." She threw her slender arms over our shoulders. I could smell her then—soap mostly, and that vaguely sweet, wet, woolly scent she always gave off. She seemed almost gleeful now. "Your father's probably sleeping in a hotel room in Oregon," she went on. She started to hum "California, Here I Come," which seemed inappropriate. Then she looked down at me. "God, I feel silly. But that was nice, what you said about Grandma's. That you liked it there. You never told me that before."

I shrugged. "It was interesting."

"You should tell me things more," she went on. "Especially when your father is away like this. We should stick together, like a family. He would want it that way." She looked over at the fireplace for a moment, thinking of something. "My brother and I used to talk every night. We slept in the same bedroom of our house in El Paso, the first one, you never saw it. We'd lie in bed, talking across the room." She looked down at me and then suddenly unwrapped her arms from us and placed them both on the knees of her black shepherd-check pajamas. "But it's late." She got up from the couch and turned to us. "You two are my valiant protectors."

I found this funny, the thought of me and my half-conscious sister actually protecting my mother from harm. I got up and pulled Elise toward the stairs, where my mother already stood with one foot on the bottom step. My mother looked very young then, her hair pulled back, the pajama cuffs hanging low over her hands.

She started up the stairs, but turned back to us. "Let's not say anything to your father about this when he comes home," she said. "Cliff, Elise, OK? It'll be one of our secrets."

We both nodded, accustomed to this request. We had lots of secrets, the three of us.

"Now we can all sleep more soundly," she said as she snapped off the downstairs lights.

It became a ritual after that. Each night before our bedtime, the three of us, weapons in hand, would make the rounds of potential hiding places in the house, talking to each other with feigned nonchalance. We checked the kitchen pantry, the utility closet in the dining room, the little room where the washing machine and drier stood surrounded by shelves of thick terrycloth towels. It turned into a joke. Each night, the weapons we carried on our rounds would change, becoming increasingly ridiculous. Elise would wield a ceramic teapot, holding it by the spout; my mother would get the old phone receiver from the closet and hold it like a blackjack, while I'd make as if to poke the intruder with the plastic dish-drying rack from the kitchen. The whole routine amused Elise particularly. She would giggle uncontrollably, hilarious with half-real fear, as we talked our way toward each closet. My mother would sometimes have to calm her down, taking away her weapon before she really hit or stabbed something with it.

Afterward, sure of our safety, we would collapse again onto the living-room couch. My mother would pull a cigarette from the pack she kept on the end table and light it with her silver lighter. Then she would say the words to us, the ones I waited for: "See, kids? Talking will keep us safe."

And that's when we would talk some more, my mother and me—for real now, not just to keep the burglars away. We would slouch against the cushions, Elise falling asleep between us, and just stare straight ahead, as if mesmerized by the harvest-gold curtains pulled across the picture window. My mother would ask me questions—odd questions, like whether I thought of us as a wealthy family, whether I knew the name of the mayor or the Secretary of State, whether I was sad that I didn't have a younger brother. She seemed intrigued by the fact that she could ask me things like this, that I was old enough now to have ideas and feelings that were not put there by her or my father. Sensing this, I tried to answer honestly. But I didn't yet know what I felt about everything, so I would improvise as I sat there. I concocted things—a vivid hatred for a fictional girl in my class, a firm conviction that we as a family were special in some strong but unknowable way. I was afraid that if my responses were too vague or uncertain, my mother would rise from the couch, stretch in her oversized pajamas, and say, "Well, it's time for bed, I think," which is what she would eventually say anyway. But I figured that as long as I told her things, as long as I could keep her listening, we could continue sitting there, safe amid the hissing radiators, the thick carpets and upholstery soaking up our voices in the dark room.

It was on the last night of that business trip—the fourth or fifth night my father was away—that my mother first asked me about God. On our closet-checking rounds that night, we had been talking about new cars, about the '64 Plymouth station wagon my father had his eye on, but now that we had established ourselves on the couch, she turned suddenly to this new topic. "I guess I should know this about you," she said, Elise's sleeping blond head resting against her breast, "but what do you believe? I mean, we never really talk about that, do we."

I turned to her, puzzled. "I thought we were Lutheran," I said.

My mother stared at the burning end of her cigarette. "Well, *you* are, you two kids. Officially, at least."

This thought was bizarre to me, that my mother wasn't the same religion as we were. I thought at first that she might be lying.

"I was raised a Catholic," she continued. She closed her eyes and put her head back against the cushions. Her bare feet rested on the kidney-shaped coffee table. "I used to go to Saint Theresa in El Paso. A big orange church on a busy corner." She laughed, a flippant, self-conscious laugh I had never heard before. "I was a passionate little Catholic girl. That was Rosa's doing. She convinced me that the bread was real flesh, and the wine was blood. I shivered every time we took communion." She opened her eyes and looked at me. "We were all supposed to believe in that—transubstantiation—but I don't think most people really did."

"I don't understand," I said quietly.

"All good Catholics believe that the bread and wine really, literally, turn into the body and blood of Christ. They call it transubstantiation."

I found myself excited by this idea. I was uncommonly interested in blood at the time—its viscousness, its smell. But this fascination embarrassed me, so I said nothing. I just sat there and watched the ash on my mother's cigarette burn down, the paper igniting silently along the edge.

"I used to go every Wednesday afternoon with Rosa, the woman who looked after me when my mother was at work. I was your age, I guess. This was long after my father left." She leaned forward and tapped the ash from her cigarette into a ceramic ashtray. "I used to love the smell of that place," she said. "They burned some kind of incense. Blue smoke pouring out of a censer the Mexican priest swung around. I remember watching that, and smelling Rosa's sweaty clothes beside me. It was all so *much* somehow, with the faces in the pictures on the altar." My mother looked over at me suddenly. "But here I am, talking when I'm supposed to be the one asking the questions."

"Why is it supposed to be that way?" I asked, the first words hoarse. "Me answering the questions."

My mother didn't respond at first. She looked thoughtful for a second, pulling at the edge of her mouth with the pinky of her smoking hand. I sensed that I had made a tactical mistake. My question had allowed the conversation to take its gentle, inevitable turn toward conclusion. My mother leaned forward and stubbed out her cigarette. "Well," she said, "it's time for bed, I think."

"Not yet. Please."

She chuckled softly to herself, staring at me. Then: "Dad's coming home tomorrow. We'll have to get this house back into shape before he does." She got up, slipped her arms under my sister's small body, and hoisted her to her chest. "Coming?"

I didn't answer. I just sat there in the dim light, my body seeming to fill with sadness, like a pitcher filling with hot milk.

"We'll talk again tomorrow," she said. "I promise."

I shook my head. "We won't. Tomorrow he'll be back. Tomorrow we won't have to check the closets."

I looked up. My mother was standing over me. She was pursing her lips. She knew that I was right.

My father came back the next evening, shortly before dinner. He had been to Portland, to visit some paper mills for an annual report he was writing. "It's gorgeous up there," he told us as we gathered around him in the living room, ceremonially welcoming him home. "Pine trees, mountains, lakes." My father seemed to have brought home the smell of the Pacific Northwest—a faint odor of pine that clung to his clothing. He pulled a small wrapped box out of his carry-on bag. "Here," he said, handing it to me, "You won't believe this." He was huffing with enthusiasm, his eyes glassy. My mother sat to his left, watching him, smiling in a sympathetic but uncomprehending way.

"Well, open it, Cliff," my father prompted.

I unwrapped the thick glossy paper and pulled off the cardboard lid. Inside was a small stuffed owl—real, by the looks of it—perched on a ceramic log. Its eyes were plastic. Its mottled brown wing feathers looked slippery and fragile.

"It's a bird," my sister said matter-of-factly.

"Not just a bird, sweetheart, an owl. Stuffed." My father took it from my hands and showed her. The thing looked much smaller in his enormous hands.

"Is it real?" my mother asked.

"That's what they tell me. The plant manager in Hillsboro gave it to me after the tour. Shot it himself in the warehouse one morning. You can feel the bullet hole in the side. Here."

Elise put her finger where my father indicated, under the left wing. She smiled.

"Here, Cliff," my father said.

I touched the spot, which was stubbly and uneven. The whole body seemed to be hollow.

"No thanks," my mother said then, anticipating my father's offer. "Why did he shoot it?"

"I don't know. He says they're like vermin out there. Always getting in where they shouldn't be." My father put the owl down on the coffee table. He reached again into the depths of his luggage. "And I've got something for your mother here." He pulled out another package, much smaller.

"Your father and his presents," my mother said, taking the small box. I could tell that she was pleased. She opened the box and pulled out a small, reddish figure of a turtle, placing it on the palm of her hand. "Another little animal," she observed.

"It's made of pipestone," my father explained. "It's an old Indian charm. A fertility charm."

"Cal!" my mother snapped. She turned her head, as if her face had been hit, and stared at the swinging door to the kitchen.

"Just a little extra help," my father said uncertainly.

I looked up in bewilderment, at my mother, at my father.

"The kids know, Faye," he said. "You knew, didn't you, Cliff?"

A faint comprehension was slowly making its way through my brain, rearranging everything as it went. But I was too startled to answer. No one spoke for a few seconds. Finally, Elise got up from her chair. "I like the turtle better," she said, stepping up to my mother and taking it out of her tightly clenched hand.

We had dinner late that night, giving my father time to unpack. It was eight o'clock before we finished. We sat around the remains of a sauerbraten dinner, which my mother had cooked expressly for his return. "The family reunited," my father kept saying. "I missed you all."

He had coffee after the meal, a special blend he bought in Oregon. "So," he said as he sipped it, "were you all right here by yourselves? Anything to report?"

"We checked the closets at night," Elise answered without hesitation.

I stopped eating, a forkful of mashed potatoes halfway between my plate and my mouth. I was amazed at the ease of my sister's betrayal.

My father looked at my mother. "You checked the closets?"

My mother shrugged, then reached across the table to adjust the placement of the salt shaker. "I thought I heard something one night. So we all looked in the hall closet together to check."

"I had a teapot to throw at him," Elise said.

My father was nodding, looking at each of us in turn.

"It became a game after a while," my mother explained.

My father paused and wiped his mouth with a red cloth napkin. "Well, that's fine," he said, "but I want you kids to know that you're all safe in this house, whether I'm here with you or not. There's nothing to be afraid of."

"They know that," my mother said, so quietly that we barely heard.

"You understand me, Elise? Cliff? You're protected. What

happened to Aunt Rita won't happen here. And your mother knows that."

"Of course," my mother said to the salt shaker. "It was just a joke. Like telling ghost stories. Nothing."

"Like a haunted house," Elise said, tickled with this idea. She held up her fork and waved it at my mother. "Mommy thought the house had a ghost."

After dinner, my sister and I lay on the floor in the upstairs TV room, watching our old black-and-white Magnavox. My mother stood behind us, ironing at the board set up beside the half-full bookcases. She seemed pensive now that my father was home. The steam iron sighed in her hand like a sorrowful animal.

At a commercial break, I got up for something to drink. I ran down the carpeted steps to the first floor, not noticing my father in the living room until I was right on top of him. He sat in a single, amber-colored pool of light, examining the owl he had brought home. He was wearing a white oxford-cloth shirt open at the neck, so that tufts of his graying chest hair showed over the top button. The sleeves were turned up twice to reveal his bulbous forearms.

"I'm getting something to drink from the kitchen," I said, feeling that some explanation was necessary.

My father reached across the coffee table, his salt-and-pepper hair glinting in the light. "Here," he said. "Use my glass. Save Mom the trouble of washing an extra."

I took the empty tumbler from his hand. Outside, rain had started, pattering the windows. "You know," he began, looking down again at the stuffed owl. He held it like a shot put in his hand, testing its weight. "There's something to be said for a place where animals like this can be a problem, a pest. Noble birds of prey."

I nodded, not sure what kind of response he expected.

He looked up at me and said, "Sit down a minute?"

I didn't want to. I was in the middle of a show. Already, I could hear its bright, phony laugh track upstairs, muffled by the distance. But I obeyed, as I always did, lowering myself into the chair across from him.

"This trip I just took," he said, placing the owl on the coffee table and leaning back, "is going to be the first of many, I'd guess. The company I'm writing for has plants all over the country. I'll be gone—" He stopped himself, and began again: "Your mother," he said, "is sort of a fearful person." His eyes shot up to mine quickly, to see if his words had caused any reaction. "I don't mean this as a criticism of her or of anybody. God knows, there are a lot of things to be afraid of in this world." He placed his fingers together and tapped them once, twice, before continuing. "But there are different ways of looking at the world, or approaching . . . matters of substance."

I stared down at the carpet. I could hear him breathing. My father was always a heavy breather. A husky man.

"I want you to grow up ready to grab the world by the balls, if you know what I mean. A boy needs someone to teach him. Me being away sometimes could be a problem."

"It's not a problem," I said. I began to get up, but my father put his hand out to stop me.

"Don't be timid," he said, almost fervently. His hand gripped my arm. "I want you to remember not to be timid. Your mother . . ." He stopped again mid-sentence.

"OK," I said finally.

My father was watching me carefully. Then his eyes softened. "OK is right," he said, laughing. He took a handful of my shirt-front and twisted it playfully, so that the shirttails pulled out of my waistband. "I love you, Cliff," he said. "Remember *that* too."

"I will."

My father smiled. He put his arm around me and squeezed me tight against his chest. "You've got your mother's eyes," he said then, boozily.

The next day, my mother picked us up from school in our light-blue Impala. It was a brisk November afternoon. Fingers of dark cloud scudded across a gunmetal sky. My mother, in her ginger-colored winter coat, had pulled a plaid scarf over her head. She wore dark sunglasses and enormous suede gloves—men's gloves, belonging to my father.

"A slight change in procedure today, kids," she said, checking her rearview after we got in and slammed the doors. "Elise, honey, I'm dropping you off at Frances's for an hour or two, OK? Cliff and I have an errand to run."

This was the first I'd heard of any errand. But there was something in my mother's voice, an artificial, songish tone, that kept me from saying anything. Elise's comment to my father about checking the closets, perhaps, had changed things; my mother now realized that Elise could not be told everything.

We drove from the school to Aunt Frances's house, the silence between my mother and me conspicuous as Elise prattled on about recess and mucilage. Aunt Frances—not our real aunt, just a close friend of my parents—lived a few blocks from us, in a house surrounded by bony forsythia bushes. "Go right in, Elise. Frances will have something for you to do."

Elise, expelling an exaggerated sigh, got out of the car. We watched as she stepped up to the front door, trailing her bookbag behind her. After a moment, Aunt Frances opened the door. She peered out at us, waved, and bundled Elise into the house.

"I told Frances I needed you to carry something from the hardware store, something for Dad's birthday," my mother said, her eyes invisible behind the dark-green lenses. "But we're going somewhere else." She put the car in gear and pulled away from the curb.

"Where are we going?" I asked when it became clear she wasn't going to continue on her own.

She didn't take her eyes off the road. "Church," she said.

After a few minutes, we pulled up across the street from a large, black-brick Catholic church in a part of town I didn't know. The enormous building stood at the top of a flight of concrete steps. Its weather-worn facade, without decoration except for a round stained-glass window over the doorway, seemed to rise ominously above the street, topped by a plain white cross that was almost obscured by crisscrossing telephone wires. A sign at the door read ST. NICHOLAS CHURCH.

"I thought you might be interested," my mother said then. Her gloved hand was on the ignition key, waiting for a sign from me. "If you're not, we can just go home."

I looked at the mountainous church for a moment before saying, "I'm interested."

My mother's hand turned the ignition key, silencing the engine.

We got out of the car and crossed the busy street. My mother took my hand as we climbed the cracked steps and pushed open the heavy wooden front door. Suddenly we were inside, out of the cold, in what seemed almost total darkness and quiet. It took a while for my eyes to adjust, but when they did, I could make out a long aisle with empty pews on both sides. At the end of the aisle was a raised area broken up by wooden pulpits, a few bunches of flowers in standing vases, a statue. The church was entirely empty.

I dropped my mother's gloved hand. On a stark metal rack near the entrance stood scores of candles, in every stage of burning.

"This is the nave," my mother whispered, her voice alarmingly loud in the vault of the church. She pulled off her sunglasses, scarf, and heavy gloves and stuffed them all into the deep pockets of her overcoat. "There's no mass now, but we can at least have a look around."

I nodded and peered into the gloom. The damp, open space smelled musty, waxy, exotic. I had never been inside a Catholic church before, and was amazed, above all, by the darkness. The Lutheran church I'd attended a few times was bright, full of blond wood and clean white walls and modern rest rooms with dishes of baking soda instead of soap.

"Take off your hat."

I pulled off my navy wool cap. Grasping it in my hand, I followed as my mother, moving suddenly, made her way down the long aisle of the church. I was wearing sneakers, but she wore black shoes that creaked as we went toward the altar. The whole building seemed to fan around us. The vaulted ceiling was impossibly high overhead, lost in shadows.

My mother stopped at the bottom of the altar steps. There were two long tapers on the marble slab, framing a dark painting. Jesus was barely visible in the painting, a pale figure nailed on the cross in an awkward, unnatural position, posed against a dramatic mackerel sky. Above the picture, a stained-glass window glowed faintly.

My mother made the sign of the cross, her fingertips touching four places on her body. I wondered whether I was expected to do the same, and even began raising my right hand to my head, but I stopped short, at chest level. I didn't know how to do it, really, and my mother wasn't watching me.

She was staring up at the painting of Jesus above the altar.

"I've always wondered what the inside of this place looked like," my mother said, as much to herself as to me. "Not the same at all."

I heard the creak of her shoes a few feet away before I realized that she had left my side. She was going toward a side chapel. Another, smaller rack of candles stood beside an iron grate here. I watched my mother reach into her pocket and step up to the rack. A coin fell into the box, making a metallic thud of such clarity and volume that I expected someone to emerge from the shadows, angry at the noise.

I quickly followed her. By the time I reached her side, she had taken a white candle out of the bin and was lighting it from the flame of another that had burned almost to the bottom. "You have to pay?" I asked her.

She glanced sideways with a little grin on her face. "You have to pay," she said. She pushed the bottom of the candle onto an empty spike. She brushed the curls of wax from her fingers and spent a moment staring at the burning taper, looking satisfied.

She began unbuttoning her overcoat. I thought this meant that we were going to stay a while, maybe a long while, in this dark church. "Mom," I began, but she silenced me with a finger to her lips. She stepped over to the black prayer rail and—awkwardly, almost as if she had to force herself to do it—knelt. I felt something like panic rising in me as I watched this behavior. She clasped her hands together, fingers interlacing, and pressed them against her forehead. Her lips began moving silently. I turned away and looked around, mortified that someone might see her. When I heard the dull impact of the door at the back of the church, I couldn't help myself; I stepped up to my mother's kneeling figure and pushed her shoulder. She looked up at me, her eyes red and surprised, as if I had just roused her from sleep. "Someone's coming," I whispered.

She stood up quickly, gathering her overcoat around herself, her thin, cold fingers groping for the buttons. She looked as guilty as I did. Coughing once, she grabbed my wrist, and we started walking down the side aisle to the back of the church. We could see the people who had come in—two ancient, white-haired ladies, both dressed in deep black. They were helping each other down the central aisle. "It's Angela," I heard one of them whisper in a loud, hissing voice. Then the taller one waved. "Hoo, Angela!" she said, her voice reverberating in the rafters.

My mother stopped short. She was about to open her mouth, to tell the woman that she was mistaking us for someone else, but she said nothing. She nodded at the two women.

"How's your aunt, dear? Better?"

My mother made a vague gesture with her free hand. "Much better, thank you," she said, squeezing my wrist to silence me.

The two old women bobbed their heads. Then the taller one spoke again: "Tell her we were asking about her. It's Lucille and Antonia. She'll know. Send her our love."

"I'll tell her that, thank you," my mother said. "God bless you." She started walking again, pulling me along. Just as we reached the back of the church, I heard the taller woman's raspy stage whisper again: "I heard it was breast cancer. Such a terrible, terrible thing."

My mother's lips were pursed as we made our way down the concrete steps. She hadn't bothered to put her scarf back on. Her hair moved like a sea creature in the sharp wind. I had a hard time keeping up as she crossed the street.

"Well, Cliff," she said when we had settled into the car.

Her cheeks were flushed. "That was something, wasn't it?"

"Why did you pretend to be that other woman?" I asked, appalled by what I had just seen.

"Oh, I don't know. They were trying to be kind." She leaned forward and turned the ignition, revving the engine twice to warm it up. "But they were cute, weren't they, those two old women? Old Catholic ladies."

I said nothing, just stared out the window at a dime store opposite the church. Two or three blots of rain hit the windshield. "What did you pray for?" I asked finally.

My mother pulled her overcoat tighter around her neck. She heaved a deep breath. "I prayed that things would turn out all right," she said. "The way your father wants them to."

I turned to her. "The way *he* wants them to?"

She paused a moment. "Yes, the way *he* wants them to," she said finally. "But it doesn't matter what you pray for. It's the way praying makes you feel."

She took out a cigarette and lit it with her lighter, the tobacco crackling as it ignited. "And it made me feel pretty damn good," she said then, smoke coming out of her mouth with each word.

The noises were coming from my parents' room again that night. I lay in bed, listening, trying not to listen, as I had done for several weeks now, before and after my father's trip. How will they know when it has happened? I wondered. Or do they know already? Is this just my father compulsively making sure—making sure things turn out the way he wants them?

A late harvest moon was pouring light into my window, turning everything the color of parchment. I kept staring at my beige sweater on the chair across the room, willing it to move.

The noises stopped shortly after midnight. I turned over

in bed and pulled the blanket up to my neck. The image of blood, of wine turning into blood, wheeled through my mind. I thought of the neighbor's dog that was run over in our street, an old dachshund with cloudy eyes. The back tire of the car had rolled over its hindquarters. I remembered seeing it afterward. It was still alive, lying at the edge of the curb, looking around almost nonchalantly while a fan-shaped pool of blood spread out from its abdomen.

Did my mother not want this? I asked myself.

I turned over again. Outside, the wind gusted, rolling dead leaves with a sound like running water. The sound blended with another—footsteps on the landing outside, footsteps descending the stairs. Someone was up, probably my mother. I got out of bed.

A light went on downstairs as I tiptoed to my bedroom door. I stood in the doorway and listened. The sound of a cigarette lighting would tell me who it was downstairs. My father used book matches—a snap followed by a hiss; my mother, on the other hand, had a silver lighter that made a metallic clink and then two or three sibilant scrapes. I waited a full minute for either sound.

Finally I decided to chance it. I crossed the dark hallway and took the first few steps downstairs. The living room revealed itself to me gradually. I saw my mother on the couch in her flannel pajamas. She was lying back in a ball, hugging her knees up to her chest, her face buried.

I stopped short on the stairs. She began stuffing pillows under her to elevate her hips. For a moment I thought that my father had hurt her, that she was lying on the couch that way to soothe an aching back. But she didn't seem hurt to me, just absorbed in what she was doing.

I took another step down the carpeted staircase. She must have heard me, because her face shot up, impossibly white.

Her eyes looked like those of an animal caught in headlights.

"Hi," I said uncertainly. "You want to talk now?"

"Go to bed!" she hissed at me. "For God's sake, Cliff, go to sleep!"

The Impala pulled up in front of our school as usual the next afternoon. Elise and I pulled open the doors and got in, muttering our greetings. It wasn't until I was settled inside that I saw it was my father behind the wheel.

"Dad?" I said. My father rarely picked us up at school. That was one of my mother's jobs.

"Mom is sick," he told us. He was paler than usual, and unbelievably subdued for my father—which sent a jagged slice of fear through me.

"What happened?" I asked.

"She's all right. The doctor's been already and he says she's all right."

"She's all right," Elise repeated from the back seat, turning the words into a charm.

We pulled away into traffic, my mind racing from one awful possibility to another. Then I became aware of my father looking at me sidelong between glances at the road. "She was in church when she took sick," he said carefully. "St. Nicholas Church. Know anything about that?"

I moved my tongue inside my mouth. "No," I said finally.

My father nodded slowly, taking note of the lie.

We got to the house at last. Unraked leaves littered the wet lawn. I jumped out of the car and slammed the door. "Go up and see her, both of you," my father said through the closed window.

I went inside and climbed the stairs to my parents' bedroom, leaving Elise struggling at the front closet with her coat. My mother was lying in bed, surrounded by magazines. She looked up when she heard me, then down again almost immediately. Her hair was loose around her shoulders.

Something told me not to go near her. "Are you sick?" I asked from across the room.

She lifted her head and brushed a wet strand of hair away from her cheek. "Fine, fine." Her voice was low, unrecognizable.

A blue dress—the dress my mother had been wearing that morning—was soaking in the master bathroom. I could see a drowned sleeve of it draped over the edge of the sink.

"I should have told you," my mother was saying then. "If we had talked about it, it would have been all right."

The words seemed lost in the dense air, in the metallic scent of blood that hung, sodden and thick, in the room.

"Cliff . . ."

My father was in the room now, behind me. I didn't turn to look at him, but I could see his presence in my mother's closing face.

"There's no reason to be afraid, Cliff," he said, placing his big hands on my shoulders. I could feel him—the insistent heat of him—on my back. "We'll try again," he whispered, as if to reassure me, as if I were an accomplice in what he had done to her. "She's a little shaken up, but there's nothing to stop us from trying again."

Giant Step

MY MOTHER announced her intention to find a job on the night the Apollo II astronauts landed on the moon. She and my father had roused us from our beds at I A.M. and had carried us to the couch in front of the new color television. "This is world history," my father told Elise and me, arranging blankets around our legs even though it was mid-July. I'm glad he said that, because his words made me pay attention. "This is world history," I repeated as I watched the bulky white figure bounce around the screen. I forced my groggy brain to lock in on that image. Even so, the thing I remember most vividly about the broadcast was that the reception was terrible.

It was after the moonwalk—after the staticky voice had spoken its famous line—that my mother made her announcement. "I was thinking of finding some kind of employment," she said, curled up in the tattered armchair. She was drinking a mug of tea. I could see her watching the three of us through the rising steam, checking our reactions to this idea. "You know, a job. Once you kids go back to school in September."

My sister Elise began to cry quietly.

"We'll talk about it tomorrow," my father said quickly. He, who seemed as surprised as we were, was bouncing around the room like that astronaut on television, turning off lights, resettling cushions in armchairs. "We'll have a family meeting after dinner, OK? Until then, we should all think about the incredible thing we've just witnessed tonight, OK?"

We went to bed again soon after the broadcast. My father, tapping his watch loudly, insisted upon it. But I couldn't fall asleep for hours. My mind kept racing. That night, a new chapter in the history of mankind had begun, but all I could think of was one thing: My mother wanted to find a job.

The family meeting began at 6:30 the next evening, after dinner. We all sat around the empty fireplace in the living room—my sister, my parents, and me—prepared to discuss. My father was the first to speak.

"This idea of your mother's," he began, talking into his steepled fingertips, "is good. I mean, I think it's a great idea for her to expand a little." He got up from the chair and walked to the starburst clock over the mantel. "New possibilities, new attitudes, new—"

"What we want to know," my mother interrupted, "is how you kids feel about it."

My father frowned. "Right," he said.

I turned to Elise, my stare forbidding her to cry again. But she seemed more composed today. "Would you still be able to pick us up at school?" she asked. My sister was going into fifth grade in the fall, at the local grammar school about a mile away. I'd be starting junior high, which in our town was called Intermediate School.

My mother seemed relieved by Elise's question. "We'd arrange it so either your father or I would pick you up. You know, Dad's writing jobs give him a lot of flexibility. We're an unusual family in that respect." She paused. Her eyes darted from Elise to me to Elise again. "Of course, when he's traveling, we may have to arrange something with Aunt Frances."

"What about you, Cliff?" my father said. "Do you have anything to say?"

I did. "What would you *do*?" I asked, letting a little too much blatant incredulity leak into my voice. But the question had been nagging me for an entire night and day now.

"Well," my mother said, "Aunt Helene thinks she'll need somebody at the candle store once school starts. I could begin with that. But eventually I want to move on to something . . . more challenging."

"A lot of women are working these days," my father added. "Look, the new prime minister of Israel is a woman, right? It's a new world out there. This will be good for Mom."

I tried to imagine my mother working in the Candle Corner, a small, cramped storefront on Anderson Avenue. It was filled with candles in the shape of mushrooms, candles in the shape of high-topped shoes, candles in the shape of peace signs. The store always reeked of lavender and rose. Our Aunt Helene made everyone who worked for her wear a frilly red apron.

"How long will you have to work there before you find something else?" I asked.

"Not long."

"Your mother's on the way." My father was rubbing his hands together, a desperately optimistic look on his face. "This'll be good, this'll be good for all of us," he said, trying to sound convincing.

School started that September, as it seemed to start every year, on a dark, rainy morning shaken by gusty winds. It had been a long August, during which my mother, who had previously been content to wear my father's old castoff clothing, bought an entirely new wardrobe. She now had a closet full of flowery dresses, pleated skirts, and pumps in shades unknown to nature.

"How do I look?" she asked me on that first day. She wore a long grayish dress patterned with small daisies, topped with a white lace collar. The look reminded me of wagon-train women, the ones who churned butter and spun thread and could shoe a horse in a pinch.

"Great," I lied.

"Well, good, because I'm too late to change."

She piled us into the car, Elise in the front and me in the back. My sister and I were completely silent on the drive to school, each of us succumbing to that heart-squeezing combination of dread, excitement, and nervousness the first day of school always inspired. The fact that my mother was starting a job the same day just made the feeling sharper, more piquant.

We stopped at Elise's school first—what had been *my* school, too, until this year. "Dad will be waiting here at three," my mother assured her, kissing the top of her head. We watched my sister slam the car door and walk hesitantly toward the front of the colonial brick building.

"Now get up here, Cliff," my mother said, without looking back at me. "I want to talk."

I climbed over the headrest into the front seat.

She gave me a comic panicky look. "I'm nervous," she began.

It was the kind of admission I was used to hearing from her. We were confidants, my mother and I, although most of the confiding in the past few years had gone in one direction—from her to me. Fortunately, I knew that no response was required of me now, so I just looked down at the virgin notebooks in my lap, each one emblazoned with my name in black Magic Marker. School.

"I've never done anything like this before," she went on. She reached into the pocket of her new wool jacket for a cigarette, but decided against it. "I *did* work in high school, I guess. I babysat for some neighbors in El Paso. But nothing like this."

"You're selling candles, Mom. It won't be hard."

This hurt her. She didn't speak for a minute or so, to punish me. She pretended to concentrate on traffic.

"I'm nervous, too," I said finally.

My mother made no reply to this; she merely nodded at the road in front of us, silently accepting my apology.

We pulled up in front of the Intermediate School. It was a nondescript modern building, flat and bunkerlike, with newer wings at both ends whose orange brick didn't quite match the brick of the original structure. There were crowds of seventh and eighth graders milling around the front steps. I recognized none of them.

We sat in the car a moment, just gazing at the building pensively. "You'll be stopping at that church on the way to Aunt Helene's?" I asked then.

Her head snapped toward me. It was understood in the family that my mother hadn't been to church in several years, since her miscarriage. I'd always suspected otherwise.

Still staring at me, she heaved a sigh and reached for her cigarettes again. "Sometimes I think you can read minds," she said, almost resentfully.

"Like Mr. Spock."

"Like Houdini, is more like it." She crushed the cigarette she had just taken out of the pack and tossed it into the back seat. "Might as well change that habit, too," she said, brushing flakes of pale tobacco from her fingertips. "While I'm at it."

My father was late picking us up that afternoon. I eventually decided to walk home with my friends Kyle and Peter, but my sister stood in front of her school for forty-five minutes before he arrived. She was furious. At dinner that night, she pushed the green beans around her plate with an expression of passionate indignation on her face. My father had already been through his excuses. He'd been tied up at a meeting, an important meeting with the president of the chemical company whose annual report he was writing. This did not satisfy my sister. Elise's sensitivity to injustice was extraordinarily keen.

"So nobody's really said much about their first day," my father said. When no one seemed inclined to respond, he turned to me. "You first, Cliff."

I paused before answering. My day had been confusing, filled with novel impressions—of my tall, resonant metal locker, of the buzzing cafeteria, the industrial arts room, the science lab with actual marble-topped tables and Bunsen burners. I had walked through the halls all afternoon in a trance, trying to grasp my new territory. People said hello to me as I passed, people I had hardly counted among my friends at School 4. My happiness had astonished me.

"It was good," I said finally. "Different. My shop teacher is insane."

My father was nodding his head. "You're taking shop now," was all he said. He stole a quick glance at Elise, then looked at my mother. "And you, Faye? Mom? How was your day?"

My mother, who had been strangely quiet ever since she got back from work at five-thirty, took a sip of orange juice before noticing the question. "Probably not as interesting as your day, Cal," she said, in a voice so odd that even Elise looked up from her plate.

"What do you mean?" my father asked.

"Just what I said." My mother licked her lips and threw a fistful of hair back behind her shoulder. "No, not nearly as interesting as yours." She put her palms flat on the table in front of her. The knuckles seemed red and swollen. "And anyway," she added finally, "I quit."

The jobs followed in rapid succession after that. She tried secretarial work first, answering phones for a company in Ridgefield that made car batteries, but left after a week. She tried selling antique clocks at Bambergers, lingerie at Alexanders, and eventually resorted to that standby of all suburban wives, real estate. But she quit each job with a breezy casualness that left us all slightly breathless. My mother was not herself, it seemed; she was itchy, impatient, distracted. I remembered what she had said the first morning of school, about my being able to read her mind, so I would sit across from her in the TV room, while we were supposed to be watching Bonanza, and try to get a bead on her thoughts. Once she caught me at it. "What are you staring at, Cliff?" she asked.

"Your hair," I improvised. "It seems darker."

"Nice of you to say so, but it's going gray if anything."

The only job that seemed to give her any satisfaction was bookbinding. Somewhere between car batteries and antique clocks, she had taken up with a master bookbinder named Orson. She had seen Orson's ad for an assistant in the newspaper and without consulting any of us had given him a call. She had no experience, of course, but he hired her the next day, agreeing to train her in lieu of pay for the first month.

Orson was an extremely tall man—six-foot-seven, at least—thin, oldish, and utterly incapable of looking a person in the eye. He kept his coarse, gray hair closely cropped, a hairstyle that exaggerated the deep lines radiating from every sense organ on his head, even his ears. He wore rumpled wool suits and frayed ties. I saw him for the first time on the day after Christmas, and I hated him instantly.

But my mother seemed determined to find Orson tolerable, even likable, so she started working at his studio three mornings a week. After her training period, Orson talked her into buying her own screw press so she could work at home. My father, sensing the importance of this, agreed to foot the bill. He even helped my mother set up the awkward wooden press in the basement near the deep freezer.

"I've come with another assignment for Mrs. Erikson," Orson said one snowy day, turning up at our doorstep with a ratty cardboard box full of uncut pages and strips of glove leather. We all stared at him as he moved majestically over the threshold, his enormous galoshes streaking slush across the carpet. "Orson!" my mother called out, appearing suddenly in the living room. She snatched the box from his fragile arms. "Thank God you've come. I'm almost done with that awful family history thing you gave me last week." My mother had been spending hours in the basement, stooped over her screw press. She had left us to fend for ourselves at meals all week, though no one dared to object. She was a bookbinder now. She had even begun to smell of paper dust, library paste, and potassium lactate.

Then, as early spring rolled around, just when we thought she had finally found her place with bookbinding, my mother heard about a job at Jungle Habitat. Jungle Habitat was a zoo about forty-five minutes from our house. It was, according to the ads, a new concept in zoos—a vast enclosed area that people could drive through to observe wildlife. The animals walked around freely; if you were lucky, they would walk right up to your car and stare into your side windows. Some animals—gibbons, for one—would actually climb onto your roof and jump around, making a metallic pounding noise more terrifying than anything the tigers or panthers could do.

The particular job my mother had her eye on was an

assistantship in the petting zoo. She had found the position listed in the want ads under the heading "Animal Handler," which told me how hard she must have been looking, even though Orson was keeping her as busy as he could. My mother thought the job was perfect for her. She had once been a volunteer at an animal shelter in El Paso. This, she figured, at least gave her some relevant experience. She was right. The zoo hired her immediately, sight unseen.

She had to wear a uniform: a navy-blue jumpsuit with the Jungle Habitat logo, a highly stylized zebra, sewn on the left breast pocket. She pinned her dark hair up whenever she wore it, stuffing the loose ends into a matching navy-blue cap with a longish brim. I remember thinking that my mother looked like a janitor in the outfit, a very slender, very pretty janitor.

"So it sounds like you've found something you like," my father said to her one morning over breakfast. It was the beginning of her second week at the zoo.

"Finally," she said, as if completing his sentence.

"I wasn't going to say that."

She got up from the table. "But you were thinking it." She carried her cereal bowl to the sink. "We all were thinking it."

My father stared into his coffee cup. He seemed about to say something, but stopped himself. I caught him sneaking a glance at me. "None of us thought that," he said at last.

It was the type of exchange that was becoming increasingly common in our house. This new, prickly mother of the last six months was still something of a mystery to us all. I suppose I accepted it as a necessary part of her new incarnation as working woman. But I could tell that my father was disturbed by it. And, strangely, nervous.

One day after school in mid-May, Aunt Frances came to

get me at the Intermediate School. The daily pickup had by this time turned into a lottery—sometimes my father would show up, sometimes Aunt Frances, more rarely my mother. I had already decided that next year I would take the school bus home.

Aunt Frances was unusually prickly herself that afternoon. "Watch out for those clothes hanging in the back!" she shouted as I climbed into the back seat of her station wagon. Elise was already in the front. "I just got them back from the cleaners and if you knock them off the hook I'll crown you. Your Uncle Bob is taking me out to dinner tonight."

Aunt Frances wore a headful of blue plastic curlers covered by a flowery kerchief. I saw Elise examining the curlers intently. "What, are they falling out?" Aunt Frances asked, patting her kerchief.

"We're going to see Mom," Elise informed me then. "At work."

"I can't believe your mother wants me to bring you all the way out there," Aunt Frances said. She started pulling away from the curb but stopped short, nearly throwing me into the front headrest. "All right, wise guy. I see you, I see you." She made a gesture of annoyance at the car that went by slowly on our left. "It's my anniversary, you know. That's why your uncle is taking me out."

"Happy anniversary," I said.

"Thank you." She threw the car into gear again, made a U-turn, and started off down the road to Jungle Habitat.

She dropped us at the front gate. "Your mother says to tell the cashier who you are and they won't charge you admission," Aunt Frances said. "Now scoot. I've still got my eyebrows to do."

We watched Aunt Frances drive away. "So this is where Mom works," I said to Elise. We stood at the front gate, looking up at the plywood representations of giraffes and ze-bras over the turnstiles. The cashier's booth had a thatched roof and was made of concrete painted to look like mud.

Elise shook her head. "She'll want me to touch the animals, I know it," she said bitterly.

The cashier, a chubby blonde not much older than me, circled the petting zoo on a map and pointed us in the right direction. On the way there, we passed three parking lots, a handful of concession stands, and a small enclosure containing something that looked like a giant rat.

"There you are, at last," my mother called out when we reached the corral of the petting zoo. She had her arm around a tiny chestnut colt that seemed to have trouble coordinating its ridiculously thin legs. She was trying to feed it from a bottle. "Come on and meet Pumpkin."

My sister and I stepped over to her, though we stopped about six feet away. The colt was in a kind of feeding frenzy, poking desperately at the nipple with its long, mobile lips. "Take it easy now, little one," my mother crooned. She looked up at us, a broad smile on her flushed face, and said, "He's hungry."

Later she showed us around the petting zoo, introducing us to animals and colleagues in the same voice, as if there were no distinction between life forms. Then, after she punched out, she asked us if we wanted to drive through the habitats before going home. "Sure," I said, knowing that this was the answer she wanted.

We joined the sparse line of cars winding through the pseudo-African savannah. Most of the animals we saw—ba-boons, antelope, lions in the distance—were asleep. "It's still early," my mother told us, biting her lip. "They get more active around dusk." Elise, ostentatiously bored, took out her social studies textbook and started her homework in the back seat.

We passed into another habitat that was more active. White goats were gathered around the car in front of us, begging potato chips from a hand at the back window. "They shouldn't feed them," my mother said huffily. She hit the horn twice. This scattered the goats for a moment, but they soon reconverged on the same car. One of them started chewing on the front tire. When the driver saw that, he hit his own horn, but the goats didn't move. Finally he put the car into gear and raced forward, screeching his tires on the roadway.

I looked over at my mother. "What are you *doing* in a place like this?" I asked.

"What do you mean, a place like this? It's where I work now." She shifted the car into drive and pulled up among the goats.

"You really like this?" I asked her.

She shrugged. "It's something to do," she answered after a moment. "And it's gratifying, really. You feed the animals and they love you. It's that simple."

Just then a hairy, blind-eyed, incomprehensibly stupid face appeared at the window next to me and began gumming the glass.

My mother watched it, then turned to me again and swallowed. "It makes me feel useful," she said. "It's like having babies again."

Three days later, while I was fixing my bicycle in the driveway, my mother called me into the house. It was after dinner. The sun was sinking lower in the sky, illuminating clouds of gnats over the back lawn.

"I want you to come with me," she said, handing me my jacket.

"Where?" I asked.

"Someplace special."

My father was upstairs watching the news. "Cal, could you keep an eye on Elise for an hour or so?" my mother called up to him.

"Where you going?"

"Cliff and I are going shopping," she said, staring at me with eyes that forbade contradiction.

We got into the car and started driving. When my mother veered onto Route 17, I knew where we were headed. "You're taking me to work?" I asked.

"The zoo will be closed. But there's a place I want you to see."

We drove, mostly in silence, to the Jungle Habitat. I looked out the window as we went past the closed front gate, a wall of metal bars drawn down over the entrance. At a booth just beyond the main parking lot, my mother turned off onto a small service road that paralleled the high wooden fence. We drove another quarter of a mile, passing a wide, grassy field and some wooden outbuildings surrounded by chicken wire. Finally she parked on the side of the road, a few feet away from the high fence, and turned off the engine.

"The lion compound is just on the other side of the fence here," she said, not looking at me. "Sometimes you can hear them roaring at this time of day."

I took a deep breath and waited—not for the roaring, but for whatever it was my mother had to tell me.

I didn't have to wait long. "Your father's having an affair, Cliff," she said at last, looking down. "It's been going on for months now. Maybe longer, but I've known about it for months. I saw them together the day I started at Aunt Helene's store. The day I quit."

I felt as if something inside me was being slowly and carefully torn open. "Is it somebody we know?" I asked quietly.

"No, thank God." She turned to me. Her eyes were dry

and clear. "Sorry I've been so strange recently. It's been kind of hard to live with."

"Does Dad know that you know?"

"Not yet," she said. "But I've decided to tell him tonight. Finally. That's why I'm saying this to you now. To warn you that things might be . . . even stranger for a while."

"Stranger how?"

She crossed her arms in front of her, squeezing both elbows. "I can't imagine things will be the same after I talk to him. Things will change." She heaved a deep, shaky breath. "It's exciting. A little. I have no idea what's going to come next."

Something was happening on the other side of the fence. My mother's finger went up. "Listen!" she said breathlessly.

I heard a low rumbling from someplace close by. It didn't seem possible that such a noise could come from an animal. The sound hacked painfully, like a saw against tough wood, but it grew in volume until it turned suddenly, astonishingly, into a full-lunged roar, a deep bellow that echoed off the trees and filled the car.

"I think it's the big shaggy one they just brought in," my mother shouted, smiling in spite of herself. "God, Cliff, isn't it glorious?"

I put my hand out to brace myself against the dashboard. "Are you going to get a divorce?"

"Just listen," she whispered. She put her hand to her throat and stared straight up at the roof of the car. For the first time in months, she seemed happy to be still, to be motionless. Fear was sizzling in my own gut, but my mother seemed totally content just to sit there, listening, while the light drained away from the hills and the first stars appeared, one by one, like wobbly hatchlings in the sky above our heads.

Numbers

I T WAS the summer of the third Vietnam draft lottery —August 1971—and no one, absolutely no one, wanted to fight in the war. Wesley, the bagger at Esposito's Market, announced that he would blow off a toe with his father's shotgun if his birthday came out lower than 125, and a few of the older lifeguards at the first-aid station took to making vague, pregnant statements about the hunting in Canada. Anxiety was almost palpable in the air that summer. You could feel it emanating from every nineteen-year-old as you paced the boardwalk at night. The boys were a little more reckless, the girls a little more pliant and forgiving. People said that the tiny jail in Seaside Heights was full to overflowing all summer long, so that on weekends the extra drunks and vandals had to be kept in a locked trailer in the sheriff's boat-cluttered back yard.

The beach house our family was renting that year was a rundown white clapboard bungalow. It was bigger than our usual rental, but its most notable features—a temperamental refrigerator and a huge screened-in porch overlooking the street—were familiar to us from a long history of similar places at the Jersey shore. The bungalow had a problem with crickets; they chirped from somewhere under the sink every night after we went to bed. And there were holes in the front screens that would occasionally let in mosquitoes from the nearby marshes.

But these were beach-house flaws, easy to live with, almost desirable. We were a thirty-second walk from the beach, after all. And, most important for me, there was room enough in the back yard to set up my weights.

My friend Kyle was down with us for most of that August, while his parents stayed home to run the family deli. He and I shared the small back bedroom, which was furnished with two narrow beds, always damp and sandy, and a single wooden bureau topped by a cracked mirror. At night, as we lay in our beds talking, the sea breezes would blow through the windows, making the plastic shades float in and out. It was as if the house was breathing.

We were fourteen that summer, Kyle and I—not quite immune to the erotic desperation in the air, but not that susceptible to it either. For one thing, our turn at the draft lottery wouldn't come for several years; with the war winding down and Congress threatening to repeal the draft laws, it might never come at all. And to be honest, we were far more interested in weightlifting than anything else that summer. During the previous school year we had both discovered body-building at the local YMCA. Now we were fanatics. It was our version of sex.

"Don't stop pushing till you can bench-press your girl-friend's bod," Kyle would say, sprawled out on the weight bench, straining for an extra rep. It was one of the little rit-ualized lines he'd repeat again and again during our back-yard workouts, like a gambler's charm. "Pectorals, the male mam-maries," he'd say. Or: "There's only one muscle that gets hard without work, man, and it isn't the biceps."

The makeshift gym we set up every afternoon consisted of two pairs of dumbbells, a barbell with removable weights, and a bench, its black vinyl cover split in two places, revealing the cotton padding beneath. We had brought down the entire set from home and now kept it behind the bungalow, chained to the outdoor shower stall at night with a series of bicycle locks. Every afternoon at four or five, Kyle and I would come back to the bungalow from the beach, unlock the equipment, and work out. We were both adolescent-skinny and had trouble putting on muscle, but that didn't faze us. We spotted for each other, shouting encouragement, while the gulls cried out like babies overhead.

My mother would occasionally watch us from the back door, shaking her head in amusement. She was in charge of us—and of my sister and her friend Jill, who both slept in the bedroom next to ours—for most of that summer. My father, who still pretended to have a real job like other men his age, would come down on weekends, usually with a bagful of Silver Queen corn and a litany of mock complaints about the necessity of some people having to work for a living. He and my mother were on rockier ground than ever that summer; everyone in the house knew it, but we all had an unspoken agreement not to see it. Divorce and separation were unthinkable at the time—to me, at least. And the only noticeable effect of my parents' discord was an extra awkwardness on weekends, after which my mother would fall into a Monday-morning funk, staring out at the ocean while twisting strands of her dark hair around a sandy index finger. We had nothing *really* to worry about, I'd tell myself, watching her, my old ally. We weren't like those other families, the ones with sons who could be sent to the swamps of Vietnam at any minute. *Those* were the families in trouble.

And so we became accustomed to the weekly rhythm of my father's visits. The beach was unlike itself on weekends in any case—more crowded, somehow less our own. Weekends at the shore were for outsiders, for the serious adults, for my father. During the rest of the week we were a more natural and coherent group—four kids and my mother, who still didn't look very much older than a kid herself.

It was during one of those weekday intervals between my father's visits that we first met Hank. Hank was older—twenty-one, he said—and therefore far beyond our normal circle of acquaintance at the shore. He was living for the summer with three of his pot-smoking friends in a pink stucco bungalow at the other end of our block. We had seen him several times before—in his neon-green flipflops, padding to the beach with his housemates—but we hadn't yet acknowledged each other's existence. We knew his name only because his friends kept shouting to him as they passed, calling him Kemosabe Hank, which was some arcane reference that only heightened our fascination with him. He was about six feet tall, with enviable upper-torso definition and longish dirty-blond hair that he sometimes tied back in a ragged ponytail.

One afternoon, as Kyle and I worked out, Hank appeared in our back yard, standing amid the damp bathing suits that flapped continuously on the chest-high clotheslines. He was carrying a beach chair and a tube of suntan lotion. His hair was streaked with sun, and his muscular thighs shone like polished copper. "Hey," he said, lifting his chin to us. "I saw you from the street. Pretty sweet setup."

Kyle could hardly speak for a moment. "You work out?" he asked.

"During the school year. I play hockey for Rutgers, varsity." He took off his sunglasses, showing his steely gray eyes. "Name's Hank."

Kyle and I introduced ourselves, feeling skinny and young and utterly inferior. We shook his hand.

"Anyway, when I saw you two freaks out here, I thought it might not be a bad thing to do a little pre-season training." He looked around at my weights, scattered in the sand. "I might teach you a few things, too. Give you some workout tips. What do you say?"

Kyle looked at me. There was a kind of passion in his eyes, the fervor he felt for anyone or anything that was inarguably cool. But since it was my equipment, I had to give the final word. "Sure," I said, though there was something about Hank's manner that gave me pause.

"Good." Hank put down his beach things, leaning the chair against the house. He pulled off his tie-dyed T-shirt and threw it over the railing of the back steps. His rounded deltoids moved in the sun like a greased hinge. "First of all," he said, straddling the bench and picking up one of the twenty-pound dumbbells, "your form's for shit, both of you, probably because you're trying to pull too much weight for your size." He curled the dumbbell twice, making his biceps jump. He looked up at us then and smiled, like someone who had just performed a magic trick. "Less weight can do more, if your form is right."

Hank dropped the twenty-pound dumbbell and picked up the fifteen-pounders. He demonstrated a proper curl and then got up from the bench. "Now you try," he said, pointing to Kyle.

Hank stood beside me as we watched Kyle try a few controlled movements with the weights. "That's right," he said, nodding. He rubbed his wrist slowly and then spoke to me. "That your mother?" he asked, gesturing with his head toward the house.

"Yeah," I said, knowing whom he meant.

"Where's your dad?"

"At home. He has to work."

"So that's really your mom," he said, shaking his head.

We watched Kyle do his last few reps. I could tell that he was really pushing—to impress Hank, although Hank didn't look easy to impress. He seemed preoccupied, and a little wary.

I noticed that there was a fine net of dead skin hugging the curve of his shoulders, the remnants of a sunburn.

"Now you," Hank said. "Cliff," he added after a second, like a salesman remembering to use the name.

I took Kyle's place on the bench and picked up the dumbbells. We had hardly used the fifteen-pounders, thinking them too light to do us any good. But now that I tried a few repetitions with the technique Hank had demonstrated—slowly, not allowing the arms to swing—I could see that Hank was right. The movement isolated the target muscle, concentrating the strain in the heart of the biceps. It made the entire exercise seem more wholesome somehow, more correct.

Hank spent a half hour with us that first day, coaching us between sets of his own program. Kyle, who normally kept up a constant patter, was silent. Hank did all the talking. He told us about flexibility, warmup and cooldown exercises, pumping for strength versus size. By the end of the workout, we were all three sweating profusely. Drops of our perspiration dotted the sand around the weight bench.

"OK, enough for today, freaks," Hank said finally, shaking our hands Black-Panther style—a palm-to-palm grip, as in arm wrestling, ending with a smack on the other person's shoulder. "This time tomorrow, OK?"

"Five o'clock," Kyle said, still panting.

Hank pulled his T-shirt from the railing and draped it over his damp shoulder. He picked up his beach chair, towel, and suntan lotion. "I'll bring over this booklet I have, about tailoring your workout." Then, without saying good-bye, he turned and headed down the alley, glancing into each window of our bungalow as he passed.

That night after dinner, as we made our way in the sand to the Casino Pier of the boardwalk, Kyle couldn't stop talking about Hank. "That guy knows what he's talking about," he said, "he *knows*." The pier jutted into the ocean about a half-mile ahead of us, its lights reflecting off the rippled surface. "Fuck, Cliff," Kyle shouted, getting out in front of me and walking backward to make his point, "I bet he could get us some dope, do you think he could get us some dope? I know those guys in that house smoke *all* the time."

"I bet he could."

"I'm *sure* he could get us some dope," Kyle went on. He picked up a piece of driftwood and flung it into a breaking wave. "He could even get us some girls, probably. We lucked *out*, man. This could be fuckin' beautiful, I know it."

We reached the boardwalk at about nine, just as the shift was changing. The families with strollers and gaping five-year-olds, the old people who hovered around the Pokerino tables, the chain-smoking middle-aged women who tried to win even more cigarettes at the wheels of chance—they were leaving now, ceding the boardwalk to the young. Kyle and I liked to roam among the rides on the Casino Pier, which was where our kind of people congregated—the high-school girls with twisted blond hair, the freaks, the tough boys, the hesitant coeds from Rider and Glassboro. They all wore short shorts and bathing suits, showing lots of tanned flesh. And they all watched each other, hypnotized by the same chapped noses and luminous teeth they'd seen in their own mirrors before setting out that night.

"Let's see what's going on at the Himalaya," Kyle shouted to me over the snaps and pings of a shooting gallery. We headed farther out on the pier. The Himalaya ride—a line of open compartments that snaked around in a circle, very fast —had a definite glamour that year, primarily because of Wolfgang, the man who ran it. Wolfgang sat in a small glass booth under the furiously blinking bulbs that spelled out HIMALAYA.

He spoke into a microphone in a heavy German accent. "Do you vant to go faster?" he would ask in his deep, Big-Brother voice. The riders would answer with a howl of assent.

Kyle and I made our way to a partially hidden place right beside the Himalaya, where you could look over the edge of the pier to the ocean. This was where many of the older teenagers came to get drunk or high, tossing their beer bottles over the railing into the tangles of seaweed and mussels below. Kyle and I liked to hang out here. We'd make mental notes of what we saw and then discuss them later in our bedroom before falling asleep.

"Hey, it's the junior Klingons, here to cling on as usual," said one of the nineteen-year-olds, a guy who called himself Red. He was sitting on the steps with two of his sunburned friends and a couple of loose-looking druggie girls we recognized from the beach. They were passing around a bottle of cheap Chianti and seemed very drunk. "How you boys doin' tonight?" Red asked us in a fake redneck voice.

"We're good," Kyle said. "Gimme a hit of that wine, OK?"

"Shit, man, who is this pushy fuck?" said one of the other guys.

Red silenced him with a raised hand. "Hey, relax. These here are my friends." He got up from the stairs and snatched the bottle from one of the girls. "These are the guys coming to Nam with me, aren't you. Gonna hold my friggin' gun for me. I always need somebody to hold my big, friggin' gun, right, Laurie?" He gave the bottle to Kyle, slinging it by the straw handle. Kyle took a long, slow pull on it, then another. "Hey, take it easy, fuckhead," Red told him, grabbing the bottle from Kyle's fingers.

"You're not going to any war," said the girl called Laurie, from the steps.

Red looked at her, his head nodding slightly. "We'll just have to see about that, right? See how the numbers come, right?" Red had long, greasy hair down to his shoulders. He was wearing an old army jacket that smelled of cigarette smoke. "Here, it's your turn," he said, handing the bottle to me.

I put it to my lips and drank. The wine was sour and overpowering, but I drank as much as I thought I could without retching.

"Fuck, these Klingons drink like fuckin' fish!" Red shouted. He pulled the bottle away from me so that some of the wine dribbled down my chin. "It's OK, though," he went on, "they're just steelin' their nerves for Nam." He threw his arms around us. "Death, boys! Cambodia, Mekong Delta, Sai-fucking-gon. All the fucking shit those death generals want to dish out. 'Cause we're just young shits, see? We're just gonna have to take it." Pushing us away, he grabbed the bottle by the neck and flung it up. The bottle rose, end over end, into the nimbus of light thrown by the Himalaya, where it stopped in midair and then plummeted down again. It struck the boards at our feet, smashing with a dull whomp, spattering our ankles.

We all looked at the broken bottle for a moment. We began to smell wine on the breeze that blew off the ocean.

"Shit," Red mumbled. He looked over at his friends, who seemed to avoid his eye. Kyle was wiping the wine from his legs, waiting to see what would happen next. Nothing did, at least for a while. Red just stood there, running his fingers through his stringy hair. "No more wine," he said. "No more fuckin' wine."

Then Laurie, a stoop-shouldered teenager with long blond hair, came up to him. She slipped her hands under his army jacket and pushed her lips against his chest. "You're not going anywhere," she said.

Red just looked down at her head for a moment. "Shit," he whispered, and began to touch her. She lifted her face to kiss him as his hands traveled over her breasts and back.

"I want you here," the girl said to him, while Kyle and I watched.

Hank turned up as promised the next afternoon, training booklet in hand. "Today, freaks," he said, pulling off his T-shirt, "we work on pectorals. Then tonight you can read up on legs and back muscles in this booklet. Beginners always neglect the lower body." He tossed the booklet onto the sand. Hank had his hair tied back with a shoelace, the plastic tips hanging down between his tapered shoulder blades. "Today we start developing good habits too, like warmups. So give me twenty sit-ups and then some jacks."

Kyle and I obeyed. We sank to the rough pebble-studded sand and gave him the sit-ups he asked for. After twenty, we hopped back to our feet and began executing jumping jacks. I could feel the sand that had clung to my back slipping off, pattering my calves as I jumped. "You want to get the blood moving in those muscles," Hank said. "A warm muscle won't injure like a cold one."

"Well, I can see you've got these boys wrapped around your little finger already." It was my mother's voice. We all turned to find her standing on the back deck with a tray of lemonade tea. She still hadn't showered from the beach and was wearing a short white tunic over her bathing suit, cinched at the waist. "Thought you might like something cold to drink while you exercise," she went on, putting the tray down on the deck.

"You must be Cliff's mother," Hank said.

"And you're this Hank the boys were enthusing about

last night." My mother extended her hand. "I'm Faye Erikson," she said.

Hank took her hand and shook it warmly. "Hank. Glad to meet you, Faye."

My mother took her hand back awkwardly. "Would you like some lemonade tea?" she asked. "An old family recipe— half iced tea, half frozen lemonade. It's what we drink down here all summer."

"We'd love to, thanks," Hank said, "but later. I don't want Cliff and Kyle bloating up on liquids."

My mother nodded, as if she had said something foolish. "Then I'll take this back in again," she replied, bending to pick up the tray. Her knees cracked softly. "I'll put it in the refrigerator and you can have it later."

"That'd be great." Hank smiled. He bounded up to the deck to hold the back door for her. "We'll be looking forward to it, Faye," he said, following her with his eyes.

That evening, a Friday, Hank stayed for dinner. My mother was the one who asked him. I was alarmed at the invitation. When she came out after our workout and asked him to share our pork chops and corn, I wanted suddenly to go back, to start over with Hank, to keep separate things separate.

News of the invitation interested my sister Elise and especially her friend Jill. They had noticed Hank many times on his way to the beach. Jill claimed to be in love with him, and Elise taunted her mercilessly about it. "Oh God," Elise groaned when she heard he was coming to dinner, "he'll be only five feet away from her. She'll probably croak."

Jill was visibly nervous when Hank showed up at six. She sat across from him for the first half-hour of dinner, not saying a word, sneaking torrid glances between forkfuls. Jill and my sister were only twelve that summer, but Hank was careful to include them in the conversation. "Do you girls go to the boardwalk ever?" he asked as he passed Jill the platter of steaming corn.

"Every night."

"We work as go-go dancers at the Chatterbox," Elise added blandly.

My mother pretended to throw a napkin at her. "My daughter's a wag in training," she said. "Pay no attention to her." She sat at the head of the small table, making sure that everyone was supplied with an ample share of food. She had showered and changed, and wore a light-blue cotton dress and sandals. "What is it about that boardwalk anyway? What's the big appeal?"

"Bright lights and excitement," Hank said, smiling knowingly at her. Then he turned and flashed a shamelessly amorous smile at the two girls. "I'll have to keep an eye out for you two. I'm up there most nights myself."

Jill looked at Elise, who rolled her eyes and took a loud bite on her ear of corn.

"So why aren't you in Vietnam, Hank?" Kyle asked suddenly.

"Kyle . . ."

"No, Faye," Hank said, savoring the name. "It's a legitimate question." He put his fork down. "I have a college deferment, or at least I *had* one. Nixon keeps changing the rules." Then, as if the question just occurred to him, he asked: "How can you tell when Nixon is lying?"

It was the first line of a joke, but it took us all a moment to realize that. "How?" asked Kyle.

Hank lowered his eyebrows. "His lips move."

My mother let out a deep, hoarse laugh that could only have been genuine. Hank looked pleased. He put his fingers to his right sideburn and stroked it nervously.

"That is *wonderful!*" my mother said. She put out her hand and touched Hank on the forearm. "I'll have to tell Cal that one. He collects Nixon and Kissinger jokes."

"Cal is my father," I told Hank, just to let him know.

Later, Hank insisted on helping with the dishes. We all stood around the breezy, dank-smelling kitchen, trying to make short work of the job. My mother washed, Hank dried, and Kyle and I put everything away in the heavily painted yellow cabinets. Elise and Jill wrapped leftovers.

"You mentioned losing your deferment," my mother said. She was finishing up, rooting around in the basin for renegade pieces of silverware. "That doesn't mean you're in the lottery next Thursday, does it? Or is that just for nineteen-year-olds?"

Hank paused a moment before answering. "Yes. I mean, I am in it. Most of the guys in my house are, too. Though a couple of them say they won't go, no matter what."

My mother nodded. "You would?"

I could see Jill watching him closely.

Hank sighed. "I honestly don't know, Faye," he said. He was about a half-head taller than my mother and looked down at her when he spoke. "Besides, it may all be over soon, with Vietnamization and everything."

"We've heard that before," my mother said quietly, looking down into the basin. "Peace with honor."

"Let the death generals fight their own war," said Kyle, slamming a cabinet closed.

"Kyle thinks if he's anti-war, he can smoke pot," Elise said.

"Shut up."

My mother put her wet hand over my sister's mouth. "We're opposed to the war in this household, as you can see," she said.

"I can see. It's great, really. At least there's one family in this country where the two generations are in agreement." Hank handed me the last batch of forks and then folded the dish towel. "But anyway, it's a decision I probably won't have to make. They're saying anybody with a number of 125 or higher won't be called. Two out of three."

"What's your birthday?" Kyle asked him. "So we can listen for it. Next Thursday."

Hank pulled the dishtowel through the handle of the refrigerator. "I'll tell you next Thursday."

"Why can't you tell us now?" I asked.

Hank ignored me. He was looking at my mother. "Everybody loves a little suspense," he said. He reached out and tugged the string of my mother's apron. "Even you, right, Faye?"

My father arrived late that night. Kyle and I were playing gin rummy with my mother on the screened-in porch; the girls were already asleep. I was about to quit and go to bed myself when my father's car pulled up. The tires murmured to a stop on the gravel drive beside the bungalow. "Your father, finally," my mother said, glancing up from her hand.

He walked through the screen door with his small canvas suitcase. "Sorry I'm so late," he said, kissing my mother, who had risen to greet him. "Just had to finish up some things. Hello, kids." He came over and shook our hands, so tired that he didn't realize he was falling into his business manners. "How's everything down here?"

"Fine," my mother said.

"There's this new guy we know," I told him. "Hank. We had him to dinner tonight."

My father was rubbing his eyes with his thumb and forefinger. "So you've met some neighbors," he said.

Just then my sister ran onto the porch. She was wearing her worn cotton nightgown, frayed at the elbows and collar. "I heard the car," she said, pushing past Kyle's chair and into my father's arms. He held her head against his chest. "Elise," he said simply, his eyes brightening for a moment. He pushed a few strands of her dirty-blond hair away from her temples.

"I thought you were asleep ages ago, young lady," my mother said, gently taking her from my father's arms. "Your father's just come in. He's tired now." She held my sister's shoulders and pointed her back to the bedroom.

"No." She returned to my father's arms, planting her feet on the bare plank floor. "I'm not through yet."

My father smiled. In the distance, a car roared off across the marshes, bellowing in the night. "It's a full moon out," he said. "It followed me the whole way down the Parkway. Kept me company."

I stared at my father as he said this, wondering how much, if anything, I should tell him about Hank. I had regarded my father for so long as the opposition—as the one from whom secrets were kept—that it was almost unthinkable to go to him now with something like this. And what would I tell him anyway? A twenty-one-year-old had been invited for dinner. If I confided my fears to him, my father would probably laugh.

We all went to bed after that. Kyle and I talked, as usual, for about an hour in the darkness, half-listening to each other, half-listening to the sounds from other bungalows—the far-off muttering of a television, the occasional voice raised in query or anger, and sometimes, if the wind was right, the sound of a wave breaking beyond the dunes. Kyle talked about the war, asked me if I thought Hank would go if he was called. "Fuck, can you see Hank in Vietnam?" he asked, staring up at the ceiling. "Can you see Hank digging latrines for some asshole lieutenant with a crewcut?"

I told him I couldn't.

"Me neither," he said.

The plastic shade billowed slowly into the room and then tapped twice against the sill.

"I bet he'd have no problem getting laid over there," Kyle went on. "They say there are whorehouses everywhere in Vietnam. Saigon, everywhere. Shit, they'd like him, too. A guy with his build? They'd probably not charge him anything, do it as a personal favor. Don't you think, Cliff?"

"Like shit, Kyle," I said. "They'd charge him. Just like everybody else."

Kyle, sighing, didn't contest the point. He just turned over in bed. "I bet he doesn't go, though. I bet he gets a high number, 300 or something." Kyle coughed into his pillow. Then: "Fuck Nixon," he said. "Fuck Nixon." The sentence seemed to please him.

The sound of voices woke me—hushed, contentious voices spilling into the open windows. At first I thought they came from another bungalow, but then I recognized my father's defensive growl, my mother's accusatory hiss. My parents were fighting.

I turned on my back and stared at the ceiling, trying to make out what they were saying. It was something I had gotten used to in the last couple of years, straining in the darkness to separate words from silence, to interpret tones of voice, to guess my future from the cadence of a murmur.

I heard my name. It jumped out from the rumble of conversation like the ping of a bell. Without thinking, I threw aside the sheet and went to the door, careful not to wake Kyle. I could feel the ache in my muscles from our recent workouts, a faint satisfying burn in my chest and arms.

I pulled open the door and slipped into the shadowy living room. My parents were out on the front porch—I could locate their voices now. Silently, I moved to the back of the house, into the kitchen. The cricket under the sink was trying a few tentative creaks, but it quieted as I passed. I slipped out the back door to the sandy yard. I was barefoot, and my heels scraped against coarse bits of shore grass. But I had to see what was happening on that porch.

I picked my way carefully down the alley between our bungalow and the one next door. My father's car was parked there, still ticking from the long drive. Crouching now, I moved along the far side of the car. When I reached the tail-lights, I peered around the bumper toward the porch. My parents were sitting across the card table from each other, spotlighted by the bare bulb of the cheap fixture. They were both smoking furiously. My father was pointing his cigarette at my mother, poking the air with it. My mother was shaking her head.

"Enough!" my father said then in a louder voice. He got up from the chair he straddled. He moved away, turned, and looked back at my mother. "I don't know what you want me to say."

My mother answered with something I couldn't hear.

"I'm going for a walk," my father said. Moving with fast, sudden gestures, he pushed open the screen door. He paused a moment at the top step before taking a last pull on his cigarette and throwing it in my direction. The glowing butt hit the gravel and bounced toward the back wheel of the car. If I'd reached out, I could have touched it.

My father jumped down the three steps to the pavement. He turned and went in the direction of the beach, walking in the middle of the quiet road. I watched him go. He reached the end of the block and stepped onto the wooden ramp that led over the dunes. The light from the full moon was so bright that he cast a shadow as he went. He stood near the top for a second, looking back. I saw him light another cigarette, putting his back to the wind to protect the match. Then he continued walking, his head disappearing finally behind the hump of the dune.

My mother was still smoking on the porch, blowing javelins of smoke at the bare bulb over her head. There was something unsettling to me about the gesture—a foreignness, a sense of veiled depth. I remembered a day, years ago, when we went to church together—a Catholic church that neither of us had ever been in before—without my father's knowledge. Going there, we knew, was something he would have neither approved of nor understood. But she and I understood each other that day; we shared a like need for the waxy scents, the blood-rich colors, and the exotic, comforting darkness held within that church's walls. It was this silent understanding that had always tied us together, that had always seemed to erase the two decades that stood between us.

But now, as she blew another stream of smoke at the light bulb above her, I saw a different woman, one who had interests of her own, separate from mine, one whose secrets were no longer my secrets. I watched—for minutes, for a half-hour, perhaps—as the gray smoke exhaled by this woman crept along the ceiling, oozed through the screen mesh, and curled into the outside air.

My father drove back home Monday morning, and Hank—it seemed to me—moved right back in. We saw him on the beach after lunch. He was with some of his house-mates, playing Frisbee a few hundred feet down the beach. When he saw us, he came over to talk. "Hey, freaks," he said, standing over the blanket where Kyle and I lay on our backs. He was wearing a flowered beachcomber swimsuit with legs that came halfway down his thighs. Someone had done a bad job smearing his shoulders and chest with lotion.

We all said hello. Jill and Elise lay on another blanket a few feet from ours. They had both bought new two-piece bathing suits and were trying to tan their white stomachs.

"You've been scarce these days," my mother told him, sounding a little irritated. She sat in a short-legged beach chair, a thick novel in her lap, shading her eyes with her hand.

"I drove to Wildwood with some people for the weekend. This band was playing down there."

"You missed my father," I told him.

"Yeah," he said, fingering the rim of the Frisbee. "Maybe next time."

"What band?" Jill asked.

"They call themselves The Sofas." He sat down in the sand next to my mother's chair and rested his arms on his knees. "Pretty intense down there. The last weekend before the lottery, I guess."

"Still not going to tell us your birthday?" my mother asked.

"Still not." Hank looked down and began idly shoveling hot sand over his feet.

"Hey, Hank," Kyle called to him. "You gonna work out with us again or what?"

Hank threw a little sand over at Jill's legs. "I guess I might, Kyle. I guess I just might be there today."

"Are you going to stay for dinner too?" Jill asked. Smiling, she brushed the sand off her legs, not even pretending to be annoyed.

"I haven't been asked."

My sister grunted. "Well, if you don't come over soon," she said, "Jill's head might explode."

Jill, mortified, grabbed my sister's wrist and squeezed it. Hank laughed. No one said anything for a moment.

"Well, I don't know, Elise," Hank went on. "I guess it's up to Faye."

We all looked over at my mother, whose eyes remained hidden behind her reflective sunglasses. "Oh, is it up to me?" she asked. She tilted her beach chair back, rocking slightly on the short back legs, inspecting Hank. Finally, she added: "OK, consider yourself asked."

Hank nodded and smiled. "Thank you, Faye," he said. "I'd like that. I'd like that very much indeed." And then he started tossing sand onto my mother's legs.

Hank ate with us for the next three nights. At five, he would join Kyle and me in the back yard for our daily training sessions. We'd work out with him for about an hour, listening to his instructions, watching his demonstrations, giving him sit-ups and push-ups whenever he asked for them. I didn't really want him there anymore, but I didn't know how to stop him from coming. It was expected that he would stay for dinner every day. No one had to ask him anymore. It was as if he belonged there, at the head of the table, teasing us, casting knowing glances at my mother whenever we said something foolish or young.

It was Wednesday, the night before the draft lottery, that Kyle and I came back to the bungalow later than usual. The atmosphere on the boardwalk that night had been electric. Everyone was hyped up and drunk. Teenagers in high-slung cars raced down the shore roads, blasting music through their open windows. Toward the end of the night, a fight broke out at the Funhouse Arcade between some nineteen-year-olds and a group of volunteer firemen from Toms River. One of the kids pushed over a pinball machine, smashing the glass top and sending a half-dozen metal balls tumbling across the arcade floor. Kyle and I stayed to watch.

My mother wasn't alone when we got back. Hank was there. The two of them sat out on the screened-in porch. My mother was lying on the tattered sofa with an old blanket wrapped around her shoulders. Hank sat across from her, his bare legs up on the cushions beside her. The radio was playing—classical music, something for solo piano. Hank and my mother were drinking beers. His feet were almost touching her thighs.

"Hey, freaks," Hank said as we came through the screen door.

My mother frowned. "You two are late. It's eleven-fifteen. After your curfew."

"There was this fight," Kyle said. "We couldn't leave."

My mother sighed. "Just as long as you weren't in it yourselves. But go to bed now. It's late."

"It's Hank's last night before the lottery!" Kyle said.

"Are you nervous?" I asked him.

Hank thought about this for a moment. "Shit yes," he said, stealing a quick look at my mother. "I know it'll hit some of us. Maybe me, maybe some of my friends. Maybe all of us."

Kyle burst out, "They should send Nixon. Nixon should have to put his fuckin' birthday in the thing."

"Your mouth, Kyle," my mother warned. Then: "Enough politics. Nobody's staying up with Hank, understood? Go on to bed now."

Hank winked at us. "Better listen to the lady, freaks. She's not somebody you want to argue with." He took a pull on his beer and put it down on the floor next to him. He seemed to be avoiding my eye.

Kyle and I reluctantly obeyed. But the moment we shut the door of our room behind us, Kyle turned to me. "Jesus Christ!" he said in a loud whisper. "Did you smell it?"

"Smell what?"

"The dope, you asshole! They're smoking dope out there. Your mother and Hank are smoking dope!"

"No," I told him. This could not be true.

"I swear I smelled it!"

I turned to the door. I considered finding some excuse to go back out there, but I was afraid that if I did, I might find that Kyle was right.

"Jesus," Kyle said, shaking his head. "Cliff's mother smoking dope."

We undressed in silence. I went through the motions—folding my clothes, throwing my underwear into the laundry bag, pulling on my sleeping shorts and T-shirt—all the time trying not to come to the conclusion that now seemed inevitable: That my mother had slipped beyond my reach. That my mother was no longer to be trusted.

Kyle turned out the light and got into his bed. "Fuck, if he'll smoke with your mother, he'll probably smoke with us," he said. "Do you think?"

"Don't be a shithead, Kyle. They're not smoking anything. It's your imagination."

"Fuck you, Cliff." Kyle was offended. He wouldn't say anything more to me that night.

I lay back against my pillow, watching the shadows thrown by the streetlight on the window shades. I tried a few times to force my eyes closed, to force myself to sleep, but it wouldn't work. I couldn't stop thinking. It was what thousands of nineteen-year-olds and their families were doing at that very same time, all across the country—thinking, unable to fall asleep. An epidemic of insomnia.

I bolted awake in a room full of dead air. The house was utterly silent. The wind had stopped, leaving the shades motionless against the windowsills.

I jumped out of bed. I tore open the bedroom door and crossed the living room to my mother's bedroom, my parents' bedroom. Without knocking, I pushed open the door.

My mother was in bed, alone. "Cliff?" she asked sleepily. Then, some urgency creeping into her voice, "Cliff, are you all right?"

"I'm fine," I told her. I looked once around the room, at her clothing piled on a wicker chair near the closet, at her brushes on the bureau. A pile of curl-edged paperbacks lay on the floor in a corner. "I couldn't sleep," I said, confused. "I was thinking about Dad."

My mother was silent for a moment in the bed. Her face looked grim in the pale light. "I was, too," she whispered then. "I was thinking about him, too."

She was gone the next morning. We found a note taped to the refrigerator: "Had some business to see to today. Back sometime this afternoon. P.S. Elise and Jill, you two are responsible for dinner prep. Put the chicken in the oven at 5 if I'm not back yet. Sorry."

"She won't be here for the lottery," Jill said.

"Christ," Elise muttered. "What kind of business can she be 'seeing to'? I hate doing dinner prep."

"Let's make something special for Hank," Jill went on. "He'll be surprised. Come on, I'll do all the work."

"Hank might not come tonight," I said to them.

"He'll come. We'll make sure he does."

We had a few rolls and doughnuts for breakfast and then set out for the beach. As we walked down our street, we could hear cars roaring on the highway over by the bay. They were blasting their horns—in defiance of the lottery, which was due to start in fifteen minutes.

We set up our beachhead at our usual place. It was a hot, cloudless day. The ocean was rough and opaque; long shreds of seaweed rolled around in the milky water at the breakline. Three fishing boats, following a school of blues, bobbed on the gray-green surface a few hundred yards from shore.

"Did your mother get new batteries for the radio?" Kyle asked. We were smoothing out the big maroon blanket, anchoring the ends with sneakers.

"I don't know who's more in love," Elise said. "Kyle or Jill."

"Fuck you, Elise," Kyle spat. "Anyway, Hank won't go, no matter what his number is. He'll join the Peace Corps or something, help natives with their agriculture." I could see him smiling to himself as he rocked a beach chair back and forth, digging its legs into the sand. "Hank's an expert on weeds, you know," he said, then made a face at me.

We had arranged—days ago—to listen to the draft lottery with Hank that morning. He said he'd rather hear it with us than with his housemates, which would have been too weird for comfort. What if his number came out high while his friend Steve's came out low? But now it was ten o'clock, time for the lottery to begin, and Hank still hadn't arrived. I kept peering at the line of dunes behind us, willing his form to appear. If he showed up, nervous and ready to listen to his fate on the radio, then I would know that I was wrong, that my fears were ridiculous. But he didn't appear on the dunes. There were just a few gulls on the walkway, squabbling over a candy wrapper.

"Let's put it on," Jill said. "He's probably on his way." She reached into her straw carryall and brought out a pen and a pad of paper. "I'll keep track of the numbers and birthdays. He could be one of the first they call, and then he'd have to wait until tomorrow to find out."

"We don't even know his birthday," Kyle reminded her.

"So I'll write them all down."

"Shit," Kyle said, apropos of nothing.

The lottery began. According to the radio announcer, capsules would be drawn from two different drums. The capsules in one contained birthdates; those in the other contained numbers from 1 to 366.

"He didn't say anything about older guys like Hank," Kyle said. "The ones who lost deferments."

"Be quiet," Jill said, holding up a palm.

The first capsules were drawn. "June 20. June two-zero," said a curt, hoarse voice. Then another, younger voice: "Thirty. Zero-three-zero."

Jill wrote the information on the pad. I wondered if this was Hank's birthday, Hank's number. Anyone with a 125 or under, I told myself. A 30 would make it definite. A 30 would leave no doubt.

"March 28 . . . March two-eight . . . Two hundred fifteen . . . Two-one-five."

The process went on, the slow monotony of birthdays and numbers announced in passionless voices. After the first twenty were called, the drums were turned to scramble the remaining capsules. It seemed like an intentionally torturous process, the droning old men taking silent glee in the power they wielded over thousands of panicked young men.

A car horn sounded in the distance, dopplering wildly as

it passed along the beach road on the other side of the dunes.

"God, where is he?" Jill said finally, lifting her sunglasses and peering at the walkway.

They were together, I knew it now. They were listening together somewhere, my mother's arms around him, comforting him, while we sat on that beach, idiotically recording the numbers. We were the stooges, the squares, the children. I got up from the blanket. "I'm going back to the house," I said, stabbing my feet into my blue plastic sandals. "It's stupid if we don't even know his birthday."

"He'll be here in a minute, Cliff," Kyle said. "Come on, it just started."

"He won't be here in a minute, asshole."

"Asshole," he answered back.

"Oh God," Elise taunted. "Now Cliff is in love with him too."

I grabbed my towel and headed for the walkway.

"Go fuck yourself, Cliff, OK?" Kyle shouted after me.

I made my way over the dunes and down to the soft, hot asphalt. It was quiet on the street now. As I walked past the bungalows, I could hear a door slam somewhere, and a woman's voice calling "Tim?" from deep inside one of the larger places. I came to our bungalow and stopped in, just to check, just to make sure she wasn't there, unloading groceries into the yellow cabinets. She wasn't. So I went out again and continued walking. I walked to the end of the street. I walked to Hank's bungalow.

I could hear the radio calling numbers and dates through the screens of the small pink house. Some male voices were talking above the words of the announcers, joking. I listened for my mother's voice, or for a voice that might conceivably be addressing my mother, a woman in that house of young men. I listened for ten, fifteen, twenty minutes before deciding finally to go up to the screen door and knock.

The quiet one with the goatee—Pete, I think his name was—appeared at the door. His eyes locked with mine through the screen. He made no move to open the door.

"Who is it?" asked a voice behind him.

He turned and called back, "Faye's kid."

The voices blossomed into laughter, shouts, whistles. Someone clapped his hands three times, like three shots from an air rifle. "Where's my mother?" I asked Pete.

He shrugged. "How would I know?"

"What about Hank?"

He shook his head. "Not here."

"Hey!" called a voice from the kitchen. "Tell him to try the Sand Dollar Motel! Studly would love a visit!"

Pete spun around. "Asshole!" he shouted. "Keep your fucking mouth shut, all right?"

More laughter and whistling from the kitchen. Pete turned back to me. "Why don't you just go to the beach or something? Hank's busy." He reached into the pocket of his shorts and pulled out some bills. "Here," he said. He pushed open the door and tried to hand me a few dollars. "Go to the boardwalk or something, OK? On me."

I took the bills from his hand. I could use it, I thought. I'd use it to take a taxi to the Sand Dollar Motel.

The bay side of the Long Beach peninsula was a stagnant place, torpid and foul. There was rarely a breeze off the water here, and the air always seemed a few degrees hotter than nearer the ocean. The bay itself smelled perpetually of crab shells, dead fish, algae. Even the bungalows on this side seemed smaller and more decrepit. No one swam here. Only gulls wandered along the water's edge, picking at the debris that washed up on the ginger sand.

The taxi left me off on a corner opposite the Sand Dollar Motel. It was a two-story stucco building with all the doors painted blue. The rooms all faced the back, where a long cement balcony overlooked the smooth bay and, to the south, the causeway that led to the mainland.

I stood there for a long time, watching the building, wondering what to do next. I couldn't go to the manager. I didn't even know Hank's last name. So I decided just to watch, to wait until Hank or my mother appeared in one of the blue doors, like a figure in an Advent calendar. I would bide my time.

I crossed the street and went around to the parking lot of the motel. The sun was now high in the sky, eradicating shadows. A pair of green dumpsters baked in the heat beneath the balcony. Above them, the whole building seemed to resonate with the hum of air conditioners.

I found a place in the shade of some salt-burned trees, where I could see down the long row of blue doors. And I waited. I watched as people came in and out of the rooms— some to go to their cars, some to hang wet towels over the metal railing, others just to look regretfully out across the water at the sinking sun. It struck me as I watched them how many people there were in the world, all of them going about their business in ignorance of each other, not caring, not even wondering about each other. I closed my eyes, counted to ten, opened them. Nothing was changed. The dumpsters still baked in the heat. I did push-ups, twenty, then twenty more, feeling the burn deep in my arms and chest. I tried to keep from crying.

Then Hank appeared. He emerged from the room at the very end of the row, next to the stairs, wearing nothing but a pair of red gym shorts. His hair was untied and fell sloppily around his shoulders. As I watched, he stepped across the balcony, yawned, and leaned against the railing, looking out at the bay.

I broke from my place under the trees. Hank didn't notice me until I was halfway up the stairs. When he saw me, a look of surprise, but not panic, crossed his face. I stopped.

"Cliff, my man," he said. "What brings you to these parts?"

I tried to look him in the eye. "Did you fuck her yet?" I asked.

He gave me a look of mock outrage. "What a question, freak! Did I fuck her?"

I pushed past him into the room. It was cool and dark inside. The bed, its sheets twisted and rumpled, was empty. But then someone came out of the bathroom. It was a woman, a girl—blond, young, not my mother. She looked stunned by my presence, frightened.

"What the fuck are you up to?" Hank said behind me, grabbing my shoulders.

I turned and took a swing at him. He tried to block the punch, but my knuckles caught the top of his cheek. He grabbed my arm and pulled me to one side. Shouting curses, I tried to push him off balance. Our legs hit the side of the bed and we spun, falling. As we went down, my arm caught the sharp corner of the dresser. I fainted from the pain.

I was admitted to the Ocean County Hospital in Toms River. It was a small hospital, not much larger than a school, but there was a feeling of barely controlled chaos about the place. The drivers of the hospital's linen service had gone out on strike, and no other service would cross the picket lines. The high bed I lay on was covered with hospital gowns—the only clean linen in the place, according to the nurses. The gowns left little open corners where the cool plastic of the mattress showed through.

My arm was broken. My shoulder had been dislocated as well, but that had been easily fixed—a quick pull by the emergency room doctor, and that was that. The fractured humerus was more serious; the bone had been broken so badly that shards of white had pierced my flesh. The puncture required scores of stitches to close. But the damage was all hidden away in a cast now, a huge white cocoon enveloping my shoulder and arm.

My mother was standing beside the bed when I awoke. She wore a loose muslin blouse and had her hair pulled back so tight that it shone in the fluorescent light.

"Where's Hank?" I asked. My tongue tasted metallic from the anesthesia.

"What on earth happened between you two? He wouldn't say. Just said you had fought."

"Is he here?"

"He left. After he found me and brought me here. He said he would explain everything later."

I turned from her and looked past the curtained partition at the window. It was dark outside. "I thought you two were together," I said.

She didn't answer. I turned back to her. Her mouth was a thin, straight line, a hyphen.

I went on: "Maybe I just hit the wrong day. Maybe I was off by twelve hours or so. Is that it?"

Something hard and distant passed over her face then. It was as if those familiar features, the ones that had looked to me confidingly, collusively, for as long as I could remember, turned subtly strange. "That's none of your business, Cliff," she said at last.

So now it was none of my business. I understood. I said

nothing more to her, just turned my back to her, untucking all the gowns on the bed.

My father, looking drawn and exhausted, arrived late that night, with Kyle and the girls behind him. There had been trouble in town, he said—some rioting in Seaside Heights. Groups of drunken teenagers went on a rampage, protesting the draft lottery. They broke windows and overturned cars. One of the rides on the Casino Pier had been set on fire.

He looked at the two of us, evaluating our fitness to hear this news, before going on. The gangs had been on our block, he said. He had arrived at the bungalow to find Elise, Jill, and Kyle dazed and scared. Kyle couldn't stop talking about what had happened. A group of teenagers had roared down the street, breaking things as they went. There were pebbles of broken glass all over the street now—some from the side window of my mother's car, which had been smashed. Someone had defecated on the front seat. My father seemed shaken by all of this, and by the sight of his son lying wounded in a hospital bed in front of him. How did it happen, he asked.

My mother spoke quickly, sternly. "He fell, Cal. That was all. An accident."

My father looked at me. "Christ. I thought it had something to do with this lottery business."

I shook my head. But of course, in a way my father wasn't far off. My injury and the riots *were* related. And now, like those hundreds of families across the country whose numbers had come up so awfully wrong that afternoon, we Eriksons would have to pay. Like them, we would know dissension and suspicion and resentment in our house. Like them, we would now have to gird ourselves for loss.

We never saw Hank again. His bungalow was empty the next day, and the next. The landlord, when we contacted him, had no idea where his tenants had gone, and didn't much care, since the rent was paid and the house had not been damaged. Maybe the damn kids were involved in the rioting, he suggested. More likely Hank just knew that it was time to leave —to get out of sight before my father came down and asked questions.

The story my mother and I created for my father—the cover story of my injury—was ingenious in its sheer banality. We collaborated on it early the next morning, before the others arrived at the hospital. I would say that I was carrying my weights into the house—worried that it might rain and that they would rust—when I lost my footing on the steps and fell. That was all. There would be no Sand Dollar Motel in the story, and no fight with Hank. The story, we both thought, was simple, believable, effective.

That morning, as we worked together on the story— putting our heads together and whispering, the way we had done when I was a child—I thought of asking my mother again whether what I suspected about Hank was true. But I never did, not only because I felt she wouldn't answer me (she was a stubborn woman), but also because I knew that her answer would have been irrelevant. The damage was done, no matter what she told me. The actual truth was beside the point.

The story of my broken arm: Cliff fell on the deck and fractured his humerus. It was a lie that said nothing, but that said everything. And it was ours. That lie, in fact, was the last thing my mother and I ever truly shared.

During one of our afternoon workouts that summer, Hank had told Kyle and me how lifting weights builds muscle. The strain and trauma of repeated heavy lifting, he said, destroys muscle cells, actually kills tissue. That may seem like something bad, but it's actually good. The tissue regenerates overnight. It grows back—larger, harder, stronger than before.

I remember thinking about this in the months following the lottery and our return from the beach. It was an attractive idea, I thought—an analogy I could derive comfort from. Yes, I would tell myself, there is no damage that cannot be repaired, no trauma that cannot be healed.

But then I couldn't help thinking of another analogy. When I finally got the cast off my broken arm, the doctor told me that the humerus had healed nicely, but that I would have to be more careful with my shoulder from then on. The joint would always be relatively weak and vulnerable where it had dislocated. Fourteen months later, I was tackled in freshman football practice and dislocated the very same shoulder.

That's the trouble with analogies: they're seductive. If they sound good enough, you can sometimes mistake them for the truth.

PART THREE

Bone by Bone

I'M AN INDEXER. I compile indexes. For books: biography, history, science. "Aztecs, farming techniques of"—that sort of thing. Some, of course, would say that "indices" is the correct plural.

I took the job because I had to. I left my husband fourteen months ago. Before that, I was by profession the wife of my husband. I provided moral support, bought the appropriate furniture and appliances, and gave parties—not too many parties, since we both disliked them. My husband and I disliked many things. It was our way. But we liked children. In fact, we thought we might want children at one time. We had met in college and had fallen in love. His hair was thick and my neck was long and tapered, he said, like the handle of a porcelain pitcher. We shared an interest in fine French and British clocks of the eighteenth and nineteenth centuries. We had clocks all over the house. Three in the kitchen alone. Four, if you count the silver-plated Louis Quatorze egg timer.

No, I'm joking. There is no such thing as a Louis Quatorze egg timer.

I will begin by describing the afternoon I went downtown to pick up a manuscript to index, a manuscript that is before me now—*Middle Management in the Middle Kingdom*, a book about the economics of modern-day China by Stuart Villington-Hedgeworth. It was delivered into my hands by my editor, Timothy Winston, of Hamilton & Fee, Publishers. Timothy affects a waxed handlebar mustache and oversized gray suits with unobtrusive bow ties. He drinks Russian Caravan tea by the potful. Like many of the most intelligent people I have encountered in my life, he speaks with a slight stammer, which has an air of censure about it. I don't like Timothy.

"This is a rush," he told me, gesturing flamboyantly over a stack of page proofs. I was standing before his majestic oak desk. Chill air emanated from the vile machine in his office window. "By the third W-wednesday in August."

Arabesques of steam rose from the spout of the small green teapot on his desk. The steam reached a certain altitude, where it was caught in the draft from the air conditioner and thrown in my direction. "You've forgotten an author contact," I told him as I looked over the assignment sheet.

"No help from the author on this one, I'm afraid. Last w-word is he's laid up in a hospital in Shandong Province with a bad case of hepatitis A." Timothy placed a fingertip against his watch, indicating that he had no more time for me. "Call if there are questions."

I gathered the page proofs and stuffed them into my leather briefcase. "My check?" I reminded him.

"You can collect it from Miss Hathaway on your way out."

Miss Hathaway, Timothy's large-breasted administrative assistant, was holding the check in her hand as I closed Timothy's office door behind me. "I hadn't forgotten, Ms. Velk," she oozed.

I took the check from her crimson-nailed fingers and muttered thanks.

"See you again, Ms. Velk."

My name is Vlieck, Hilma Vlieck. It's right there on the check. My maiden name.

It was then that I came up with the notion of a Louis Quatorze egg timer. Perhaps it had something to do with Miss Hathaway's somewhat exaggerated hourglass figure. The image amused me. My little joke on Miss Hathaway.

I left the offices of Hamilton & Fee at precisely 3:43 by my watch, which is fast.

I must explain how I work. Others work differently, I know. Timothy says that my methods are outdated, inefficient, and incompatible with the chosen system of Hamilton & Fee.

I use a word-processing program. As I read through the page proofs, I decide what subjects on a particular page are sufficiently important to be included in the index. I then use a global search command to find that subject on my already input list. For instance: FIND? Long March, The <RETURN>. If "Long March, The" is already present on the list, the cursor will pause there, and I will type in the appropriate page number. If "Long March, The" has not already been added to the list, the program will tell me LONG MARCH, THE NOT FOUND. I will then PageUp to the L's and add it to my list, not forgetting, of course, to include the page number where it first appears.

Timothy informs me that there are indexing programs available that will "cut my turnover time in half." He has even given me a pirated diskette of one such program, complete with illegally photocopied documentation. The entire package sits in my study on the mahogany chest with the pleasingly vulgar studs, the chest my husband and I bought one autumn at a flea market in Rye, New York. Someday I will read the documentation. My reluctance to do so is not intended as the defiant statement it may appear to be.

I began work on the Villington-Hedgeworth book soon after I picked it up—that very evening, in fact, after dinner. I set up my computer on the kitchen table, since I hadn't yet found a fuse to replace the one I had blown by attempting to word-process a business letter and dry my hair at the same time. The entire front of my apartment is without electricity. I take long, weepy candles to bed at night, like a Victorian heroine.

The work went slowly, as it usually does when I am just beginning an index. I must do a substantial amount of typing at first, as the list of subjects is created. Once I get a certain distance into the book, subjects start repeating, and I type only page numbers. Usually this begins to happen by page 10 or 12. Mr. Villington-Hedgeworth's book, however, was particularly recalcitrant in this respect. By page 15 there were still no repeats. I kept adding subjects to the list, typing, typing.

Of course, you will say that the slowness with which I worked had to do with the fact that I was thinking of my husband that night. He had telephoned me just before dinner from the house in Armonk—from the wall telephone in the kitchen, if my sense of the acoustics of that house has not already deserted me. My husband was tipsy after his usual pair of pre-dinner gimlets.

"Hilma," he stated flatly when I picked up the phone.

I didn't answer him. He knew it was me.

"Hilma, I have a question."

The pendulum of the Alsatian mantle clock on the Formica counter swept back and forth three times.

"Hilma, do you think we made a mistake? Hilma?"

I placed the receiver gently back into its cradle.

That, you see, is something my husband cannot stand.

———

I am writing this file on the same diskette as the file containing the Villington-Hedgeworth index. In fact, I can toggle between the two files almost instantaneously by pressing a preprogrammed function key. Whenever I tire of Mr. V-H and his endless analyses of business ventures in Tianjin, I can just hit my program button and be here, in this other file.

Timothy called me today. "Just ch-checking to see how you're coming along," he said. I thought I could hear the stiff hairs of his mustache brushing the mouthpiece of his beige telephone.

"This book is atrocious, Timothy," I told him, affecting my magnificent raging Harpy voice. "I'm on page 30 and he still hasn't returned to a single topic. He's wandering."

"He's an academic," Timothy said blandly, as if this explained everything. "But what I'm calling to say is that we need the book a few days earlier than I said."

I waited a moment before stating: "I quit."

"Oh stop it," he said. "Try to get it in on Friday. That's five days. All right?"

"I quit."

"Yes, do. But finish the index first. I'll see if I can sq-squeeze a little extra out of the budget for your trouble. Bye." Timothy hung up.

Timothy is fond of saying that he and I have an understanding. He knows that I desperately need this freelance work. The job I previously had involved writing the Police Blotter column for a Westside weekly. I had to think of clever titles for the items: "Senior K.O.'d on West 79th" and "Your Money or Your Wife!" I can't go back there, and Timothy knows it. This is what he regards as the understanding between us.

I have begun to wonder whether Timothy gave me this manuscript (page 40 and still no repetition of subject) as some kind of subtle joke. One of my first assignments for him was a biography of a Mexican composer best known for his concept of nonrepetitiveness. I remember one line by heart: "His creative instincts favored the continuous unfolding of musical ideas—the element of renewal rather than repetition." I indexed the reference under "Nonrepetitiveness, as aesthetic technique." Perhaps Timothy is sitting there in his air-blown office, waiting for me to call up and say, "Oh Timothy, you clever man. Now may I have the real assignment?" Perhaps that's why he called me, to find out if the realization was beginning to dawn on me.

This is something I have learned about men—they are devious. One must always be alert to the subtext of what they are saying. Truth is a game to them. This distinguishes them from women, who, in my experience, simply lie.

"Hilma, do you think we made a mistake?"

Can that, my husband's question, have something to do with the fact that Renata Daley, our next-door neighbor in Armonk, refuses to leave her husband after all? Is this his devious response to that other woman's lie? "Did we make a mistake?" he asks. My neck was long and tapered, he said, like the handle of a porcelain pitcher.

I have unplugged the telephone from the wall jack. I have an entire index to complete by Friday.

I was in the dry, lint-smelling laundry room in the basement of my apartment house this morning, trying to stuff three weeks of clothing into the inadequate dryer, when Jamie Jesperson and her daughters came in. Jamie's long, wheat-colored hair was pulled back in a casual ponytail that spilled over her shoulder and into the hamper of miniature pants and shirts in her arms. Deenie and Wanda, her twin three-year-olds, stood behind her thighs and stared up at me like those saucer-eyed children in the terrifying old paintings.

"Well, am I glad to see you, Hilma," Jamie said, swinging the hamper onto the washer. "I haven't seen anybody my own age in days."

This was a kindness. Jamie is ten years my junior. In her late twenties and already the mother of five—the two with her and three boys of school age. She lives across the hall from me in 3B.

"Philip away again?" I asked. Her husband is a photographer for the Associated Press.

Jamie frowned, wrinkles of exhaustion appearing around the edges of her mouth. "Iraq this time. For God knows how long."

"IranIraqIranIraq," said Deenie (or Wanda) from behind her mother's leg.

"I'm going crazy," Jamie said.

We went upstairs to have some tea. Jamie sat across from me at the kitchen table. I pushed my laptop computer and the manuscript to one side and set a tray of cookies and a pot of tea in the center of the table. The twins, cookies disintegrating in their hands, stood hypnotized by the figure of Artemis, my Siamese, basking on the windowsill.

"I got a call from him last night," Jamie said, using a fingertip to push a crumb daintily from her lip into her mouth. "From Baghdad, he said. There was so much static I could hardly hear him. He said something about a stomach virus."

"Iraq!" said one of the twins, without taking her eyes off Artemis.

"You must be terribly worried," I told her.

"Yes," she answered, and ducked her head to take a sip of tea.

The cookie fell from Deenie's hand and hit the floor with a tiny sound.

"You have such a full life," I said.

Jamie laughed at this so hard and so suddenly that the twins turned away from Artemis and stared at their mother.

"Excuse me," Jamie said, grabbing for her children.

"Hello, Hilma?"

I could hear his slow breathing.

"Why are you calling me?"

"Hilma, have you ever felt that you've made an enormous mistake? That you've done something and, unless you undo it, you'll regret it for the rest of your life?"

"No."

He chuckled. "You're being difficult."

"Life is too short and confusing for regrets. That's something *you* always said."

"I *was* confused," he confessed, as if conceding a point. "You're right, I was confused."

The light from the screen of my laptop threw a blue glow over the refrigerator, the stove. It was the only light in the apartment.

"Listen," my husband said, "how about we get together for dinner tomorrow and talk things over?"

"I'm working under deadline. I can't."

"One hour, for a little dinner!"

"You've heard my answer."

He sighed. "You're determined to hold this thing against me," he said.

I turned one of the knobs on the stove and watched the blue flame flare up and burn quietly in the dark kitchen.

"You're still willing to listen to me," my husband said.

I passed my hand back and forth through the cool flame.

"I notice you're not hanging up."

I placed the phone down on the countertop and left the

room. I could hear his narrow, metallic voice saying more words as I slid the kitchen door closed.

The children in 3B are making noise. I can hear the murmur of their voices, punctuated occasionally by Jamie's frantic contralto. If I were another kind of neighbor, I would complain. "How is a person supposed to get any work done with that racket!" Or: "I don't care if your husband's in Timbuktu, for Christ's sake!" It is amusing to think of a woman—any woman—saying those male lines.

I sit here wondering what Stuart Villington-Hedgeworth looks like. I imagine a tall, gaunt man with a wan complexion—I don't know why. He affects a Mao suit, thinking himself a scholar yet a man of the people. He smokes filterless cigarettes, the local brand. He has small ears.

He comes from money, of course. In fact, it would not surprise me if his family were major stockholders of Hamilton & Fee. I don't see any other way he could have gotten the book published. It is not even Hamilton & Fee's sort of book; H&F is known for publishing illustrated biographies of obscure French artists and inept mysteries by aging professors of literature.

Sometimes I imagine Villington-Hedgeworth looking like my husband. This is the kind of book my husband would write—seemingly innocuous, discursive, but with an ulterior, subversive motive.

He has returned to nothing. He moves from a discussion of capital creation under Deng's regime to joint ventures in Guangzhou to an anecdote about an entrepreneur in Harbin who bought an old factory from the government and then sold it back three months later at a 50% markup. "Capital, creation of." "Harbin, swindler of." HARBIN NOT FOUND.

I have moved all of the clocks in the apartment into the kitchen. I must remind myself constantly of my deadlines.

Jamie rang my buzzer today. I opened the door to find her with her youngest son, Bob, who wore a baseball cap with a letter on it that signified no city or team I could remember. He clutched his mother's hand. "Is that your laundry down there in the laundry room?" Jamie asked. "Somebody piled it in a corner of the folding table. It's getting all dirty again."

I told her that I was terribly busy and couldn't really think about it now.

"If you'd like, I'll bring it up for you," she said.

I told her that I didn't even believe it was my laundry.

"Oh," she said, and I caught her looking up and down at what I was wearing.

Fortunately the phone rang. I closed the door.

"If you'd like, you can come in with what you've done so far and we can see what the problem is," Timothy said over the phone. "But I can't do it until M-monday, I'm booked solid."

The heat is getting worse. Car alarms are sounding in the street below my windows.

HARBIN NOT FOUND.

There are children all around this place. They stand in the vestibule, in the halls, beyond the doors. Towheads, brunettes. They stand outside my door and breathe. They are all waiting for me to give in.

Morning. I have thrown away the liquor bottles in this apartment. They interfere with my work, and I can't afford any more delays. Like last night's. There was nothing in the house to eat, so I had champagne and beef jerky for dinner.

The beef jerky was called "Bear Butte Brand," from Sturgis Meat Service, Sturgis, South Dakota. One wonders how such things get into the house.

Yes, I had dinner with him today. My husband. My husband is a large man who wears impeccable suits. He was wearing one this evening, one I did not recognize, a silk blend perhaps, gray, with a subtle warm glow. His hair is thick and silver. My husband can be surprisingly, aggressively handsome.

He stared at me over the nimbus of a single candle flame. As I sat across from him, it occurred to me that no one can tell you how difficult certain eyes can be, or how a certain kind of light can be a reproach.

I moistened my fingertips with my tongue, reached over, and pinched out the candle flame. It sizzled wetly.

"Does that mean something?" he asked me.

"It means that I should not be here."

"And yet you're here."

"I'm here as an observer," I said, picking up my glass of wine.

"Of whom? Of me? Of us?"

"Of myself," I said. I felt, suddenly, deeply pleased with this remark.

My husband signaled to the waiter to relight the candle. "I don't understand," he said. "I don't know what that means."

The waiter came over and touched a match to the black wick of the candle. The candle seemed to jump at the flame.

"That's better," my husband said.

I reached forward again and pinched the wick. I felt pain in my fingertips. When I pulled back my hand, I saw that the pads of my thumb and index finger were black. The candle was still lit.

He said: "There are certain things you must admit to yourself."

I pressed my fingertips together to stop the pain. "My lawyer says that you and your lawyer are not returning her phone calls," I said. "Why is this?"

My husband put down his fork. "We're moving too fast, Hilma. I think we should slow down, rethink."

There were two elegantly dressed women at the next table, eating in silence. I noticed that they did not look at each other. They were in their forties, with big, thick hands. They were, both of them, watching their hands as they ate.

"You're not even listening to me, are you?"

I looked back at him. "How many stars does this restaurant have?"

My husband frowned. "I don't know. Two, I think."

"If you had really wanted me back, you would have taken me to a three-star restaurant, to woo me, or to a one-star restaurant, to impress me with your lack of desperation. Not to a two-star restaurant." I was certain of this.

"That's ridiculous," he said.

"And if I had wanted you back, I would not have come."

My husband sighed. He looked down and rearranged the napkin in his lap. When he looked up again, his eyes were hard. "We could try to find what we've lost," he whispered.

My arm shot out and pushed the lit candlestick into his entree. It rolled to the side of the table and fell to the thickly carpeted floor.

I rose from the table. "I was never wrong about you," I said, fumbling with my napkin.

I left the restaurant, apparently having made one of those scenes I purportedly make from time to time.

It was—I checked—8:17 P.M.

———

Night. I spent the entire afternoon and early evening cat-aloging the clothes in my closet while the light was still good. I possess too many things. Jamie says that her husband owns two suits, two sports jackets, a dozen shirts, and five pairs of pants. He takes half of what he owns on his assignments around the world. That is the kind of life I could lead—flying off to Baghdad and knowing that I have only one suit to lose if my apartment should burn down in my absence.

I have put several old dresses and a silk blouse into a shopping bag. I will take them down to the thrift shop in my neighborhood that sells such things to the poor at reasonable prices. It will be pleasant to imagine a poor woman wearing my clothes.

The phone has been ringing all day. I have let the machine answer. Timothy, leaving urgent messages: "Where is the China index, Hilma? Today's the deadline. Call me." Two calls from my bank. And then my husband: "Hilma? Hilma, pick up."

I will say nothing to them.

This I have decided.

I will not be found.

The contents of my bedroom closet:

Cocktail dress, lavender silk blend, with black markings
Suit, brown tweed, sensible
Bolero, black felt with embroidered lining (never worn)
Frock, beige cotton
Gown, black satin, accompanying jacket
Middy blouse

There is a knocking at my door. I hear knocking, and sirens in the distance. As if this building were on fire.

Jumper, navy corduroy
Skirt, navy polyester blend
Housedress, nondescript
Tea gown, yellow cotton
Kimono, blue cotton, with parasol design

I imagine a woman in old China. Only she is not a woman, she is a man, a surprisingly handsome man. His eyes have been brightened with drops and his beard hairs have been plucked from his face. His feet have been broken, bone by bone, and wrapped in bandages smelling of eucalyptus and perfume. They have put him in a small house by a stream, under a magnolia tree, and he wanders through the rooms all night, singing faint songs of men who have gone to war in far-off lands. He watches the moon rise. He drinks wine made of haw and plums.

The pounding at my door continues. It is my husband. He is drunk. He repeats my name, over and over again.

I take a sip of tea. As if this building were on fire.

Cardigan, red cotton
Overcoat, fawn-colored wool

Bludgeon

W<small>E</small> W<small>ANTED</small> to reach Utica by morning but God apparently had other plans. We'd been driving since midnight, since making our quiet escape from Jake Hiller's drying-out facility in Cape May. Brady was asleep by this time, hunched over in the passenger seat, which was just as well, since my driving wasn't up to close scrutiny. I was tired, distracted, maybe still a little drunk from the Wild Turkey we had bought on the way north. But I didn't want to stop. The road was empty in front of us, like a perfect silver path to someplace clean and far.

At first I thought that what I saw in the roadside brush was human. But when the thing swiveled into motion, I knew. I recognized the curve of the breastline, the long muscles of the legs. The antlers, turning in the headlights, came out of nowhere like a pair of claws. I hit the brake pedal.

The buck—its outline sharp now in my brights—dipped its head to meet the impact.

I could hear the dull smack of the collision, and the scrape of the buck's body as it skiddered along the side of the car.

When I finally got the vehicle to a stop, Brady was awake. "Was somebody shouting?" he asked. I twisted around in my seat. The rear window was fogged, but I could make out the deer back there in the moonlight—a heap on the shoulder of the road, two long legs pawing the air.

There was nobody else around. This was early, five-something in the morning, a Sunday morning. I remember looking at my watch: 5:38.

I waited another minute, getting my thoughts into line.

"You okay, Mikey? You tired?" Brady asked, touching my arm. He still didn't know we'd hit something.

"We've got a problem," I told him. I shifted into reverse. Cutting the wheels, I backed the vehicle onto the grass divider, so the buck would be in the headlights. When I stopped, we could see the dark bulk of the animal, like something on stage, steaming into the high beams.

"Christ," said Brady.

"Look what I've done," I said.

We both climbed out of the car. The ground was hard and slippery under my shoes. I could hear the buck breathing from there—raspy, panicky, fast.

We came around to the front of the car. The buck tried to twist its head to get a look at us, the gray bone of its antlers scrabbling on the pebbly shoulder. It tried to get to its feet, then fell back against the asphalt with a whomp. A black string hung from the open mouth, swinging back and forth. Blood, or it could have been the tongue, I guess.

"You got a cigarette?" I asked Brady.

He fished one out of the pocket of his thin leather jacket. "So what do we do?" he asked.

"I don't know. We kill it, I guess."

"With what?"

I turned around. The old Ford looked all right, hardly damaged at all. "We could hit it with something. A tire iron or a hammer, something heavy, at the base of the skull."

"You got something like that?"

"There must be a jack with the spare tire somewhere. Cars come with them now." But then I thought about it and I knew I wouldn't be able to make myself swing at the head of some terrified, half-dead animal with a car jack. I just couldn't do it.

The buck's body was pulsing fast now, like an enormous heart.

"Jesus, it's freezing out here," Brady said.

We got back into the vehicle. I started the engine and turned on the heat. Brady put his head between his knees, to get the blood circulating up there, or to sober up. I just closed my eyes and sat. What I wanted right then, more than anything else in the world, was Sam, my wife, still legally my wife. I wanted Sam, but I guess a drink would have done, too. The bottle of Wild Turkey under the seat was empty.

I remembered what Jake Hiller had said the afternoon before. "I'm not asking you to change what you want," the fat old man had told me. "I'm just asking you to change what you do."

Change what you do. The first time I stayed out all night, my first real incident, I came back in the morning to find the house empty. A note lay on the table in the hall. It was sliding away from me in the draft from the open doorway. "They've left me," I said aloud as I grabbed it. Sam had written twelve words on the slip of paper: "We're out of lemons and bread. Have gone to the Shop-Rite. —S." It was an unbearably cruel note. When she came back a half-hour later, Clare in the Snuggly, little Ellen struggling with her own half-filled bag of groceries, I almost ran into the bedroom to hide. I couldn't speak to them for an hour. That was the first time I told my wife, "Never again."

I opened my eyes in time to see a car go by on the highway in front of me. It was a station wagon, red. It didn't even see us. Or else it just didn't care.

Brady's head popped up. "Did something go by?"

"We need something to kill this deer," I told him.

Brady was looking longingly at my cigarette. He was trying to quit, but still carried around a pack—for me, he said. "Let's just go and leave the thing, all right? We could think about this later."

"Look, I won't leave it out there to die like that." I had decided this. The new person I was going to be when I came back—after the weeks we would spend at Brady's mother's house getting a handle on the booze thing without all the dewy-eyed sermons—would not drive away from something like this. The new person would be a man who made damn sure that the deer's suffering ended quickly.

"I don't want to have to think about this," Brady said. He was younger than me, in his twenties. A kid, really. I don't know how we got to be friends. All we had in common, I think, was the knowledge that Jake Hiller was not the answer to our problems.

I looked again at my watch: 5:53. Somebody had to be up somewhere. There were lights showing through the trees beyond the southbound lanes of the road—not too far away. Do it, I told myself. I turned off the lights and the engine. "I'm going to look for somebody in those houses. You want to come?"

"Fuck no. I'll wait here." He crossed his arms. "I'll watch over the deer. Make sure the devil doesn't grab its soul or anything."

I got out of the car and started across the grass divider. I crossed the two southbound lanes and entered the woods on the other side. There was a huge moon, thank God, so I could see where I was going, through a bunch of dogwood and maple, some snow still hanging on in pockets. It would be Easter in a couple of weeks. Easter was when I promised Sam

I'd stay until. I told her I wouldn't set foot out of Jake's huge, rundown Victorian mansion until she came to get me, the kids and a potted hyacinth in the back seat. Now I'd have some explaining to do. I could see Sam on the phone with Jake, twisting her red hair, the anger rising in her gorge. Her mind would already be going over the ways of breaking the news to Ellen and Clare.

I was on the other side of the woods now, standing on somebody's lawn, which was the color of bone in the moonlight. It looked like a brand-new subdivision of houses on a dead end. You could tell the sod was just put in—there were hatchmarks in the lawn—and the trees around the house were hardly more than saplings.

"Christ Jesus, this is ugly. This is worse than my mother's place." It was Brady, coming up behind me. He had a lit cigarette in his mouth. I guess he didn't want to sit by himself with the deer.

"They're houses," I told him. "At least these people have houses." Across the way was a half-finished colonial, labels still on the windows. A yellow Caterpillar stood in the dirt front yard like something left behind.

I turned back. The house in front of us, a little green cedar-shingle, had a light on in the window. "OK," I told Brady, "let's see if somebody will open the door for us."

We stepped up to the dark front entrance. I pushed the doorbell button while Brady threw the cigarette aside and tidied up his hair with his palm. We could hear the muffled chime deep in the house, but then it was a long time—so long that I was ready to give up and try the next house—before the porch light came on and we heard a clatter and thunk and the brand-new door pulling open. I saw a head peering around the door—down at hip level—and I thought for a second it was a child we'd woken up, but it was a man in a wheelchair.

A young guy with glasses, rail-thin, with long bony wrists that stuck out from the cuffs of his white shirt. He was straining to look out at us in the dim light.

"Who are you?" he asked.

"I'm sorry," I said. I hadn't thought of what I would say, and I was flustered. "We're just drivers, motorists, whatever, and we hit a deer over on the road there."

"Yes?"

The point, the point. "Well, and what the problem is, the thing is suffering, and we need something to put it out completely."

"Out of its misery," Brady added.

The man gaped at us. Then his shoulders started bobbing up and down—so much, that I thought he might be having a fit. He made this little nasal gasping sound. He was laughing. "Out of its misery?" he asked.

"Well, yes, that's about the size of it," I said, a little annoyed.

He touched an electric lever on the arm of the chair, moving himself back and to the side. We could see then that he was barefoot. He had long, hairless toes that were clamped around the metal of the foot stand. "Come in, please," he said.

We stepped past him, Brady wiping his feet on the mat. The house was hot, suffocating, and there was a musty, closed-in smell to it, like the home of a very old person. The living room was filled with books. There were books on all the shelves, books piled on chairs, books shoved into corners. There was hardly any furniture at all, just a few straightback chairs and a table with a long, ratty tablecloth, heaped with books. Little parts of statues and stone ornaments were all over—a small marble lion, a cracked top from a column of some kind, a few feet of carved molding. On the floor by the door to the kitchen was the marble head of some small classical statue, eyes blank, lying on its ear. There were no rugs on any of the floors.

"Very nice," Brady muttered. I think he thought he had to be appreciative, like a visitor.

The crippled man maneuvered his chair beside me. "Just what kind of weapon do you need, Mr. . . . ?"

"Dunbar. Mike Dunbar. And this is Sean Brady. I don't know. A gun of some kind would be best, if you have one. But something heavy to hit it with would be all right."

The man was staring up at me, his eyes soupy behind the thick lenses. "You mean a *bludgeon* of some kind?" Again, he gave me the impression of being amused by this whole goddamn situation.

"An ax, a crowbar, whatever."

"I don't understand, Mr. Dunbar. Why don't you just let the animal die on its own and save yourself all this trouble?"

"This was my point, too," Brady put in. "I said the same thing to him, Mr. . . . ?"

"Spock."

Brady giggled. "Oh. Like the guy on television."

"Right, right, the pediatrician," he said impatiently. "I've heard it all before."

"The reason," I said, interrupting them, "is that it looks like the buck won't die on its own for a long while."

I could feel this man trying to figure me. "I see. You're a man of compassion, in other words. If only we were all so lucky as to be run over by a man of compassion."

What could I say to this? He didn't seem all that sympathetic. "If you don't want to help us," I said, "we'll ask next door."

The man thought a little, touching his knee with a long index finger. Then he looked up at me and said, "Well, maybe we can arrange a little exchange, Mr. Dunbar."

"OK. Whatever."

"You see, my helper, the boy who normally lives with me here, ran off last night. Something I said, apparently. He's not a very resilient person." He touched the lever, moving the chair back a foot or so. "I need help going to bed. My legs aren't much use anymore."

"You've been up all night?" I asked, staring again—stupidly—at those toes.

"It hasn't put me out. I've had things to do. But I *would* like to go to bed now. Do you think, in exchange for the weapon you need . . . ?"

"Sure, sure. Of course," I said. A man who can't go to bed without someone helping him.

"It would be our pleasure, Mr. Spock," said Brady, giggling at the name again.

"Well," Spock said, "I'm glad to see that your compassion extends beyond the animal kingdom." He swiveled the wheelchair around and puttered off to a doorway. We followed him through the kitchen—dishes and glasses piled unwashed on the counter—to the pantry door. He stopped. "You'll find a small pistol in a coffee can on the bottom shelf."

I opened the pantry door and flicked on the light. There were shelves on shelves, filled to the ceiling with cans and boxes—a year's supply of food, it looked like. On a high shelf was a fifth of Jack Daniel's, standing sentry. My excitement at seeing it embarrassed me, and I wondered if Brady saw the bottle too.

"Down on the right," Spock said.

I saw the coffee can on the bottom shelf and took it. Inside, wrapped in a chamois cloth, was the pistol. It was lighter than I expected, hardly lethal at all.

"It's loaded, so be careful." The man reversed the wheelchair and pivoted, almost running over Brady's foot. "Turn out the light and close the door. Then come with me."

I did as he told me, but with a glance up again at the Jack Daniel's bottle. Brady was looking at me with his comic, wide-eyed expression.

"Are you coming?" We'd lost sight of Spock around the bend of the kitchen, but I could hear the whine of the wheelchair. I ran, and tripped on the stone head, sending it spinning across the floor. He heard that, I guess, because when I looked up, he was fuming at me across the living room. "Pick that up!" he yelled. "Pick it up and bring it here!"

I stopped a minute, not sure how to react.

"Pick it up!"

I walked across the room and, putting the pistol down on the table, picked up the head. I brought it over to him. He took it awkwardly in his stiff, long fingers and examined it, turning it over to check all sides. "You could have broken it. Do you have any idea how valuable this is?"

"You left it on the floor."

"No, I did not. That idiot boy did." He turned it a few more times and then handed it back to me. "Put it on the table there. Carefully."

I put the head on the table, upright, on its neck, so it looked out across the living room. But the man had buzzed off again, into one of the rooms. Brady, grinning at me from the doorway, pulled aside the flap of his leather jacket and showed me the Jack Daniel's bottle nestled in the big inside pocket he had sewn there for just this kind of purpose.

I went after Spock, into his bedroom. There were more books here, a big multiband radio, and a huge painting on one wall which showed a forest of birch trunks in winter. He'd pulled his wheelchair up to the full-sized bed. The covers were rumpled, making me think that he had tried to pull himself into it earlier on, with no luck.

"Wait a minute," he said sharply when I came in. "I'm not ready to sleep yet. I want to see this dying animal of yours."

This confused me. "You want to—"

"I want you to take me to see the deer," he said impatiently. "Do as I say, or you don't get the gun."

I stared at him. It occurred to me that we could just take the gun and leave, return it after we were done with it. Or not return it. What could he do to stop us?

"This is on the road, on the other side of those trees. Your chair won't go there."

"Then you'll carry me. I weigh virtually nothing, as you can probably tell." When I hesitated, he went on, "Come on, Mr. Dunbar. Compassion sometimes means going to a little trouble. Just pretend you're taking some sick child to the zoo. Pretend I'm the local poster child and you're Jerry Lewis."

"Why do you want to do this?"

"Let's just say I have an interest in things like this. Come on now, help me with my shoes."

I thought of Brady back in the kitchen. He'd probably taken a few long hits from the bottle already. "Where are your shoes?" I asked.

The man smiled. "Beside the night table. And there are socks in the top drawer of the bureau."

I got the socks and shoes and brought them over to his wheelchair. Crouching in front of him, I took one of his long feet into my hands. It was cold, and the toes seemed curled over in some kind of muscular cramp. It reminded me of the buck on the road, its legs sticking out, stiff and cold. I slid the sock over the foot as quickly as I could, and turned to the other one.

He spoke from above me. "He won't believe that I actually

did something like this without him. Evan, I'm talking about. My helper. He'll be furious when he comes back."

"*If* he comes back," I had to say, as I tightened the laces on his strange, thick-soled shoes.

"Oh, he'll come back. Where else could he go? This is a little game Evan plays sometimes. He runs off and leaves me, to remind me that I can't get along without him. He thinks he's punishing me."

"There," I said.

"And now my coat. Let's go."

We found Brady in the dining room with the pistol in his hands, looking guilty. I could see the bulge of the whiskey bottle under his jacket. Spock must have seen it too.

"You know how to shoot one of those, I hope," the crippled man said to Brady.

Brady chuckled. I could tell that he had had a few shots. One last binge was what we had agreed on. But Brady didn't look like somebody who was going to stop in the morning. "That's for killing rabbits, Mr. Spock," he said.

"It'll do the job." Spock turned his wheelchair into the front entrance hall. The closet door was open, and he grabbed a gray snorkel coat from the low crossbar. He tried to pull the coat around himself. "Here, let me get that," I said. He stopped struggling and let me do it for him, as my three-year-old used to. I maneuvered his arms into the sleeves and pulled the coat straight on him. The man's body seemed hollow as a bird's. "Just the zipper. Never mind the buttons."

"It's cold out there, Mr. Spock, so bundle up," Brady said. He handed me the gun. "I'll wait for you here. Too cold for me."

I tried to read Brady's face, but it wasn't giving up anything. Would Brady try to raid the guy's medicine cabinet while we were gone, or look for some cash? It was the kind of thing he felt nothing about doing. He was constantly lifting twenties from Jake Hiller's wallet. It was one of the things about Brady that made me feel old-fashioned, or maybe just old.

"You'll come with us, Mr. Brady," Spock said, catching on somehow. "Now give me the gun and let's go."

I handed him the pistol. "Is there some kind of safety catch on that thing?"

"I know how to handle this gun, don't worry. Now lift me."

I nodded, then slipped one arm behind his back and one under his legs. When I hoisted him to my chest, I couldn't believe how light he was. I could smell him now too—that musty, sweaty smell I had noticed earlier, combined with a little cologne.

"Pull the door closed behind you," he snapped at Brady as I carried him outside.

The night seemed colder now. The moon hung enormous over the new houses on the street. With the man in my arms, the gun clasped tight in both of his pale hands, we crossed the lawn and entered the little stand of trees. Spock didn't say anything, just moved his head from side to side, looking at everything, as if he didn't go outside much.

I could see the Ford's dark shape on the grass island. We hadn't put the flashers on. We should have, maybe; that might have attracted another car to stop and find out what had happened. ·

We crossed the southbound lanes of the highway, white in the moonlight, and came up beside the car. I heard movement again—the deer scrabbling in panic at our approach.

"Still alive, I see," said Spock. "Good."

"So there it is, Mr. Spock," said Brady. "A beauty, isn't she?"

"I think you mean 'he,' Mr. Brady," he answered. This

was a man who obviously liked to correct people. Then, to me: "Put me down on the hood of your car."

I did. The engine was still throwing heat, the metal almost comfortable to sit on. I could see a line of something—blood or deer crap—running along the fender where the buck had hit.

"Can I have the gun now?" I asked.

"Relax, relax. Let me look at the beast for a minute."

"That's a long extra minute if you're dying on the side of a road."

"You're a regular Kierkegaard, Mr. Dunbar," he said. He was shivering in the cold as he contemplated the deer. "I see you have Jersey plates," he said. "What are you doing up here at this time of night?"

I sighed and turned away. The man seemed to enjoy dragging this out. Brady was getting pissed, too. "I think I need a drink," he said, and slipped the bottle of Jack Daniel's out from under his coat.

"Me too." I took the bottle from him after he had taken a hit, but offered it to Spock first.

He shook his head. "Thank you for offering me my own whiskey," he said. "Yes, yes, I recognize it. Now tell me what I want to know."

"You know, Mr. Spock," Brady said. "I don't think we have to tell you anything."

I saw Spock staring at him, slowly licking his lips in concentration. Brady, I thought, could have been a little more tactful, seeing as Spock had the gun. Spock probably thought so too.

"What are you running from, Mr. Dunbar. The law?"

"Christ, no," I said. "Not yet anyway."

He turned to look at me. "A family, then?"

"Mike here's a happily married man," Brady said then.

"And two kids. Two skinny little girls, who could probably push a man your size into a snowbank, come to think of it."

Spock wouldn't even look at him. He seemed intrigued by me. "You're running out on your family? Is that right?"

When I didn't answer, he cocked his head, the thick lenses of his glasses catching the moonlight. "Interesting," he said. A car passed in the southbound lanes, not seeing us on the traffic island. "What ages are your children, Mr. Dunbar?"

I sighed. The deer lay quiet in front of us, as if listening to the conversation. "Three and five."

"Well," he said. "This sheds a new light on things, doesn't it."

"Can we get this over with, please?"

"Oh right, right. You wanted to put the creature out of its misery. The man of compassion."

I reached out to take the gun. He pushed my hand away. "I'll do the mercy killing here, if you don't mind," he said. "Put on the headlights, please."

It seemed the fastest way. I fished the keys out of my pocket. When I got in, Brady banged on the passenger-side window for the Jack Daniel's. I rolled down the window and passed the bottle to him.

"Jesus, this guy's a pain in the ass," he said, leaning into the window.

I flipped on the lights. The deer startled again, flinching —weaker this time—on the shoulder of the road.

I could see the back of Spock's head through the windshield. He had a little bald spot there, covered with a few long strands of hair from the side. I watched his body move in the parka, then heard a shot, then another and another. My heart was racing as I pulled myself out of the front seat. I could see his face now, concentrating, the gun held in front of him with both hands. He fired again into the dead carcass.

"Let me take a few shots," Brady said, reaching for the gun. Spock shrugged him off. "C'mon."

Spock turned the gun in his direction.

"What are you gonna do, shoot *me* now?" Brady said.

Spock was glaring at him, the gun pointed at Brady's chest. "Probably not," he said finally. He lowered the gun. "Although I could make up something quite convincing for a jury. People are accustomed to thinking of me as a victim, Mr. Brady. Just as they are accustomed to thinking of people like you and Mr. Dunbar as criminals."

"Are you through?" I asked him.

He turned to me. "That," he said, "was an extraordinarily satisfying experience."

That's when Brady hit him—with the Jack Daniel's bottle, right on the bald spot.

"Oh Lord," I said, as the man rolled into my arms. The pistol hit the ground at my feet, and Brady scooped it up. "Are you out of your mind? He's out! The man is out."

Brady had the gun, but he looked scared. "It was justified, I thought. This is a rude man."

"What if he's dead?"

"Let's just leave him. Maybe they'll think the deer trampled him or something."

I had this little crippled man in my arms. "We've got to take him back to the house." His glasses were gone. They must have flown off when he was hit. "Where are the guy's glasses?"

"Let's *go*, Mikey. I don't want to be around when he comes to."

"Find his glasses. They must be somewhere on the road. Then come with me." I started back toward the trees, hoping that Brady would follow me, hoping that he didn't get so scared that he took off without me. Then I remembered: I had his keys.

"They're busted," Brady said, beside me suddenly. He held the broken glasses in his hand.

Spock was breathing, at least, and his head seemed to be throwing heat. I thought of my three-year-old again, when I'd carry her to her room after she fell asleep in front of the TV.

We came out onto the lawn. The moon was lower in the sky, throwing shadows across the grass. It would still be a little time before the sun rose.

Brady ran ahead to open the front door. I pushed in behind him and eased Spock into the wheelchair. The cushion gave underneath him.

I tried to push the wheelchair into the living room, but there must have been a brake on or something; it wouldn't budge. I pushed as hard as I could, but the wheels just skidded along the floor, leaving marks.

I'd lost sight of Brady, but I could hear him in one of the rooms, opening drawers. "Don't do this, Brady. This is serious stuff here, Brady."

Spock slumped in the chair. I thought he might slip out of it. I felt the back of his head. It was hot and damp, but there was no blood, thank God.

"Brady, I mean it."

He came out of one of the rooms, stuffing something into his jacket pocket. "This guy owns squat," he said, his eyes still moving around the room. "Shit, what'd I do with the bottle?" He headed back into the bedroom.

I wedged Spock up against the arm of the wheelchair. I thought I should get some water. Throw it in his face.

Brady was back, with the bottle of Jack Daniel's. "Let's go now, Mikey."

"This guy is seriously hurt maybe."

"He's fine. C'mon. That friend of his will be back, like he said. Maybe we'll be lucky and he won't remember a thing."

"We should be calling a doctor. The guy's got a serious disease."

"Give me the keys, Mikey. We gotta go." This whole thing seemed to wire him up somehow. He could hardly control his voice. Then his eye caught the carved marble head on the dining room table. He ran over and grabbed it.

I'm thinking: Oh God, tell me what to do.

"Shit, look at this thing," Brady says. "What a friggin' thing to own."

I should stay with this guy. I did nothing to him. It was Brady. I should stay with this guy.

"Let's go, Mikey. Let's go before the other one comes back."

This is it, I tell myself. This is the start—the start I was making when we left Jake Hiller's. This is where I take the first step back.

The crippled man sank another inch in the wheelchair.

I stood up. "Christ, Brady."

We left the door wide open behind us.

Brady was running ahead of me across the lawn, the head under his arm like a white football. I followed, pouring on speed until, in among the trees, I passed him. My head was a little foggy from the Jack Daniel's, but it felt good to be running.

I came out into the open and sprinted across the road. The deer lay motionless now on the shoulder, a small stream of blood running into the middle of the northbound lanes. I stopped. Brady passed me and got into the car. OK, I said. Bracing myself, I grasped the buck's antlers and pulled. The carcass was heavy, but I managed to pull the thing onto the grass divider.

"Christ Jesus, Mikey!" Brady yelled through the car window.

I eased the buck's head gently down. But the animal looked grotesque there, its limbs splayed out. I bent over and gathered the legs together, so that it looked normal, so that it looked asleep. I stood again.

Brady hit the horn.

I looked down on the deer—this animal lying there because of me—and tried to think of something to say. Brady, behind me, was leaning on the horn. "I'm sorry," I whispered.

The steam was still rising from the deer's flanks. I thought it might be the animal's soul lifting from the body and hovering there, watching me, waiting to see what I would do next.

Unique Szechuan II

THERE ARE three kinds of people in the world: those who divide everything into three kinds, those who divide everything into two kinds, and those who, like me, belong to the latter group."

Warren recites this to his mother, Lana Bentelli, as they sit over their double order of Kung Po Beef with Peanuts. It's a joke, of course—Warren has spent hours perfecting its delicate illogic—but she doesn't seem to get the point. For that matter, neither did the Mensa examiner he tried it on that afternoon, during an interview for admission to the organization. The examiner merely frowned, shook his head, and lowered his eyes mournfully to the papers in his hand. The rejection of Warren's application, of course, came as a disappointment to the young man, but it wasn't entirely unexpected. For years now, Warren has had to inure himself to the inability of his fellows to respond to what is clearly a superior, ultra-refined sense of humor. It's something he's had to learn to live with gracefully. Swirls, as he often says to himself: I cast my swirls before pine.

Lana is staring at him, her chopsticks poised halfway to her lips. "You told *that* to Mensa?" she asks. "Well, no wonder they rejected you. They probably thought you were out of your mind."

Warren frowns indulgently. He rearranges his spidery legs more comfortably under the table. "It is a paradox, Mother. Think about it and you'll get it eventually. Like the barber paradox? Who shaves the barber in the village where the barber shaves those who don't shave themselves? That's Bertrand Russell, for your information."

They are sitting in Unique Szechuan II, their Chinese restaurant of choice in Brooklyn Heights, on a foggy winter night. Warren and his mother eat here up to three times a week, whenever the Woman in White (as Warren likes to call her) comes home from the hospital too tired to cook. Lana finds the restaurant "inspiring." The waiters, as she never tires of telling him, are all physics and economics students earning their tuition—serious people, with serious plans. Warren, meanwhile, just loves the name. Its patent absurdity gives him a jolt of pleasure every time he thinks about it. Although he's not entirely sure, he believes that his mother has yet to catch on to the joke, and he, for one, is not about to squander the revelation of such a gorgeous secret. He is saving it up—for her birthday, perhaps, or for the day somebody actually offers him a job.

"So this examiner, he told you you weren't smart enough for Mensa," Lana says.

"He did no such thing, Mother!" Warren says. "The little man simply informed me that my test results indicated 'a certain deficiency in mathematical ability.' Mathematics? What does mathematics have to do with intelligence, I asked him. Machines do mathematics. Little hand-held devices from Japan do mathematics. Mathematics is to true intellectual endeavor, I told him, as bricklaying is to the art of cathedral-building."

"You said that aloud to him."

"Of course I did."

"Warren." Lana takes off her glasses. They have small

lenses, with frames the color of graphite—the kind of glasses, he once quipped, that scientists in the Manhattan Project wore. "Warren, Warren," she continues, "how many times have I told you not to be clever in interviews."

"Can I help it if these people are charlatans?" he asks, placing a slender white hand on his chest.

Warren watches his mother stir the beef on her plate. He knows that she finds him infuriating at times. But he is her own. Lana Bentelli, a large, rotund woman, is deputy head nurse in the pediatrics ward of Long Island College Hospital—a position she is justly proud to have attained. When her husband, Warren's father, died eighteen years ago, she was left with nothing but a few bad debts and himself, Warren, an underweight nine-year-old with sugar diabetes. Warren cannot even imagine having to cope with a situation like that. She was twenty-five at the time. And unemployed. Warren finds his mother enormously, stupendously impressive.

"So you're rejected. So you go on," Lana says finally. "You've got more important things to worry about, anyway."

"Such as?" Warren asks, knowing full well what she means.

"Such as your graduate-school applications. You've got your references to line up. Bill says they'll need time to write your letters."

His mother is referring to Bill Verona, her "boyfriend" (Warren always supplies the quotation marks in his mind). Bill runs the gift shop in the waiting room of Lana's hospital. Warren dislikes him intensely.

"Bill Verona, if that's whom you mean, never went to college, so how, pray tell, would he know?" Warren takes a sloppy sip of his water. "Besides, define *they*, Lana, this group of academics just clamoring to write my recommendation letters." He gestures with his hand to indicate the gaggle of waiters at the end of the room. "Do you think one of these ultraserious brain surgeons will do me the honor? Remind me, which one has the Nobel Prize?"

"Don't call me Lana," Lana says.

"Fine." Warren realigns his chopsticks with a pert tap and begins eating again.

"I was thinking," his mother goes on cautiously, "of asking Dr. Weisenborn . . ."

Warren pretends to choke on a piece of Kung Po Beef. "Hello? Hello, audience? Lana can't be suggesting that I ask Dr. As-Played-by-Richard-Chamberlain for a graduate school recommendation, can she?"

"Shut up and listen to me, Warren. He's a respected pediatrician and he *knows* you."

"The man looks younger than most of his patients. They don't accept recommendations from people who don't shave yet, Mother, it's on the application."

Lana grabs his wrist. "I've made an appointment for the two of you tomorrow afternoon, to talk. He says he would be glad to help."

Warren feels panic rising in his narrow chest. His mother seems serious about this. He may actually have to go through with these grad-school applications. Suddenly, as if in answer to a prayer, his tongue finds a bit of bone in the meat he's chewing. Bracing himself, he bites down on it with as much force as he can muster. A dagger of pain plunges up through his nasal cavities. He feels the splintered filling drop against his gum. "Oh God," he nearly screams, rising from his chair. "My tooth! My tooth!"

His mother keeps her grip on his wrist. "Sit down," she commands quietly.

"I broke a filling on this hellish Kung Po Beef!" Other diners in the restaurant are craning their necks to identify the disturbance. "We'll sue! My tooth is totally destroyed!"

One of the waiters appears suddenly at Warren's elbow. "A problem, sir?" he asks, putting a bony hand on Warren's free arm.

Warren shakes loose of both grips. "You, sir, are responsible," he says, holding his jaw. "Mother, you settle this. I'm going to assess the damage." He pushes past the grim-faced waiter and storms to the men's room.

"Wash it out with water," his mother calls after him.

Warren pushes into the tiny bathroom and locks the door behind him. He turns, bumping a knee against the sink in the limited space, and peers at his reflection in the dirty mirror. Dr. Weisenborn, he says to himself in exasperation. He stares at his face, the gaunt, colorless cheeks, the lips brimming at the corners with saliva, the enormous, bloodshot eyes. No, he will not—he *cannot*—stoop to solicit a recommendation from his mother's juvenile boss.

Remembering suddenly, he spits the half-chewed mouthful of beef into his hand and searches for the filling. When he finds the fragment of silver metal, a shard of tooth attached to it, he throws the food into the toilet and washes his hands in the sink. He pockets the filling and leaves, refusing to flush the toilet behind him.

When he returns to the dining room, his mother and several Chinese men are standing around the table, deep in discussion. "Did you get the name of their lawyer?" Warren asks loudly as he lurches up to the table.

"We've got it all settled, Warren, so keep your shirt on. The owner will pay for any necessary dental work."

"Unacceptable," Warren pronounces.

One of the waiters pats his shoulder. "We are very sorry, sir. We know you are regular customer."

"And what about the cost of the meal?" Warren asks. "I don't expect my entree to bite me back."

"Free, free, our treat," the waiter says.

Warren knows that the man despises him, but he doesn't care. "Come mother, let's leave. I've had enough of this establishment for one night."

"I was finished anyway," she says blandly. Warren and his mother gather up their coats and head for the door, Lana attempting to hush her son's *sotto voce* insults about the service.

Outside on Atlantic Avenue, the streetlights are just coming on, casting a flesh-toned glow over the sidewalks. There are big ships moving in the harbor nearby. They sound their foghorns, giving Warren the momentary impression of being in a waterfront movie from the 1950's.

He stops to fill his lungs with briny winter air. He's feeling better now. To hell with Mensa, says he. There are a few individuals, at least, who appreciate his virtues, even if they don't always appreciate his jokes. He slips his hand through his mother's arm and turns her in the direction of home. "I'll have to get this tooth looked at right away," he says to her. "If old Philip Wexler is booked, I'll have to find somebody else. It's an emergency." He pauses, and adds, "I guess this means tomorrow's meeting with your adolescent boss is off."

His mother chuckles pleasantly. "Not a chance, Warren. Your precious tooth can wait a day or two. My adolescent boss expects you at 2:15."

"So your B.A. is in musicology, with a minor in philosophy."

"Yes," Warren says through tense lips. "Just as it's written there."

Dr. Daniel Weisenborn nods ambiguously. "N.Y.U. is very strong in philosophy, I'm told."

Warren closes his eyes. Oh Lord, the things he must

endure to humor his mother. This has been an unbearable nuisance from start to finish. First sitting around for twenty-three minutes in this man's overdesigned, oversanitized waiting room, fending off the overtures of infectious little tots dressed in Oshkosh B'Gosh overalls. Then being led down sterile hallways to this plush, leather-appointed office for another twelve-minute wait. And now, worst of all, the final indignity—sitting in front of this large antique oak desk, examining his fingernails while this . . . this medical homunculus reads through Warren's curriculum vitae. His mother will pay for this, Warren tells himself. He will wreak his vengeance upon her in some subtle but effective way. By refusing to eat her lasagna, perhaps. Or forgetting his morning shot of insulin.

Warren shifts in the chair and regards the framed diplomas hanging on the office wall. Colgate, Johns Hopkins, a little citation from the Brooklyn Borough president for (unspecified) community service. Warren snorts, almost audibly. This is what his mother would love for him, a little cliché of a doctor's office and a wallful of serious academic paper. Warren turns and watches the doctor reading through his file. The man is young enough to be his brother. Look, he's practically moving his lips as he reads!

Dr. Weisenborn flips a page, a jarring sound in the muffled quiet of his office. "So you didn't get your degree until 1988. Remind me again why?"

"Medical problems. I, sir, am a diabetic."

The doctor raises an eyebrow. "Yes, I know. But your mother tells me that your case is not so serious. Nothing to keep you out of school."

"There were other problems," Warren says, making a dismissive gesture with his hands. "Rather not talk about it, you know."

"Of course." Dr. Weisenborn—or Dr. Daniel, as Warren

now decides he'd rather think of him—places a single finger against his sweatless temple.

Warren watches him closely. It was the ones like Dr. Daniel that he despised so much in high school—the little smart ones, the Most Likely to Succeeds, the fair-haired boys who barely seemed to notice his existence. Harmless, one of them —a Stanford-bound lacrosse player—had once called Warren. Harmless. The adjective has stuck with him, sizzling in his memory.

Warren shifts his weight in the tubular chair. His tongue seeks the unfamiliar hole in his second upper-left-hand molar. He presses steadily until he feels a twinge of pain. *There are three kinds of people in the world* . . . Warren begins to compose in his head.

"Work experience?" the doctor asks suddenly.

"I do not type fifty words per minute, Doctor D—, uh, Weisenborn, which apparently makes me unfit for employment at any publishing house, magazine, newspaper, or even university in this fair city of ours." Warren places his hand on the knot of the tie his mother insisted he wear. "I do occasional rewriting for an Algerian professor of economics at Brooklyn College. His English is one or two steps above atrocious."

"And you'll be getting a recommendation from him as well?"

"Oh yes. Or, as Dr. Assiz himself would put it, *sans doute.*"

Dr. Weisenborn sighs. He closes the Manila folder and taps it twice against the desktop. "You didn't want to come here, did you, Warren. Lana put you up to this."

"If you mean my mother, Mrs. Bentelli, then yes, she did arrange this meeting, as you know." *There are three categories of people in the world* . . .

Dr. Weisenborn rises to his feet, making his swivel chair

groan. "Well, let me be straight with you, Warren," he says. "Normally, I wouldn't write a recommendation for someone I know so little about. But I've known your mother for four years now—"

"And they've been the happiest four years of her life, I can tell you that, sir."

The doctor stops short. He wets his lips and puts Warren's folder down on the desk. "You may leave now, Warren. I'll have the letter for your mother when I see her at the hospital on Friday."

Warren rises from the chair. "Thank you, doctor." He stretches to his full six-feet-five, showing the man his glory.

"Looks like you could put on some weight, Warren. How much do you weigh?"

"I weighed approximately 158 pounds last time I checked, which was sometime during the Carter administration."

The doctor shakes his head. "Much too little."

"But what's there, as Spencer Tracy might say, is cherce." Warren extends his moist hand in a show of utter insincerity. *There are three groups of human beings in the world . . .*

Dr. Weisenborn shakes the hand as he leads him to the exit.

. . . and Dr. Daniel should consider joining at least one of them, Warren completes the thought as he shuts the office door behind him. He considers it for a moment, turns it over in his mind. A paltry effort, he decides finally, feeling disappointed in himself. But for now it will have to do.

Next morning, Warren, who has overslept again, is sitting on the edge of his bed, fixed in a bright diagonal of sunlight. Backlit motes of dust are rising and falling on the complex thermals of his ill-heated bedroom. The windows of the basement apartment (which he has shared with his mother for years) are high on the walls, so that the top sash is just a few inches below the ceiling.

Warren purses his lips. He presses the hypodermic needle to the inside of his thigh until the pale skin gives way with an audible pop. Breathing heavily through his nose, he presses down on the plunger, injecting the insulin into his bloodstream. The sensation, a slowly spreading burn, is familiar, luxurious, consoling. After a moment he pulls out the needle and swabs the patch of skin with a cottonball soaked in alcohol.

The telephone rings. "Oh spare me," Warren mutters, tossing the cottonball into his thatched wastebasket. He upends the hypodermic into a frozen orange-juice can, pulls up his trousers, and goes to the living room to answer the phone. He hates it when the phone rings while his mother is at work. Sometimes he doesn't bother to answer it, which annoys his mother no end. More often than not, it's she.

"Villa Bentelli," he says into the white plastic phone.

"Dr. O'Connor calling for Lana Bentelli," says a hurried female, "please hold."

Warren rolls his eyes for the benefit of his omnipresent spectators. Dr. O'Connor is a new one on him. Warren thought he knew every physician who ever set foot on his mother's floor at the hospital. She certainly talks enough about them, boring him nightly with tales of their heroism and scientific triumphs. Maybe this is a new one, Warren speculates as he waits. Another young one, wet behind the ears like our Dr. Danny.

The line clicks, and a low male voice speaks. "Mrs. Bentelli, we just got your test results back from the lab."

"A moment, a moment *please*, Dr. O'Connor. This isn't Lana Bentelli you're speaking to, this is her son."

"Oh, I'm terribly sorry." The doctor pauses. "Is Mrs. Bentelli at home?"

"Alas, no," Warren says. "She's working. In fact, you can probably find her right there at the hospital. She's a nurse in pediatrics."

Another pause. "All right. Can you have her call me, either at my office or at St. Vincent's? She has the numbers."

"St. Vincent's?"

"Sorry about the confusion. My receptionist told me she had Mrs. Bentelli on the line. Good-bye."

Warren hangs up. St. Vincent's? His mother works at Long Island College Hospital. Why would a doctor from another hospital be giving his mother tests? As he moves away from the telephone, Warren's mind lurches toward a speculation, but he pulls himself back. No, he says to himself, something else, think of something else. "The imbecile," he says then, aloud. "Doesn't he know that the woman will be at work on a Thursday morning? And these people are supposed to be doctors."

Warren glances through the kitchen doorway at the clock over the sink: 10:45. He has an eleven o'clock appointment. "I'll be late for the dentist," he says aloud. He tells himself he must think hard about the dentist. He must imagine the steel, enamel, and vinyl of the high mechanical chair, the burnished shine of the silver implements, the high imploring whine of the water-cooled drill. He reaches for the phone to call his mother, but stops himself. He is late for the dentist. There is simply no time.

"You can rinse that now." Dr. Wexler reaches across Warren's bibbed chest and presses a lever. A tiny paper cup fills with water, the stream from the chrome spigot making a wet buzz as it hits the bottom of the cup. "Swish it around real good now."

Warren takes the cup and drains it into his mouth. The lukewarm, mint-flavored water stings as it hits the broken tooth.

"Kinda quiet today, aren't you, Warren?" Dr. Wexler asks in his gentle Southern lilt. "Not mad at me, are you?"

Warren spits into the swirling waters of the enamel sink. "It never ceases to amaze me how you dentists can fill our mouths with every instrument of torture invented since the Spanish Inquisition and then expect us to discuss the weather with you."

Dr. Wexler chuckles. "Now *that's* the Warren Bentelli I know. Says it right here on your chart: 'Pugnacious as all get-out.'"

"Spare me the quaint down-home-isms, Dr. Wexler. We all know that you were born in Canarsie."

"So you keep telling me," Dr. Wexler says, a smile deepening the wrinkles around his eyes and mouth. "By the way, you've got a string of drool running down your chin."

Warren dabs himself with the paper bib. "Thank you," he says curtly.

Normally Warren enjoys sparring with this husky, sandy-haired old man (who, to be fair, really is from a place called La Grange, Tennessee), but he can hardly bring himself to play today. The call he received for his mother is bothering him, droning in his head like an ostinato of misgiving. Who is Dr. O'Connor of St. Vincent's? he keeps asking himself. His mother usually sees one of the GPs in the neighborhood, Dr. Vornov. Why now this Dr. O'Connor? All morning, Warren has worried the question, just as his tongue has worried his broken tooth—pulling away instantly at the first throb of pain. He must not think about it.

"Seems there's a little decay around the old filling," Dr. Wexler says to him, adjusting the light so that it flashes in Warren's eyes. "One shot of novocaine, a little drill action, and we'll fill it up good as new. Have you out of here in half an hour."

Warren nods, becoming aware again of the wordless assistant behind his head. She's rummaging around to prepare the injection. The Little Ghost, Warren always calls her.

"OK, open," Dr. Wexler says. He sticks a red-tipped cotton swab into Warren's mouth and lodges it between his cheek and gum. "Leave that there for a few seconds."

Warren thinks suddenly of his mother's body—a specific image. It was just before church on a Sunday morning. He walked into her bedroom to ask her about the color of a certain wool tie (Warren is partially color-blind) and found her peering at her breasts in a mirror. She turned away quickly, but Warren remembers seeing a slice of impossibly white flesh under her splayed fingers. The skin caught the morning light as she spun away. "Disappear!" she shouted at him. She had been examining her breasts for lumps.

Dr. Wexler pulls the swab from under Warren's cheek. "We're ready for the novocaine now. You'll feel a pinch." He pulls Warren's moist lip away from the upper gum. Warren feels a vague prick as the needle pierces the skin. Dr. Wexler repositions the needle several times, injecting the painkiller at different angles around the tooth. The metal syringe clicks against Warren's front teeth. Then the dentist pulls out the needle and massages Warren's gum with a fingertip.

"That'll take a few minutes to kick in," he says. He hands the syringe to his assistant and wipes his hands on a paper towel. "We'll be back. Don't go away." They leave the room, Dr. Wexler's rubber-soled shoes utterly silent on the polished linoleum floor.

Warren presses his head back against the headrest. Of course his mother was examining her breasts, he tells himself then. She's a nurse, for heaven's sake. He looks out of the dentist's window, at the male and female feet passing on the sidewalk above. The feet seem to pass with such confidence, feet encased in fine soft leather, as supple as skin. Warren glances down at the tips of his oxblood penny loafers. A tide of panic rises in his chest, up his esophagus. He puts his hand to his cheek. It seems swollen, puffy and lifeless. Warren swings his legs down to the floor just as Dr. Wexler walks in again.

"Going someplace?" the dentist asks.

"I just remembered a telephone call," Warren tells him, his words slurring from the anesthetic. "Important. Can I use your phone?"

Dr. Wexler shrugs. "Sure, if it really can't wait. Use the phone in my office."

Warren pushes past him and down the corridor to Dr. Wexler's private office. He grabs the phone and presses his mother's work number. It rings five times before someone answers. "Hello," Warren says urgently, "is Nurse Bentelli there?"

"Hold on."

Waiting, he presses the cold phone receiver against the side of his face. He can feel the cold only from his temple to a point just above his cheekbone, where all sensation stops.

"I'm sorry," the voice says. "Nurse Bentelli is with a patient now. Can I take a message?"

"Yes. Please have her meet her son for lunch at one o'clock at the Chinese restaurant. She'll know which one. Tell her it's important. Please."

"I'll give her that message."

"Thank you." Warren puts down the phone. He turns and finds Dr. Wexler standing in the doorway, watching him.

"Well, Warren," the dentist says, a little puzzled, "we'd better go back in now. Just remember you'll have a new filling, so take it easy on the Moo Shoo Pork."

Warren is sitting at their usual table near the back of Unique Szechuan II, waiting for his mother. The restaurant is busy with secretaries, lawyers, and bureaucrats from the municipal buildings in downtown Brooklyn. Warren recognizes only one or two of the waiters who normally serve at dinner. The others, he reflects, must all be off at their advanced physics seminars. He drains his second Coke and lifts his hand to order another.

Warren checks again the clock on the wall over the silverware station. His mother is late, but he is calm. He has decided that nothing like this can really happen to him. He is Warren Bentelli. The Woman in White had a few tests done, that's all. Tests are, definitionally, periodic checks, ways of making sure. Now that she has had these tests, they will be sure. "Good man," he says loudly as the waiter puts a fresh Coke in front of him. He takes a sip. The cold liquid seems to divide his mouth in two—one half chilled, the other numb. The sensation is bizarre, titillating.

Warren leans back in his chair. Today is the day, he tells himself. Today he will reveal to his mother the joke about the name of their favorite restaurant. Unique Szechuan II. Smiling, he imagines her expression as the realization flutters down over her, as a falling parachute descends on a skydiver at the completion of a jump. She will appreciate it in the way only they two can appreciate it. "I wonder which of the two restaurants is the more unique," he will quip at the appropriate moment.

Suddenly his mother appears at the glass doors of the restaurant, her nurse's uniform hidden under the flapping tails of her winter coat. He waves to attract her attention.

"I see you, I see you," she says as she walks up to the table. "I'm not blind, you know." She frees her shoulders from the arms of the coat and wriggles it off. "I'm surprised you got our usual place. They're packed today."

"They wouldn't dare give anyone else the Bentelli Table. They keep it in waiting twenty-four hours a day."

"Dream on, Warren," Lana says. She takes a seat across from him. "So tell me about your tooth."

Warren smiles, his mouth lopsided. "As good as new. And I was so benumbed by Dr. Wexler's inane banter that I didn't even need novocaine."

"He's a good dentist, you shouldn't make fun." Lana pushes her glasses up the bridge of her nose and picks up one of the plastic menus. She pretends to look over the entrées, but he can tell that she's not reading. "So tell me, Warren, what's with this lunch date?" she asks.

"I need an excuse to invite my own mother to luncheon?" Warren responds, the panic welling again.

"It's about Dr. O'Connor, isn't it. He told me about the telephone call when I talked to him."

Warren looks down at the empty soda glass in his fingers.

"Well, I have some news for you, Warren." His mother puts down the menu. She reaches forward to touch him. "I'm going to have another baby."

Warren stares at his mother. His mouth throbs noisily in his ears.

"I just got the results. I'm going to have another baby."

Warren thinks he has stopped breathing. "Another?" he manages to say.

"I mean a second one. After you. Bill and I talked it over, and we'll be getting married in the spring. The baby is due in July."

"I don't understand," Warren says.

She grabs his hand. "I'm not an old woman yet." She pinches the white skin on the back of his hand. "And don't look so tragic, Warren. Be happy for me, damn it. And for you, too. You can have the apartment to yourself." Then she adds: "Unless you decide to go to school out of state."

Warren rises slowly from the table. He feels a terrible certainty that he must do something, but he has no idea what. He unfolds himself into the steamy warmth of the crowded restaurant.

"I promise you, honey, no one can replace you," his mother is saying, trying to calm him. "You know that."

Warren picks up the empty soda glass. He can hear tug-boats in the harbor outside, sounding their horns.

"Honey," his mother says.

Warren feels a little surge of energy. Harmless, he says to himself.

His mother's face is peering at him. Her hands are moving in a vague, helpless gesture. She hardly seems to recognize him.

"You'll always be my one and only," she says finally, the fright creeping into her voice.

Safe Houses

W HEN ESTHER BOYD'S handbag disappeared in
the crowded Lark Hill Tavern one difficult November evening,
she decided one thing instantly: she would not report the loss
to the police. There seemed to be no point. The police could
hardly be expected to investigate every petty theft that came
to their attention; and if the bag ever turned up, as stolen bags
often did, cashless and cardless in the dumpster behind some
brutally lit all-night A&P, she would be notified. There hadn't
been much money in the bag—about forty dollars, Esther
guessed—and she was sensible enough to stop her credit cards
within minutes of becoming aware of the loss, calling from
the pay phone with quarters offered by the sympathetic bar-
tender. More important, her ring of keys was safe; Esther had
recently developed the habit of stuffing them into the pocket
of her camel-colored overcoat, after once too often losing the
whole ring in the arcane folds of her utterly impractical Mexican handbag. So the loss was minor, really, more an inconvenience than a calamity, except for the letter.

The letter was the reason she had come to the Lark Hill
Tavern in the first place. Esther was not in the habit of visiting
bars by herself, particularly not bars like the Lark Hill, with
its tired nostalgic décor (fly-specked Coke advertisements from

the 50's, neon jukeboxes) and its large-screen color television tuned to some obscure cable sports channel. But she drove past the bar every evening on her way home from work, and on this particular day she decided to stop for a drink. The letter—the very proximity of it to her person—was troubling her. She had received it the day before. She still hadn't opened it.

The letter was from Ann-Ellen Gluck, Esther's former colleague, former housemate, and former—though this last former a result more of distance than of choice—lover. They had parted eight months earlier, when Esther left New Mexico to accept her long-awaited administration job at Vassar College. There had since been an understanding between the two women. It was an admission of realism, or, as Ann-Ellen preferred to call it, a clear-eyed recognition of the 2,500 miles between them. Perhaps because this understanding was so sensible—so brisk and rational—Esther had never quite been able to believe in it. In her mind, Ann-Ellen was always there, in that little stucco house in the desert hills, preserving the life that Esther had left behind, keeping it whole and unchanged: a sanctuary, a reassuring presence, an option. But then the letter came. Ann-Ellen never sent letters; she called, as everyone did nowadays. In fact, the two women spoke on the phone religiously twice a month, every other Friday night, complaining fondly to each other about the inane bureaucratic morasses into which their profession inevitably and repeatedly tossed them. That's why Esther hadn't been able to bring herself to open the letter immediately. A letter, unlike a scheduled phone call, smacked of moment and weight. It carried with it connotations of official change. The letter frightened her.

And now, Esther told herself as she drove home from the bar along the empty country roads, the letter was gone. She shook her head in the slick, engineered comfort of her new car's dark interior. The Lark Hill Tavern. It probably served her right.

Feeling warm, uneasy, the unaccustomed vodka tonic spreading a dimly voluptuous fuzz over her perceptions, Esther tried to think about the calls she would have to make, the forms she would have to fill out, in order to replace the contents of her bag. Her credit cards were already taken care of, but she would have to reapply for a university ID, a library card, her Blue Cross/Blue Shield, her driver's license—Oh God, she thought suddenly, I'm driving without a license. Esther eased her foot slightly on the accelerator, allowing the speedometer needle to settle back below 40. She took a deep, slow breath. "Too much to think about," she said aloud to the luminous dashboard.

Esther turned off the main road onto an unlighted street. After a few hundred yards, the houses on either side began thinning out, moving farther and farther back into the tangles of leafless shrubbery and pine. When she reached the little yellow house with black shutters, she turned into the curving driveway. The house, which she had been renting for the past three months, stood amid oaks and Japanese maples along the edge of a tiny, rock-strewn brook. The small property had seemed almost tropical in the lushness of August when Esther signed the lease, but now winter had leached most of the color and texture from the surroundings, giving the house an austere aspect that she thought of as somehow Scandinavian. She loved the way the house looked now—the sheer *seriousness* of it— but that love was still mostly aesthetic. This was where she lived now; that was all.

Esther parked the car, extinguished the lights, and reached for her bag. Strange, she thought to herself when, of course, her hand found nothing. Strange how the body had a memory of its own. Her mind knew, but her hand had to be reminded. If she closed her eyes (which she did now, wearily), she could almost feel the Mexican bag in her hand, the smooth, dermal patches of thick leather, the knobbled stitching, the cold metal ring that bound the bag to its long shoulder strap. She'd had the bag for years. It was a souvenir of a desperate, ill-planned trip to Cozumel, the winter before she met Ann-Ellen. An awful winter, she told herself now, getting out of the car and heading up the walk. A winter that would always be troubling for her to think about.

She unlocked the front door and pushed into her chilly kitchen, making the shades on every window in the house tap once against the frames. The brick-and-flagstone kitchen (one of the major reasons she had taken the house) assembled itself around her as she flipped on the brass wall sconce, the counter lamp, the amber light above the sink. A pile of mail had been placed neatly on the counter—a small courtesy of William, the owner of the house, who was doing some plastering in the basement on his week off. He was gone now, leaving, as usual, little sign of his presence.

Esther picked up the mail and shuffled through it quickly, relieved to find nothing of importance. She put it aside and then stepped into the dining room, slipping out of her long coat as she moved. This room was warmer, but almost empty of furniture. A lonely oak table and four chairs stood in the middle of it. A single floor lamp loomed behind them, its shade rakishly askew.

A light was blinking on her answering machine in the dim living room beyond. A quick, optimistic thought flashed through Esther's mind: they had found her bag, whoever they were, and only the money was missing. But, of course, it was too soon for that. She pressed the replay button and waited while the tape rewound its two messages. The first was from her landlord: "Hi, it's William. I've got a few more days of plastering downstairs, I think, but I won't be coming tomorrow. My daughter's got this thing, this school thing that needs to be taken care of, so, I'm not sure, but I think I'll be back on Thursday, if that's all right. Bye."

The tape ran silently for a few moments before the second message began. Esther knew the voice immediately. "Hello Es, I thought you'd be home by now. I didn't know if— Well, I wondered if you'd gotten my letter yet. I was just wondering. Anyway. So, if you want to talk or something, call. OK? It's 6:20 your time. Anyway. Love you. Bye."

Esther imagined Ann-Ellen in the house, calling from the small octagonal table in the study. Her long, prematurely graying hair would be pulled back and held in a rubber band. Her knees would be drawn to her chest, her feet in thick red socks, the eccentric house unfolding out around her like a Japanese fan . . .

"I should call her," Esther said aloud, shifting on her feet. The letter would have to be sent again. Or, better yet, Ann-Ellen could simply tell her what had to be told, over the phone, now. Esther would just admit to Ann-Ellen that she was in that bar—they would laugh about that, The Lark Hill Tavern—and that she had lost the letter. That it had been stolen. That she hadn't been able to open it.

She walked back across the room to hang her coat in the hall closet. "I should call her," she said again. But she knew, as she pushed the coat deep in among the cool, fragrant sweaters and overcoats and down jackets, that she would not call Ann-Ellen. Not tonight.

Esther closed the closet door and turned to stand with her back against it. She looked across the shadowy room at the floor lamp by the stark, uncurtained window. She breathed.

———

It was two days later that Esther received the first postcard in the mail. She recognized the image the moment she saw it, sandwiched in among the bills and catalogues that William had piled on the kitchen counter. She had bought a postcard of this very same painting—the Alex Katz of a woman in a white bathing suit, awkward but frank, standing at the center of a field of marine blue—at the university bookstore just days ago, along with several others. She marveled at the coincidence for a moment before—a jagged realization, a sudden shifting inside her—she understood.

The message on the other side was written in red ink in a large, immature hand: "God sees Everything in life and Death. You must Pray to God for He shall be Forgivness and Mercy. I and God are Your JUDGES. Embrace the Love."

Esther groaned and sank onto a kitchen stool. He had read the letter. Guessing her relationship with Ann-Ellen from its contents had probably not been difficult for him. And then he, whoever he was, had pawed through everything else in her bag. He had her postcards, her driver's license. Esther crossed her arms over her chest. Of course he had those things, she told herself, he had stolen her bag. Why hadn't she thought of this before? The man knew who she was, knew her address.

Esther looked down at the card. She tried to read the postmark. It was half-obscured by the ink scrawl, but she could make out the letters "PA" near the edge of the stamp. He wrote from Pennsylvania. Far away. Far *enough* away, she hoped.

Esther rose from the stool. She should call the police, perhaps. The man had opened a letter addressed to her. Unless she was mistaken, that was a federal offense, a felony. And now this postcard. Was it a threat? She reread the message, the words almost fluid on the card in front of her eyes.

She placed the card on the corner of the counter and

walked to the window. Outside, the bony fingers of two Japanese maples quavered in the wind. Her car sat in the driveway beside them, looking calm and solid and expectant, like a confident bride. The wind pulverized the light dusting of snow beneath the wheels, blowing it out across the white lawn.

For two days, Esther had been filling out forms. "Lost" she had explained on each one. Not stolen, but lost. It had been easier that way. Less bother, less sympathy. That way, it was her own fault. What would she tell the police now? How much would she be required to explain?

She moved away from the window, went back to the postcard. It was a hateful thing; she didn't even want it in the same house with her. Acting on impulse, she turned on the front left burner of the stove and, her lips taut, held the card over the flame. It caught after a moment or two, the flame sliding up the edge like thick amber syrup. Panicking slightly, she threw the card into the sink. She watched the blue-and-white image twist and consume itself, the pale-skinned figure blackening from the head down.

At 11:15 that night, the phone rang. Esther was already in bed in the front bedroom upstairs, lying in the dark. She listened to the phone croon once, twice. The answering machine clicked on downstairs. Not moving from the bed, she waited to hear the voice on the speaker. There was a slight pause, then Ann-Ellen's voice filled the house, as if she were calling from the foot of the stairs: "Esther? Es, are you there? I know you've gotten it by now. Please just talk to me. Please."

Esther called in sick the next morning. She slept late—until ten, which she rarely did, even on Sundays—and rose to make herself some coffee. It was a bright morning, the low sun melting the snow on the paint-spattered rhododendrons outside. She carried her cup into the dining room and sat at the table. The belt of her terrycloth robe squeezed the flesh around her waist, so she loosened it and retied it. She had gained some weight, just a few pounds, since her move east.

A car, William's flesh-toned jeep, bounced into the driveway and pulled up next to hers. She closed her eyes momentarily, only now remembering that William would be coming today. She watched her balding, ample-bellied landlord extricate himself from the jeep. He glanced briefly at her car, then peered toward the house, as if reluctant to come closer. Esther got up and waved to him from the dining-room window. Seeing her, he returned the wave with an ironic, self-deprecating smile. He grabbed a brown-paper shopping bag from the back seat and made his way up the front walk.

They met at the door. "I didn't expect to find you here today!" William said too loudly as he pulled open the glass storm door. He came in, bringing with him the cold, resiny smell of outdoors.

"I wasn't feeling so well," Esther explained. "To be honest, I forgot you were coming. I hardly know when you've been here. You leave no trace. Like a little mouse."

"Like a little mouse," he repeated, tickled by the comparison. He stamped his work boots energetically, leaving hieroglyphs of snow on the doormat. William moved fast and angularly, like something mechanical that had been wound up too tight. "But don't let me bother you. I'll go right down."

"Don't be ridiculous. Would you like some coffee?"

"Thanks anyway. I brought my own." He pulled a little plaid thermos from the shopping bag. "Didn't want to make any dishes to wash."

"William," she said, scolding. "This is *your* house, you know."

He chuckled. "Your house now, Esther. That's what rent

means." He smiled impishly, his forehead gleaming. "Oh Christ, though," he said then, "the mail. I pulled it from your box." He turned and pushed back out the frost-fogged door. Esther watched him return to his jeep and retrieve a stack of mail from the front seat. He habitually collected it from the box on the main road as he came in. A thought occurred to her: Had William seen the postcard yesterday? Had he read the message? She tried to decipher the answer in his face as he returned to the house, his breath vapor curling around his head. When he saw her staring at him, he smiled and waved again, looking embarrassed.

"Christmas catalogues already," he said, bringing in another block of frigid air. "They start earlier every year!"

Esther put down her coffee cup to receive the bundle of mail.

"Anyway, I'd like to start right away," he said, picking up his shopping bag again. Then, looking slightly abashed, he added, "Gangway," and slipped past her to the basement door.

Esther put the mail on the high kitchen table. She looked at it for a moment, then walked calmly to the counter to retrieve her coffee. The postcard was right on top of the pile—the Richard Avedon photograph of Isak Dinesen, her ancient face bright with energy and possibility. What had she been thinking that day, Esther wondered, to choose this particular picture, or the Alex Katz of the day before? She was in the habit of posting favored images—postcards, advertisements, photographs—on the door of her refrigerator. That's what she had intended to do with the cards she bought that day: to create a gallery of hopeful, strong women on the front of William's aging Frigidaire.

Esther poured the rest of her coffee into the sink. She told herself that she would not read this postcard. It would only frighten her. Or anger her. Returning to the table, she coolly removed it from the top of the pile and laid it aside. She sorted through the rest of the mail. William was right; it was mostly catalogues, along with her replacement American Express card, a few odd bills, and one or two fundraising solicitations. Ironic, she thought, that the only personal message was the one on the postcard. She stared at it again, at the lurid white face whose vitality seemed almost like a reproach now. She should at least look at the postmark, to make sure. Before any part of her could object, she grabbed the card and turned it over. The postmark, much clearer this time, said, "Lansdowne PA." It was then inevitable that she read the message, printed again in red ink: "Do you know the Word of the Living God? For He is Our Judge and Savier, the Rhyme and Reason of ALL THINGS!"

"So," Esther said aloud, putting down the card. She cleared her throat awkwardly, self-consciously. So this was what needed to be said to her today. Her message from the world. Esther's eyes filled suddenly, without warning, and she turned from the table, pressing a hand against her face. It was impossible to know what to do. How could she have left Ann-Ellen and come to this place, alone?

"Esther?" It was William behind her, standing at the entrance to the kitchen.

"I'm sorry," she said, engineering a quick smile for him.

William didn't appear to notice the tears. "Did you know about the leak down there?" he asked. "Toward the back of the house. There's water seeping down the plaster. Looks like it's been that way a while."

"No," Esther said, "or I would have called you."

William frowned. "Could be from the bathroom on this floor. The location's right. I'll have to get somebody."

"Of course, of course." A plumber was what he meant.

"I'm sorry," he said, spreading his large hands. "I'd do it

myself, only plumbing is a little out of my league. They may have to tear up the bathroom wall to find it." He sighed sympathetically. "More inconvenience."

"William, please, it's not your fault. Anyway, I hardly use that bathroom."

William was nodding. "Well, I might as well call now, if I can use your phone. I can call somebody I know, he'll come tomorrow if I ask him. Unless you think you'll be here tomorrow?"

"No, no," Esther told him, looking away involuntarily. "I'm much better already. I probably should have gone in today after all."

"You just don't worry about it. I'll be here to let the guy in and out. Can I call him?"

She smiled with as much warmth as she could muster and directed him to his own telephone in the living room. She watched as he dialed his plumber friend and spoke into the phone. The two men began joking with each other. William made mock complaints about some work the plumber friend had previously done in the house. Esther wondered if the friend was a widower too, like William. She wondered if they drank beer together after work—at a bar like the Lark Hill Tavern —and moaned about their teenaged daughters.

The rhyme and reason of all things. Esther turned and gathered the mail, carrying it upstairs into the half-furnished master bedroom.

That evening, Esther spent an hour in the rope hammock on the glassed-in back porch. This was where—in late summer, when she was new to the house—she had passed most of her evenings, listening to the intense throb of insects outside as she read thick, undemanding novels from the local library. She was training herself to be courageous, to not mind being alone in a house engulfed by dense foliage. At first, of course, she had started at every little noise, but by autumn, by the time William came to replace the screens with streaky glass panels, she had succeeded in hardening herself to the resonant darkness outside. Her mind, she told herself, had tamed her heart's irrational terrors. She could read in the hammock for hours at a time and not be frightened.

Now, in the chill of a Hudson Valley November, she was mostly confined to the interior of the house. The electric heater installed beneath the hammock was vastly expensive to run, and it never did more than make the porch just bearable. But she still liked to spend at least a little time out here. On all but the coldest nights, she'd put on a thick cable sweater and down vest, brew herself a cup of something hot, and go to the hammock to think.

Tonight, the arrival of the second postcard still preying on her mind, Esther found herself missing her stolen handbag. The Mexican bag, for all its gaudy absurdity, had been important to her. The story behind it was one that she told only to her closest friends, and even they were not privy to all of the details. There were parts of the story, in fact, that Esther had kept from everyone except Ann-Ellen.

That trip to Mexico had been a marker in her life. She had left her husband, Neal, the summer before and moved in with Annette, the woman whom Neal, with his usual obtuse tenacity, regarded as single-handedly responsible for the destruction of his marriage. Annette was two decades older, nearing fifty-eight, a blunt-featured woman with a close-cropped helmet of gray hair and an air of studied superiority that many people found difficult to bear. But for Esther, at that time, Annette had seemed a haven. She knew everything that Esther was going through—she had seen it all a hundred times before, she liked to say—and proved almost frighteningly adept at predicting every move that Neal and his lawyer would make in their long psychological and legal campaign to get Esther back. Eventually, Esther came to resent Annette's omniscience; she didn't like the idea that her ratchety course of self-discovery—so vivid and novel and unpredictable to herself—was in Annette's weary eyes almost a cliché. And the smugness with which Annette greeted every new development in Esther's radical makeover, the little nod that said, "Ah yes, this is what happens next, you see," eventually became intolerable. Before long, the two of them quarreled. Esther turned sullen, irritable. She began to spend longer hours at her job in the admissions office of New Mexico State University–Las Cruces, a job that Annette disapproved of as lacking progressive social value. Affronted by Esther's contrariness, Annette accused her of ingratitude, of stupidity, of not knowing what was good for her. What's more, all of their mutual friends—sour, tight-lipped women, as Esther now saw them—sided with Annette (whom, of course, they had known much longer). Esther began to wonder if she'd made an enormous mistake. Perhaps the feelings that had driven her from her previous life were more a reaction to Neal than anything else. Who could say whether she was not merely replacing an old false self with a new one, equally false, equally manufactured?

Eventually, she left the country. She arranged for a two-month leave of absence from the university, inventing a terminally ill mother whom she had to care for (her mother had actually died a decade earlier, of ovarian cancer), and took the next plane to Mexico. Why Mexico? It was inexpensive, for one thing. And she knew that no one—not Neal, not Annette—would follow her there. She set herself up in the cheapest clean hotel in Cozumel and simply lived for a while, breathing in the air of this safe house, where no one knew who or what she was or had been. Most days, she sat on the beach, reading in the sun, avoiding the fond but insistent questions of the obese widow who ran the hotel. Sometimes she wrote postcards, brief nasty things to Neal mostly, which she would regret immediately upon sliding them through the mail slot in the hotel's gloomy lobby. At night, if she felt incapable of sitting alone in her room, she went to bars and talked with the tourists.

Esther slept with three people that winter, two men and a woman. All were younger than she, and the woman was quite drunk. They all seemed to regard her as some kind of local institution—a part of the exotic scenery that had to be experienced before going home. It was the woman who gave her the handbag. She had bought it, she said, at the market in Chichén Itzá, near the pyramids, but now she wanted Esther to have it.

Finally Esther's money and patience ran out. She had decided nothing. She just felt tired now, and older, much older. So she returned to New Mexico—but not to Las Cruces, where there were too many remnants of her former lives lurking. She found a small efficiency apartment in Albuquerque, not far from her sister Helen's house. Helen was sympathetic, stable, the closest thing to a friend Esther had now.

Esther applied for a job at the University of New Mexico in Albuquerque and at several other schools in the area. Nothing was immediately available, so she took a job as a travel agent, sending her clients to, among other places, Cozumel. Then, after almost a year in Albuquerque, she got a call. Her résumé had crossed the desk of the dean of students at a small women's college outside Taos. Could she come up to discuss an opening on the staff?

The interview took place on a Tuesday. Esther drove her used hatchback up into the chilly mountains around Taos. She was wearing a new linen suit—an older style than she was accustomed to, but one that made her look more capable, less desperate. She was nervous, of course, but tried to show confidence. The woman she was to speak to, the dean herself, was named Ann-Ellen Gluck—her new life.

Next day, the day after the second postcard, Esther went shopping for a new handbag. She had been using an old bag since the theft—a brown zippered lozenge that reeked embarrassingly of the late 1970's—but now she decided that she really needed a new one. Taking an early lunch hour, she drove out to the Poughkeepsie Galleria to find one.

This was only the third or fourth time she had shopped at the glittery, generic mall. The first few times were last spring, shortly after she started her new job as dean of student affairs. The clothes she'd purchased in New Mexico had proved hopelessly inadequate for her new situation. All of those Indian motifs, the turquoises and siennas, seemed an aggressive affectation—even an anachronism—out here where Santa Fe style had apparently come and gone briskly a decade ago. So she had scoured Lord & Taylor and Bloomingdale's in search of things plainer, darker, more urban. She did continue to wear the Mexican bag, however. Despite its hideousness, she had grown fond of it. And she liked to think that it kept her honest, a palpable reminder of the wreck she had once made of her life.

Entering through the glass doors of the mall, Esther went straight down the cobbled walkway to a leather boutique that had caught her eye on a previous visit. It was a quiet, gray-carpeted place, with scores of handbags hanging like ripe fruit from free-standing chrome racks. A smartly dressed saleswoman smiled at her inquisitively from behind the glass counter.

Esther returned the smile but quickly made for the chrome racks. She never liked dealing with salespeople—their frankly evaluative glances, their brittle friendliness, their expectation. She preferred to shop undisturbed, in department stores, where clerks wouldn't burden her with their attention. One of the things she most admired about Ann-Ellen, in fact, was how she never seemed at all intimidated by salespeople, or by taxi drivers, waiters, telephone operators—all of whom cowed Esther with their subtle tyrannies.

Even now, under the watchful gaze of the handbag saleswoman, a sleek, pampered brunette with a pair of eyeglasses hanging from a chain, Esther began to feel the familiar discomfort. She examined the bags on the rack in front of her, running her fingers over their buttery surfaces with a plunging sense of hopelessness. None of these bags were for her. For one thing, the prices were astronomical. And the bags themselves, their restrained beauty, irritated her. Would she feel like an impostor, wearing one of these?

I and God are your judges. That sentence came back to her suddenly, planting its ragged thorn of misgiving. There were times in the past few days when everything, all of the recent events of her new life in New York, seemed to be pointed somehow. First the letter from Ann-Ellen, then the theft, and now the postcards, thrown back into her face like encoded rebukes for past misdeeds—all seemed part of some obscure punishment. But punishment for what? For changing her life? For leaving the person she loved? Ann-Ellen had encouraged Esther to take this job; it was she who suggested applying for it in the first place, she who wrote the glowing letter of recommendation.

Esther thought of the two messages Ann-Ellen had left on her answering machine. Could it be that she was reading too much into them? Maybe Ann-Ellen was merely selling the house—a piece of news she'd know Esther would find disturbing. Esther became so attached to houses. When she left

Neal back in Las Cruces, it had been the little cape with the pink-roofed dormers that she missed most. Would the same be true now, with Ann-Ellen's house? Esther remembered the day she moved into that ocher house surrounded by junipers. There had been a powerful sense of expansion in her chest—but whether the feeling came from bare stone floors and light-filled skylights or simply from the prospect of living with Ann-Ellen, Esther couldn't be sure. The house and Ann-Ellen, in fact, were inseparable in her mind. Ann-Ellen's warmth, her good-natured acuity, her surprisingly earthy sense of humor—all of the things that Esther loved about her—seemed embodied in those walls. That was why, at unexpected moments, a certain angle of light in a doorway, or even a familiar weave of coarse wool upholstery, could suddenly spill cold trickles of regret through Esther's body, reminding her of what she had given up to come here.

"A bag, a bag," Esther muttered to herself. She must decide on one quickly. There was work to be done back at the office. Finally, she put out her hand and touched one of the bags, her fingertips catching on the cold silver clasp. The bag was black leather, simple, tasteful, exuding a comforting sense of quiet. This is the one, she told herself. She sighed, grateful to have made a decision.

Esther returned to her office a few minutes after one o'clock. "Aha," said Judith, her secretary, as she walked through the door. "Now I know why you lost that other bag—so you'd have an excuse to buy a new one!"

Esther smiled and looked down at her new handbag. "Do you like it?" she asked.

"Very elegant," Judith said, nodding. She was older than Esther, a rotund divorced mother who seemed to derive a generous amusement from everything her new boss did and said. Esther wasn't yet sure how to respond to this woman.

She knew she should have a plan, a consistent attitude—warmth, a willingness to joke around, but just enough distance to keep the hierarchy clear?—but as yet she was still improvising.

Judith completed her examination of the new handbag. "Very nice, but not as much character as that Mexican bag. Guess you couldn't find one like it."

"I'm not sure there *is* one like it in the world, Judith, or at least not north of the Rio Grande." Esther picked up her pile of messages. "Anything important?"

"Two flunking students looking for sympathy," Judith said, "and a call from Ann-Ellen Gluck in Taos. Just left her number."

"Thanks." Esther carried the yellow squares of paper into her office and shut the door behind her. She dropped the bag into a chair and slipped out of her overcoat. Ann-Ellen. Ann-Ellen would laugh at the bag she had bought. "Oh, Es," she'd say, her knuckles raised to her lips to suppress the smile. "It looks so serious, so Republican."

Esther threw her overcoat over the chair, covering the bag. Tonight she would return Ann-Ellen's call. If that life was over, then it was over. There was nothing to be gained by continuing this game of hide-and-seek. She looked at her calendar. Today was Friday. They would have the entire weekend to discuss it, if need be; they would have as much time as they needed. She and Ann-Ellen could run up their phone bills, the way they used to in the first weeks after Esther left.

A third postcard was waiting for her when she arrived home that evening. The mail, as usual, was piled neatly on the kitchen counter. But today the card was buried under several bills and a note from William: "My plumber friend found the leak and fixed it, but we didn't have time to sheetrock the wall.

OK to come on Sunday to finish up? I'll call. SORRY ABOUT THE MESS!!"

She put William's note aside and examined the postcard. It was another photograph—the old Lartigue of a woman sitting alone on the top of a London double-decker bus. Esther stared at the image with a nagging sense of confusion. Had she really wanted to buy *this* card for her refrigerator door? The woman seemed so isolated, alone up there above the passing street. Esther could barely remember choosing it.

The message on the back was written in pencil this time: "Sinners. Sinners, Both of us. We are the same, to Them we are the same, to HIM we are the same. May be there IS no forgivness for us except *from* us." Esther felt weak. This was different, this message was different, she thought. He had mentioned himself. What could it mean? She brought the card closer to her eyes to read the postmark. It, too, was different. New York, New York.

A wave of nausea swept through Esther's chest. The card still in her hand, she hurried back through the house to the ground-floor bathroom. Her shoes crackled on some plaster grit before she even reached the door. There were three long gashes in the walls behind the toilet, the shower stall, the sink. The black-and-white tile floor was littered with rubble. The air smelled of chalk and plaster. Two corrugated footprints, large and grimy, marked the terrycloth throw rug in front of the sink.

She stopped in the doorway. The nausea passed, lingering for a few long seconds before disappearing.

Esther made her decision. Moving quickly, she backed out of the doorway and went into the living room. Then—standing, unable even to sit down—she picked up the telephone and dialed Ann-Ellen's number.

————

Saturday morning. The day was brighter but still cold, an intermittent wind rattling the old windows in their frames. The sun, bloated and watery, flashed through the wagging branches of the oaks that lined the little stream.

Esther got up at nine. Tying the turquoise robe around herself, she descended the uncarpeted stairs, slipped past the open bathroom door without looking in, and padded into the kitchen to make some coffee. She lit the flame under the kettle and then just stood there, watching it, before thinking to put a filter in the cone and spoon some coffee into it.

They had talked last night, finally. Esther had called Ann-Ellen at the office—it was two hours earlier in New Mexico —and told her straight out that the letter had been lost, unopened. Ann-Ellen seemed relieved, as if this explained Esther's elusiveness of the past few days. And then, while Esther listened quietly, Ann-Ellen explained what she had written in the letter. Although she wasn't able to talk as freely as she would have liked (her assistant, she whispered, was staying late today), she said enough to confirm Esther's fears. There was someone else, someone Esther had met once or twice but didn't know well, someone who would be taking her place in the juniper-scented house in the desert hills.

Esther was surprised at how calmly she took this news. She wondered if perhaps her subconscious mind, suspecting such a revelation, had been silently shoring up its defenses. In fact, Esther was even able to convince herself that this was a positive development. Perhaps she needed this abrupt closure to get on with things, to enter truly into the course of action she had chosen by moving east three months ago. Everything had to change, evolve, transform itself. And yet, she had remarked to Ann-Ellen, at least one thing hadn't changed. The two of them still loved each other. They were still soul mates.

It was only after they hung up that Esther realized she

had said nothing about the anonymous postcards, or even about her bag being stolen. But she did not call Ann-Ellen back. It seemed unnecessary. There would be things now that she and Ann-Ellen would not share.

The water in the kettle was nearing a boil. Esther turned off the burner and poured water over the coffee grounds. While it ran through, she went into the living room to get her brief-case. There was work she had to do this weekend, work she never had time for in the office. She would take care of it this morning, before driving to the police station in the village to make her report. That, too, she had finally decided to take care of. She would tell the police everything they needed to know.

A car pulled up as she was returning to the kitchen. At first she thought it was William, but when she looked through the kitchen window, she saw it was a taxi—the dusty green wagon that stood sentry at the small train station every day, waiting to serve the few arriving passengers who had no one picking them up. Esther watched, puzzled, as an indistinct figure in the back seat leaned forward to pay the driver and then stepped out of the car. It was a woman—a girl, really— dressed in an oversized gray raincoat and carrying a large knap-sack. It must be a mistake; the girl had come to the wrong address. Esther went to the door, hoping to stop the taxi before it pulled away, but then caught sight of the bag. The girl was holding the Mexican handbag, adjusting the long strap on her shoulder. The bag seemed more worn than before, the little patches of colored leather looked dimmer, but there was no doubt that this was the bag that had been stolen.

Esther watched as the taxi backed up and drove away. She still could have run out and stopped it—shouting, hands waving—but she felt incapable of moving. The girl stood on the driveway, looking up mournfully at the second-floor windows of the house. She must have been sixteen or seventeen, with long stringy blond hair and pinched, sharp features. She seemed frightened and very tired. She was also pregnant.

Esther, breathing carefully, stepped to the door and pulled it open. The girl's eyes met hers through the glass door. The eyes, a faint, gelid blue, shadowed for a moment in confusion, as if Esther was not what she expected to find in the doorway.

Esther pushed the glass door open a few inches. "Who are you?" she called out.

The girl lowered her eyes. "I got your pocketbook," she said. "I'm the one who stole it, I guess."

It was as if great blocks of thought and expectation were being shifted in Esther's mind like stage scenery. The cold air crept in, crept down the front of her turquoise robe to her feet.

The girl shrugged. "Can I come in?" she said. "I already asked God's forgiveness, and now I want to ask yours."

Esther hesitated. But the girl was obviously harmless; she looked as if the faintest sign of rejection or censure would crush her. Esther pushed the door open wider. "Come in, then," she said quietly.

The girl nodded and moved toward the door. As she passed into the house, Esther caught her smell—a humid, rank herbiness. She had probably not bathed in days.

The girl put her knapsack on the floor and, slipping the handbag from her shoulder, placed it on the high kitchen table. "There it is," she said. "It's all there, except the money. I can't pay back the money."

Esther still stood by the door. She didn't want to touch the bag, not yet. "You were in the bar that night? The Lark Hill Tavern?"

"Is that what it was called?" She looked away again, at

the cup of coffee brewing on the counter, steam rising from the plastic cone. "I was on my own then. I needed to get to Pennsylvania."

"You ran away from home?"

The girl paused before answering. "I ran away three months back, when I first started showing. I stayed at my aunt's house a while. She's not as"—another pause—"as religious as my mom and other people. They're Pentecostal." The girl cleared her throat. "Me too, I guess." She looked around the kitchen, her eyes darting from one thing to another nervously. "Ma'am," she said then, "I'm gonna need to ask you for a bathroom. With this baby laying on me, I got to go ten times a day."

"Yes," Esther said, still not moving from the doorway. "There's one through there, next to the stairs."

The girl dipped her head in thanks, stepped down the hall, and disappeared into the bathroom. Esther watched her go, wondering if she should follow, if she should even have allowed this girl into her home. She briefly considered calling the police—the girl was a thief, after all—but of course she could not. The girl was in trouble, desperate. She wasn't a criminal.

Then Esther remembered about the bathroom. "Wait," she called out, and hurried down the hallway. "Excuse me," she said, pushing wider the bathroom door which the girl had left ajar. But the girl was already sitting on the toilet, her raincoat bunched up around her vast, swollen belly. Rubble from the plumber's work surrounded her. "I'm sorry," Esther continued, "I forgot there was work being done here. There's another bathroom upstairs."

The girl peered up at her from the toilet. She looked pitiful in that position, in the middle of the mess, but she smiled. "That's OK, ma'am, Miss Boyd. This is good enough for me."

"Oh," Esther said, surprised by the use of her name. She stepped awkwardly back, out of the bathroom, and pulled the door shut.

She returned to the kitchen. The Mexican bag sat on the butcher-block table, a garish, shapeless lump of leather and metal. Esther regarded it for a moment, remembering what the woman in Mexico had said when she gave it to her years ago. That had also been a Saturday morning, and the woman was leaving that day on a flight to Chicago. "You keep it," the woman had said, pulling a brush through her shoulder-length sun-bleached hair. "It belongs down here, to this life. I just can't see myself carrying it to work. You'll feel the same way, when you go back."

"*If* I go back," Esther had replied from the bed.

"When you go back." The woman looked straight at her. "This won't last forever, what you're doing here. Nothing ever does."

Esther heard the toilet flush. Then the girl, her raincoat rasping, appeared again in the kitchen. "Hi," she said, shrugging.

Esther turned to her. "Why are you here? You can't stay here, you know."

"I don't *want* to stay here," the girl said, a childish petulance entering her voice. "I'm going back to my aunt's. We talked on the phone."

"Then why did you come?"

The girl dug her hands into the deep pockets of her raincoat. "To return the bag, I guess," she said. "And to pray with you. You're a sinner like me. I thought maybe we could pray together."

Esther crossed her arms in front of her chest. "No," she said after a moment, "we won't pray together." She looked at the girl, at the long, formless hair, the eyes dull but vaguely hopeful. No, they were not alike. Esther could barely even imagine what this girl's life was like. And there was nothing —certainly not sin—binding them together, no matter what the girl thought.

Esther, awkwardly conscious of her crossed arms, unfolded them and placed her hands on her hips. She would have to decide exactly what to do about this girl. She realized, as they faced each other warily across the kitchen, that the girl would eventually ask her for more money. She realized, too, that she would give it to her—at the very last moment, just as the cab was pulling up to the house. But in the meantime, before the cab was called back, before the girl was packed off again to parts unknown, there were other things to be considered. "You must be famished," Esther said. "I should probably feed you."

The girl broke into a smile. She pulled her hands out of her pockets and wrapped them around her belly. "I was hoping you'd say that," she said. "I was hoping you'd say exactly that."

Medicated

1.

HE TOLD ME that he wanted to visit Houdini's grave.

He told me that small animals seemed attracted to him, and that this was causing problems on the job.

He told me that he was the owner of a hairbrush that had once belonged to Walt Disney.

He told me that I was the only woman whose knee he had ever touched with his tongue.

It seemed he had been talking continuously since Day One. We met at the Inverness Public Garden, where Jon worked as a landscaper, rotating the annuals, snapping the dead buds off roses, raking long, elegant strands of algae from the decorative ponds.

This was spring. I was taking one of my famous days off, one of those days when the thought of spoon-feeding Manifest Destiny to a roomful of ninth-graders was enough to make me break into a cold sweat.

Iceland poppies were in bloom. Forget-me-nots. Those cloying, throat-catching white hyacinths.

He approached me from behind in the Blaise Memorial Gazebo. "What do you know about watches?" he asked.

I turned, surprised by the voice so close to my ear. The person attached to it was young, sharp-featured, deep-eyed.

He wore teal overalls with the word JON stitched into the breast pocket in orange thread. A long reddish-black ponytail emerged from the back of his cap like—well, like the tail of a pony.

Jon the gardener. I recognized him. I'd seen him on previous visits, wandering distractedly among the phlox and lupines. There was something about his manner, the nervous preoccupation, that interested me.

"Watches?" I asked.

"Digital. Quartz movement. Liquid-crystal display. The world of watches."

He sat down on the bench beside me and held up a smooth-muscled arm. Strapped to his wrist was one of those cheap plastic digitals that come with magazine subscriptions. It was flashing the wrong time, on and off, on and off, on and off.

"My brother gave it to me."

I gave him my best defensive smile. "I'm sorry, but I don't know anything about watches."

"That's all right," he said. "I'll just read the directions."

He paused, sighed once deeply, and turned to gaze out at the duck pond. The mallards were parading in front of us, making flat little snickering sounds like old men telling racy stories to themselves.

Then: "Have you seen what the deer have done to the tulip display?"

Two things flashed through my mind. One of them: Don't go anywhere with this man. The other: Go anywhere with this man.

He asked again: "Have you seen what they've done?"

I hadn't. That was the truth. "Is it very bad?" I asked finally.

It was. I could see that it upset him. And so I went with the man. We walked over, Jon and I, to have a look at the carnage.

2.

There were gifts. Jon was always presenting things, little hopeful tokens. It began that first afternoon, at the tulip display. I watched as he hopped around the trampled beds, pointing out toothmarked leaves, decapitated stems. He wore thick rubber boots that probably did as much damage to the flowers as the deer had. "Here," he said, handing me the severed head of a purple tulip. It was compact and smooth, streaked with white, like an Easter egg.

After that, over the next weeks, Jon gave me:

a Chinese coin;
a chestnut, burnished to a warm shine;
a pewter paperweight in the shape of a Japanese beetle;
a children's calendar from the makers of Jell-O brand
    pudding;
a pair of slipper-socks, slightly used;
two snapdragons;
a homemade cassette tape featuring himself playing Christ-
    mas carols on the flutophone;
a tailfeather from a mallard duck;
a postcard depicting the Blaise Memorial Gazebo with the
    words "A Place Near to Both Our Hearts" printed on
    the back;
another Chinese coin;
a cough drop.

What I gave Jon:

an extra pair of shoelaces;
a copy of Howard Belkin's Essential Guide for Home
   Video Rentals;
my word that I would not throw out anything he had given
   me.

One can impersonate a citadel for only so long.

3.

I had a husband who died when I was twenty-four years old. We were in graduate school together at Penn, I in Early American History, he in Classics. We married on a midterm break—foolishly, of course, since we had no money and no reason, really, to make our union legal. A justice of the peace performed the ceremony in his hideous green ranch house in Vermont, where I and my husband-to-be had driven on a whim to see the leaves changing. We were too early—most of the leaves hadn't even begun to blush pink at their centers—so we got married instead.

My husband had a nest of fine blond hair and a spray of birthmarks over his shoulders and back. He had a boyish smile and a very bad temper. He wore wire-rimmed glasses, one arm of which he scotch-taped to the rest of the frame.

One night, four months into our marriage, he went out to the Wawa Market for a bag of pretzels and was shot in the head by a jumpy crack-addict whose robbery seemed not to be going as smoothly as he would have liked. My husband was dead before anyone could call 911.

In an earlier century, of course, I would have known what to do. I would have returned to my father's house, to salve my grief with hard work and the care of younger siblings, playing the part of the stoic aunt who has known tragedy too soon. But this was impossible. My father had disappeared soon after my seventh birthday. My mother had since devoted her life and what was left of her emotions to another man, the little knock-kneed bagpiper on the bottle of Beefeater Gin. I had no choice but to put myself in the hands of the doctors.

Some of them, I should mention in the interest of fairness, were very kind.

But I don't deceive myself; it was the little green-and-white capsules that brought me back. That, and several years of distance. Pills and time.

Which is all to say that I did not go into this blindly. I knew what it was like to owe my soul to Pfizer Chemical. I knew what it was like to check the time whenever I felt the heaviness descending (4:30 every afternoon, like clockwork). I knew, in other words, what I was getting myself into with Jon.

4.

He wouldn't open his eyes the first time we made love. He said that my bare shoulders reminded him of something, but he couldn't remember what. I decided to take that as a compliment. I hadn't gotten too many of those over the years.

This was summer now. School was out, my only teaching obligation a summer-school class in American history, meeting three mornings a week. "America," I would tell my students, "is about the replacement of kings by money, of oppression by abandonment, of poverty by emptiness." They would actually write this in their notebooks. A few—God love them— would even adore me for it.

Summer. It was all right. I was all right. I was a resident of this little New York town complete with firehouse and aluminum-sided diner and old school building that smelled comfortingly of marijuana and library paste. I was an active member of three organizations: the teacher's union, the local library association, and Women Against Illegal Dumping (WAID). And I had two friends: Amy, the calculus teacher at school, and Mr. Donnapolis, my pharmacist.

And Jon. A third friend, now in my bed. He had let his hair down, so that it fell around his shoulders in damp curls. He looked like a figure from one of those brightly colored Bible illustrations—an unnamed shepherd, perhaps, or one of those dreamy olive sellers whose faces shine with the knowledge of routine miracles.

(Except for the watch. The watch was still strapped to his wrist, still blinking on and off, on and off, on and off. He hadn't read the directions yet.)

My mother would not approve, I told myself silently.

Afterward, he opened his eyes. "You won't hurt me in any of this, I hope," he said.

"Hurt you?" I'm sorry, but imagine someone looking at St. Sebastian and pleading: Don't shoot, please don't shoot. "No," I told him. "I'll try not to hurt you."

This seemed to confirm something in his mind. He closed his eyes again. He licked his lips and used them to kiss my navel.

5.

We went swimming together at a pond near the private boys' school. Jon wore cutoff jeans the color of rusted metal. His thighs were long—long, hairless, and smooth.

"Jon," I asked him, rubbing sunscreen onto the curves of his shoulders, "let me see the pills you're taking."

I felt his muscles rumple under my fingers. He pulled away from me and lay down on the bedspread we had set out on the grass. "You can't take them, you know. They're not that kind of pill. They won't do anything interesting."

I flinched at the misunderstanding. "No," I said quickly. "I just want to see them, see what they look like."

He stared up at a scrap of cloud that was inching along the tops of the maples. He reached for his sunglasses and put them up on the top of his head.

"Don't even tell me what they are," I said. "I don't want to know. I just want to see them. Please."

He relented. Sighing, he pulled the bottle from his knapsack. The tablets were pink, with an odd dumbell-shaped hole in the center. He held them out to me in his palm. I worried them back and forth with an index finger. I had no idea what they were.

"And now," he said, watching me with a sly little smile, "you have to show me yours."

I looked at him sidelong, but of course I should have known that he knew. The brotherhood of the scarlet letter. M, this time, for medicated.

I hemmed a bit. But what's fair is fair. "Sure," I said finally. I opened my canvas bag and fished out my little Sucrets tin.

"Prozac," he announced, identifying the pills immediately. "You've taken them?"

He chuckled. Then he frowned. "I've taken everything," he said.

6.

Jon's scent was of garlic and bell peppers whenever he worked out in my garden apartment. Sometimes I'd sit in the black armchair and watch him, his body soaked with the cold white light of my glowing Esso sign as he eked out a set of twenty push-ups. He was so slender, so sinewy. His body was like a mast, a floorbeam, something a person could cling to until the lifeboats reached her.

I introduced him to Amy (Mr. Donnapolis, the pharmacist, he already knew). The three of us got together at the diner in town for lunch one Saturday. Jon brought us gifts—three crocus bulbs each. He made us promise not to plant them until the recommended time in the fall.

Amy was cautious at first. I'd told her about Jon, and what I'd told her worried her. Amy knew all about what she called "unstable" men. She'd been married to a few.

"I've seen you before," Jon said to her after we ordered. "At the A&P. You asked me if I knew where the hell they kept the endive in that place."

Amy was surprised. "That was you?"

"You must have thought I worked there. I was wearing my garden overalls."

"That *was* you."

Jon turned to me. "I told her that the A&P didn't carry endive, that she should try the Shop-Rite."

"I was amazed," Amy said. "I thought it was just like Kriss Kringle in that old Christmas movie, where the Macy's Santa sends people over to Gimbel's."

"Miracle on 34th Street," he told her.

"Exactly."

I started breathing a little easier. Amy, I knew, would be well disposed to someone who knew where to buy endive.

I was right. "He's earnest," she said to me later that afternoon, after Jon returned to work. "Earnest and sexy and somehow innocent-seeming—not a combination you find very often. Just be careful, all right?"

I promised her I would be careful.

The summer turned hot. Jon cooked for me almost every weekend—at my place, which was air-conditioned. He had a heavy hand with ground cloves, and would throw a dash into the most unlikely dishes—tomato sauce, hamburgers, anything that struck him as too bland. Sometimes he'd bring me handfuls of gladiolas, irises, or even freesia from the Inverness greenhouses, and their smells would mingle with the cloves. I liked the effect. It made me think of us as refugees from an obscure spice island, reconstructing in this foreign town a tiny oasis of home.

Yes, there were episodes. Or whatever the medical term. There were days when Jon would mope, cry, eat doughnuts by the dozen. I learned to associate doughnuts with frustration—my own sense of helplessness when I found him that way, hunched over the white Entenmann's carton in the glow of my back porch light. One learned not to try to bring him out of such episodes. One learned to avoid the cloaked eyes, the whispered awfulnesses. The words he called one were like cornered animals—small, brutal things, capable of great hurt.

But it would pass. Balance would be restored.

I can *help* him, I told myself. And he can help me.

One evening, we lay naked on the floor in the dark, letting the warm breeze from the bedroom window sweep the smell of night over our bodies. Jon slid between my legs and rested his head on. my belly, his hands raised to cup my breasts. He fell asleep that way. And I, after an hour, after two hours, watching the sheer curtains billow in and out like someone's indecisive ghost—I fell asleep too.

7.

A few weeks after starting on my first antidepressants, they began to work so well—lifting the gloom like a dentist's X-ray vest off my shoulders—that I almost felt depressed all over again. How could this be, I asked myself. Was my despair such a trivial thing that a few well-chosen chemicals could dispel it? Apparently my doctors thought so. I was cured, they said eventually, though not in so many words. And I suppose

I believed them. I would occasionally miss one of my therapy sessions with Dr. Hagler, but I always made sure to keep the bottle of Prozac full to the brim.

One morning, about two years after my husband's death, I entered the Wawa Market—the very same one. I purchased a loaf of white bread and a quart of milk and a Kit-Kat bar. Then I left. I had breathed normally the whole time.

The next fall, I went back to school. I took up my old subject, everyday life in the Puritan era, with a special interest in the Salem witch trials. When I earned enough credits for my master's, I was done. My mother even managed to stumble her way to the commencement exercises—eyeliner smudged, silk dress askew, but there. She had found just the right dosage of Beefeater to get her through the event.

The miracles of modern science.

8.

We were fine until the evening of July 4th. Jon and I went to the fireworks at the high-school ballfield. We sat side by side on the blanket, drinking identical plastic glasses of lemonade. I kept scanning the crowds for Amy, who had promised to meet us there. Jon, I noticed, couldn't seem to keep still. His foot waggled continuously, like a fish on a hook.

"Jon," I said, "are you warm enough?"

"Fire works," he answered, not looking at me. He was twisting a hank of his long hair around an index finger. "It's a pun. Fire works. Kaleidoscope. This is really interesting."

A couple of eyes from other blankets strayed in our direction.

I moved closer to him and put a hand on his foot, stopping it. "Should we go home now, you think?"

One of my summer-school kids walked by then, one of

my smarter, more conscientious kids. "Hey, Ms. Downey. Happy anniversary of the Declaration of Independence."

A clever line. I gave him an approving smile. "The same to you, Kevin."

Jon's head swiveled in my direction. His eyes seemed intense, but at the same time distant. "Happy anniversary of what?" he asked loudly.

"Just some history department humor," I told him. "One of my students."

"Is that what this is all about? Is that all? Shit!" He lay back and grasped his head. "Shit, shit, shit," he kept muttering, rocking back and forth.

The bombs bursting in air . . .

He was in the hospital two days later. The doctors had called his brother Larry in Connecticut, who then called me with the news. Jon had stopped taking his pills, Larry told me. Nobody knew why.

We met at the hospital. We had heard about each other, of course. Larry was the close brother. The far brother, Mike, lived in San Diego. The parents were dead.

Larry looked a lot like Jon, I thought as I shook his hand, except for the hair, which was short. And the eyes, which carried a weariness which told me that this was not the first time he was meeting his brother's new friend in the waiting room of a strange hospital.

"There's supposed to be a system for this," Larry said, leading me to the check-in desk. "There's supposed to be a system for making sure he takes his pills."

I knew that system. You have your regular appointments with the doctors. If you show up, they ask you if you're taking your pills. If you don't show up, they call you. If you don't answer the phone, they wait for the next appointment. That's the system.

Larry and I went upstairs. Jon seemed sedated, foggy. He managed a smile from the depths of the bed. "Sarah," he whispered.

"There," Larry said loudly, stepping toward him. "I brought her. Happy now?"

"Happy."

Larry began rearranging the pillows behind Jon's neck. Now that I saw them together, the resemblance was remarkable. Jon looked like an older, gaunter, more ravaged version of his brother, as if they were two formerly-identical lab mice, one of which had been injected with massive doses of caffeine over a long period of time.

"I won't be in here long, not long at all," Jon assured me while Larry fooled with his pillows.

"This is the second time in a year. Last time they found him running barefoot through the garage at the Milbrook DPW."

Jon looked at me. "Things—shitshitshit. OK. I mean, things don't always work the way they're supposed to."

"An obvious point," his brother added, punching pillows.

Afterward, Larry and I had coffee at the hospital canteen. I sat across from him in one of the red vinyl booths by the window. "OK, tell me everything," I said to him. "Tell me everything I need to know."

9.

There is a scholar at the University of Michigan who believes that the witches of Salem were actually mentally ill—schizophrenics, manic-depressives, sufferers of extreme psychological trauma. The witch trials of 1692, he argues, were the Puritans' way of neutralizing the threat presented by these people to an orderly religious community. Those accused often obliged by behaving in ways that supported the prosecution's contention of supernatural influence.

I tell my students about this theory every year, during my notorious lecture on Cotton Mather. I usually see one or two of them shaking their heads in disbelief. The idea is too far-fetched for them. Such a lack of sympathy on the part of our forebears is unimaginable. Even three hundred years ago, they think, people couldn't have been *that* cruel.

Jon got out in time for my birthday. His doctor had given him a new prescription. He had lost eight pounds in the hospital.

"I'm looking for a new job," he told me as I drove him to the Red Lobster in Wappingers Falls, where we would celebrate with a king crab platter and clam stew.

I looked at him. "Why a new job?"

"They gave away my place at the garden. They said they needed somebody reliable."

I stopped the car. "You were sick," I said, the outrage seething in me. "They can't do that. It's illegal. Isn't it?"

"They gave it away before I got sick. I forgot to tell you."

My Nissan was clicking in the heat. The air wobbled over the hood in the late sunlight.

"I guess I missed some days," he went on, not looking at me, looking out the window. "The squirrels were really bothering me for a while there. So I didn't go in. I never really told you about that."

I didn't answer for a moment or two. How could I be angry with him? Who was I, after all, to scold someone who had stayed home from work for reasons that others would regard as nebulous? "So what will you do?" I asked.

"I've applied for other jobs. I've applied to be a health inspector in Poughkeepsie."

"But you're not qualified, are you?"

"People find it hard to lie to me," he said, bracing his hand against the dashboard. "What more qualification can you need?"

10.

Jon was unemployed for six weeks. He all but ran out of money by the end of July. There was some kind of stipend from his father's life insurance, but he could only get so much per month. Some arrangement the brothers had set up. Jon's tiny apartment (which I had seen only twice) was fortunately under Larry's name; somebody, probably Larry, paid the rent.

During the last weeks of July, Jon ate nothing but bagels and macaroni-and-cheese. And zucchini squash, which he stole from a garden on my street and cooked with butter and nutmeg and, of course, ground cloves.

"Let me lend you something," I told him in bed one night. I tried to spend as many nights as I could with him—to feed him, to make sure he was taking his pills. I was the new system, I guess.

"I don't need anything. I can live on almost nothing." Jon was running his thumb down the curved line of my jaw. It felt eerily satisfying, as if I were being sculpted.

"You can't live on nothing," I told him.

He pulled his thigh up over my belly. "I can," he whispered to me. "I can do anything in this world. Just wait."

We would watch cheerful movies on my VCR—*Miracle at Morgan's Creek, Splash, His Girl Friday*. Amy would come over sometimes and watch with us. She would tell us which of the characters behaved exactly like one of her ex-husbands. The night we watched Peter Pan, she had a field day.

One evening, Jon told Amy that she looked just like Julie Christie in the remake of *Heaven Can Wait*. I thought she might not like that, but she did. She knew it wasn't a line, I suppose—coming from Jon.

One night, I took his watch off the night table as he slept. I carried it into the kitchen, and there, under the amber light of the range hood, I fooled with its buttons until I had the time exactly right.

11.

He got a job at McDonald's in mid-August. He was a morning chef, specializing in fries. He would come to my door in his little paper hat, the long hair bound up in a net. "Is Sydney really not the capital of Australia?" he'd ask. Or else: "Is it true that there are no midgets anymore? Ella the cashier told me they've got this growth hormone now."

We would spend the long twilight in bed. His arms were covered with tiny splash burns from the hot oil. I'd kiss each one.

"The fries I make are feeding the world," he'd say, burying his face in my hair.

We swam nearly every day at the pond now, in the early afternoon. He continued to get thinner. The skin of his belly seemed concave over the waistband of his cutoffs. The wet hair squiggled down his shoulders like something in Arabic.

"Do you see that woman over there?" he asked me suddenly one afternoon. There were several other people swimming at the pond these days. The woman he was talking about was a mother with her twin toddler boys, a harried-looking blonde with a modest one-piece racing suit. "Do you see her?"

"Yes," I said.

"That woman is making me think about her. Do you know what that means? Do you know what that feels like?"

His foot was going again—the gasping fish.

No one answered at Larry's number. Jon said Larry had gone on vacation. To the Cayman Islands. Why did I ask?

"Jon," I asked him, "are you taking your pills?"

He had a wrinkle in his forehead that deepened whenever he felt affronted. "I'm taking my pills," he said flatly, his eyes revealing nothing.

I got the doctor's number. "What makes you think he's not taking his medication?" the man asked. His name was Dalton, Dr. Edward Dalton.

"He isn't acting right," I said. "I feel like he's . . . moving out there again, if you know what I mean." (My IQ has a tendency to fall fifty points whenever I talk to a member of an arrogant profession. It is something I regret but don't apologize for.)

I could hear Dr. Dalton sighing. "A man with Jon's illness cannot be expected to act right. That he can act in any way that is acceptable to you is something of a miracle."

I was silent, trying to think of a sentence of sufficient nastiness to answer back.

"He'll be in for his appointment on Friday," the man went on. "Let's see what he has to say for himself then, OK?"

That night, Jon threw a rock through my window.

I was awake when it happened. I saw the little shards of glass bouncing on the bedspread at my feet.

"Jon?" I whispered, pulling on sneakers. I went to the broken window. Glass crackled under my feet. He was out there, standing in the moonshadow of the rhododendrons. "Jon," I called to him. "Don't be afraid."

I could see his arms swinging back and forth. He was humming to himself.

I put on my bathrobe and went out to him.

As I crossed the lawn, he lay down on the damp grass— like someone resolutely going to sleep.

"Jon?" I asked as I stood over him. "Let's go to the hospital, OK, Jon?"

"Why? Are they having a party?" His face was as pale as the face of a clock. He was staring straight up at the sky.

"I think we should go to the hospital, Jon."

"I want to sleep. I want to sleep in the deep in my sleep. Don't ask me about the water times, cunt, I don't want to know!"

"Jon . . ."

I reached down to him, to turn his face toward me. He grabbed my wrist and pulled me down. We rolled on the grass until he was on top of me, his knees on my chest. "Don't ever touch me, goddamn it!" Something came into his eyes then that I had never seen before. My mistake was suddenly clear.

The police wanted me to press charges. It was advisable, they said, to press charges—assault and battery, at least—even if I dropped them later. Charges, they told me, would make picking him up a lot simpler.

I refused. Not that it made their job any more difficult. They caught Jon the next morning, at the DPW garage. There seemed to be something he liked about that place.

Larry came to see me at the hospital. Amy was there, but I didn't bother to introduce them. "Christ" was all Larry could say when he saw me. "Nothing like this ever happened before." Then: "I'm sorry."

"Where is he?" I asked.

Larry sat with his hands planted on his knees. "There's this place down in Westchester. He'll be in the locked ward, at least for a while."

"Am I allowed to visit him?"

He looked at me, eyebrows high. "You would want to?"

I didn't have an answer to that one. "Maybe not," I said finally, feeling Amy's eyes on me from across the room.

I went home the next day. Nuprin, the doctors had told me. Nuprin was what I needed right now.

Amy and I spent the afternoon cleaning up the glass in my bedroom. A warm breeze came in through the broken window, ruffling the edges of a paperback on my night table.

There, on my bureau, lay the chestnut, the paperweight in the shape of a Japanese beetle, the duck feather. They lay where I had left them, but they were strange objects to me now—mute, vaguely sinister. It was like the old optical illusion, the one that looks like a white goblet against a black background, until something shifts in your head and you see it as two faces, two blank silhouetted faces, staring nose to nose, and then it can't be seen as a goblet anymore. Those two awful faces are there; they've commandeered your perception; they won't go away no matter how hard you try to refocus your eyes.

"What are you thinking?" Amy asked, watching me. "I don't like what you're thinking. Don't you dare tell me that you plan to forget this."

12.

School started the next Monday, before the bruises had faded. I went into my first class, facing a new score of hopeful acned faces. I stood before them with my hands buried in my aching armpits. If I were one of those old Puritan sermonizers, I could speak to them as they needed to be spoken to. O children, I would say, beware this earthly world. It is not your home, for there is no shelter in it. Your time here is a time of pain and injustice and coldness. Expect nothing more.

But what I actually said to them was this: "Good morning, class. My name is Sarah Downey and our topic this year is the story of America."